INTRUDER
IN
THE DUST

INTRUDER
IN
THE DUST

WILLIAM
FAULKNER

VINTAGE BOOKS

A Division of Random House
New York

Library of Congress Cataloging in Publication Data

Faulkner, William, 1897-1962.
    Intruder in the dust.

    I. Title.
[PZ3.F272In5]   [PS3511.A86]   813'.5'2   72-397
ISBN 0-394-71792-9

Manufactured in the United States of America

Vintage Books Edition, August 1972

INTRUDER
IN
THE DUST

Chapter One

IT WAS JUST NOON that Sunday morning when the sheriff reached the jail with Lucas Beauchamp though the whole town (the whole county too for that matter) had known since the night before that Lucas had killed a white man.

He was there, waiting. He was the first one, standing lounging trying to look occupied or at least innocent, under the shed in front of the closed blacksmith's shop across the street from the jail where his uncle would be less likely to see him if or rather when he crossed the Square toward the postoffice for the eleven oclock mail.

Because he knew Lucas Beauchamp too—as well that is as any white person knew him. Better than any maybe unless it was Carothers Edmonds on whose place Lucas lived seventeen miles from town, because he had eaten a meal in Lucas' house. It was in the early winter four years ago; he had been only twelve then and it had happened this way: Edmonds was a friend of his uncle; they had been in school at the same time at the State University, where his uncle had gone after he came back from Harvard and Heidelberg to learn enough law to get himself chosen County Attorney, and the day before Edmonds had come in to town to see his uncle on some county business and had stayed the night with them and at supper that evening Edmonds had said to him:

'Come out home with me tomorrow and go rabbit

hunting:' and then to his mother: 'I'll send him back
in tomorrow afternoon. I'll send a boy along with him
while he's out with his gun:' and then to him again:
'He's got a good dog.'

'He's got a boy,' his uncle said and Edmonds said:
'Does his boy run rabbits too?' and his uncle said:
'We'll promise he wont interfere with yours.'

So the next morning he and Aleck Sander went home
with Edmonds. It was cold that morning, the first winter
cold-snap; the hedgerows were rimed and stiff with frost
and the standing water in the roadside drainage ditches
was skimmed with ice and even the edges of the running
water in the Nine Mile branch glinted fragile and scintil-
lant like fairy glass and from the first farmyard they
passed and then again and again and again came the
windless tang of woodsmoke and they could see in the
back yards the black iron pots already steaming while
women in the sunbonnets still of summer or men's old
felt hats and long men's overcoats stoked wood under
them and the men with crokersack aprons tied with wire
over their overalls whetted knives or already moved
about the pens where hogs grunted and squealed, not
quite startled, not alarmed but just alerted as though
sensing already even though only dimly their rich and
immanent destiny; by nightfall the whole land would
be hung with their spectral intact tallowcolored empty
carcasses immobilised by the heels in attitudes of frantic
running as though full tilt at the center of the earth.

And he didn't know how it happened. The boy, one
of Edmonds' tenant's sons, older and larger than Aleck
Sander who in his turn was larger than he although they
were the same age, was waiting at the house with the
dog—a true rabbit dog, some hound, a good deal of

hound, maybe mostly hound, redbone and black-and-tan
with maybe a little pointer somewhere once, a potlicker,
a nigger dog which it took but one glance to see had an
affinity a rapport with rabbits such as people said Negroes had with mules—and Aleck Sander already had
his tapstick—one of the heavy nuts which bolt railroad
rails together, driven onto a short length of broom-
handle—which Aleck Sander could throw whirling end
over end at a running rabbit pretty near as accurately as
he could shoot the shotgun—and Aleck Sander and Edmonds' boy with tapsticks and he with the gun they went
down through the park and across a pasture to the creek
where Edmonds' boy knew the footlog was and he didn't
know how it happened, something a girl might have
been expected and even excused for doing but nobody
else, halfway over the footlog and not even thinking
about it who had walked the top rail of a fence many a
time twice that far when all of a sudden the known
familiar sunny winter earth was upside down and flat
on his face and still holding the gun he was rushing not
away from the earth but away from the bright sky and
he could remember still the thin bright tinkle of the
breaking ice and how he didn't even feel the shock of
the water but only of the air when he came up again.
He had dropped the gun too so he had to dive, sub-
merge again to find it, back out of the icy air into the
water which as yet felt neither, neither cold or not and
where even his sodden garments—boots and thick pants
and sweater and hunting coat—didn't even feel heavy
but just slow, and found the gun and tried again for
bottom then thrashed one-handed to the bank and treading water and clinging to a willow-branch he reached the
gun up until someone took it; Edmonds' boy obviously

since at that moment Aleck Sander rammed down at him
the end of a long pole, almost a log whose first pass struck
his feet out from under him and sent his head under
again and almost broke his hold on the willow until a
voice said:

'Get the pole out of his way so he can get out'—just
a voice, not because it couldn't be anybody else but
either Aleck Sander or Edmonds' boy but because it
didn't matter whose: climbing out now with both hands
among the willows, the skim ice crinkling and tinkling
against his chest, his clothes like soft cold lead which he
didn't move in but seemed rather to mount into like a
poncho or a tarpaulin: up the bank until he saw two
feet in gum boots which were neither Edmonds' boy's
nor Aleck Sander's and then the legs, the overalls rising
out of them and he climbed on and stood up and saw a
Negro man with an axe on his shoulder, in a heavy sheeplined coat and a broad pale felt hat such as his grandfather had used to wear, looking at him and that was
when he saw Lucas Beauchamp for the first time that he
remembered or rather for the first time because you
didn't forget Lucas Beauchamp; gasping, shaking and
only now feeling the shock of the cold water, he looked
up at the face which was just watching him without pity
commiseration or anything else, not even surprise: just
watching him, whose owner had made no effort whatever to help him up out of the creek, had in fact ordered
Aleck Sander to desist with the pole which had been the
one token toward help that anybody had made—a face
which in his estimation might have been under fifty or
even forty except for the hat and the eyes, and inside a
Negro's skin but that was all even to a boy of twelve
shaking with cold and still panting from shock and exer-

tion because what looked out of it had no pigment at all, not even the white man's lack of it, not arrogant, not even scornful: just intractable and composed. Then Edmonds' boy said something to the man, speaking a name: something Mister Lucas: and then he knew who the man was, remembering the rest of the story which was a piece, a fragment of the country's chronicle which few if any knew better than his uncle: how the man was son of one of old Carothers McCaslin's, Edmonds' great grandfather's, slaves who had been not just old Carothers' slave but his son too: standing and shaking steadily now for what seemed to him another whole minute while the man stood looking at him with nothing whatever in his face. Then the man turned, speaking not even back over his shoulder, already walking, not even waiting to see if they heard, let alone were going to obey:

'Come on to my house.'

'I'll go back to Mr Edmonds',' he said. The man didn't look back. He didn't even answer.

'Tote his gun, Joe,' he said.

So he followed, with Edmonds' boy and Aleck Sander following him, in single file along the creek toward the bridge and the road. Soon he had stopped shaking; he was just cold and wet now and most of that would go if he just kept moving. They crossed the bridge. Ahead now was the gate where the drive went up through the park to Edmonds' house. It was almost a mile; he would probably be dry and warm both by the time he got there and he still believed he was going to turn in at the gate and even after he knew that he wasn't or anyway hadn't, already beyond it now, he was still telling himself the reason was that, although Edmonds was a bachelor and there were no women in the house, Edmonds himself might refuse to let him out of the house again until he could be returned to his mother, still telling himself this even after he knew that the true reason was that he could no more imagine himself contradicting the man striding on ahead of him than he could his grandfather, not from any fear of nor even the threat of reprisal but because like his grandfather the man striding ahead of him was simply incapable of conceiving himself by a child contradicted and defied.

So he didn't even check when they passed the gate, he didn't even look at it and now they were in no well-used tended lane leading to tenant or servant quarters and marked by walking feet but a savage gash half gully and half road mounting a hill with an air solitary independent and intractable too and then he saw the house, the cabin and remembered the rest of the story, the legend: how Edmonds' father had deeded to his Negro first cousin and his heirs in perpetuity the house and the ten acres of land it sat in—an oblong of earth set forever in the middle of the two-thousand-acre plantation like a postage stamp in the center of an envelope—the paintless wooden house, the paintless picket fence whose paintless latchless gate the man kneed open still without stopping or once looking back and, he following and Aleck Sander and Edmonds' boy following him, strode on into the yard. It would have been grassless even in summer; he could imagine it, completely bare, no weed no sprig of anything, the dust each morning swept by some of Lucas' womenfolks with a broom made of willow switches bound together, into an intricate series of whorls and overlapping loops which as the day advanced would be gradually and slowly defaced by the droppings and the cryptic three-toed prints of chickens like (re-

membering it now at sixteen) a terrain in miniature out
of the age of the great lizards, the four of them walking
in what was less than walk because its surface was dirt
too yet more than path, the footpacked strip running
plumbline straight between two borders of tin cans and
empty bottles and shards of china and earthenware set
into the ground, up to the paintless steps and the paintless gallery along whose edge sat more cans but larger—
empty gallon buckets which had once contained molasses
or perhaps paint and wornout water or milk pails and
one five-gallon can for kerosene with its top cut off and
half of what had once been somebody's (Edmonds' without doubt) kitchen hot water tank sliced longways like
a banana—out of which flowers had grown last summer
and from which the dead stalks and the dried and brittle
tendrils still leaned and drooped, and beyond this the
house itself, gray and weathered and not so much paintless as independent of and intractable to paint so that
the house was not only the one possible continuation of
the stern untended road but was its crown too as the
carven ailanthus leaves are the Greek column's capital.

Nor did the man pause yet, up the steps and across the
gallery and opened the door and entered and he and
then Edmonds' boy and Aleck Sander followed: a hall
dim even almost dark after the bright outdoors and
already he could smell that smell which he had accepted
without question all his life as being the smell always of
the places where people with any trace of Negro blood
live as he had that all people named Mallison are Meth-
odists, then a bedroom: a bare worn quite clean paintless
rugless floor, in one corner and spread with a bright
patchwork quilt a vast shadowy tester bed which had
probably come out of old Carothers McCaslin's house,

and a battered cheap Grand Rapids dresser and then for
the moment no more or at least little more; only later
would he notice—or remember that he had seen—the
cluttered mantel on which sat a kerosene lamp hand-
painted with flowers and a vase filled with spills of twisted
newspaper and above the mantel the colored lithograph
of a three-year-old calendar in which Pocahontas in the
quilled fringed buckskins of a Sioux or Chippewa chief
stood against a balustrade of Italian marble above a
garden of formal cypresses and shadowy in the corner
opposite the bed a chromo portrait of two people framed
heavily in gold-painted wood on a gold-painted easel.
But he hadn't seen that at all yet because that was behind
him and all he now saw was the fire—the clay-daubed
fieldstone chimney in which a halfburned backlog glowed
and smoldered in the gray ashes and beside it in a rocking chair something which he thought was a child until
he saw the face, and then he did pause long enough to
look at her because he was about to remember something
else his uncle had told him about or at least in regard to
Lucas Beauchamp, and looking at her he realised for the
first time how old the man actually was, must be—a tiny
old almost doll-sized woman much darker than the man,
in a shawl and an apron, her head bound in an immac-
ulate white cloth on top of which sat a painted straw hat
bearing some kind of ornament. But he couldn't think
what it was his uncle had said or told him and then he
forgot that he had remembered even the having been
told, sitting in the chair himself now squarely before the
hearth where Edmonds' boy was building up the fire
with split logs and pine slivers and Aleck Sander squatting tugged off the wet boots and then his trousers and
standing he got out of the coat and sweater and his shirt,

both of them having to dodge around and past and under the man who stood straddled on the hearth, his back to the fire in the gum boots and the hat and only the sheepskin coat removed and then the old woman was beside him again less tall than he and Aleck Sander even at twelve, with another of the bright patchwork quilts on her arm.

'Strip off,' the man said.

'No I——' he said.

'Strip off,' the man said. So he stripped off the wet unionsuit too and then he was in the chair again in front of the now bright and swirling fire, enveloped in the quilt like a cocoon, enclosed completely now in that unmistakable odor of Negroes—that smell which if it were not for something that was going to happen to him within a space of time measurable now in minutes he would have gone to his grave never once pondering speculating if perhaps that smell were really not the odor of a race nor even actually of poverty but perhaps of a condition: an idea: a belief: an acceptance, a passive acceptance by them themselves of the idea that being Negroes they were not supposed to have facilities to wash properly or often or even to wash bathe often even without the facilities to do it with: that in fact it was a little to be preferred that they did not. But the smell meant nothing now or yet; it was still an hour yet before the thing would happen and it would be four years more before he would realise the extent of its ramifications and what it had done to him and he would be a man grown before he would realise, admit that he had accepted it. So he just smelled it and then dismissed it because he was used to it, he had smelled it off and on all his life and would continue to: who had spent a good

part of that life in Paralee's, Aleck Sander's mother's
cabin in their back yard where he and Aleck Sander
played in the bad weather when they were little and
Paralee would cook whole meals for them halfway between two meals at the house and he and Aleck Sander
would eat them together, the food tasting the same to
each; he could not even imagine an existence from which
the odor would be missing to return no more. He had
smelled it forever, he would smell it always; it was a
part of his inescapable past, it was a rich part of his
heritage as a Southerner; he didn't even have to dismiss
it, he just no longer smelled it at all as the pipe smoker
long since never did smell at all the cold pipereek which
is as much a part of his clothing as their buttons and
buttonholes, sitting drowsing a little even in the warm
huddled rankness of the quilt, rousing a little when he
heard Edmonds' boy and Aleck Sander get up from
where they had been squatting against the wall and leave
the room, but not much, sinking again into the quilt's
warm reek while there stood over him still, back to the
fire and hands clasped behind him and except for the
clasped hands and the missing axe and the sheeplined
coat exactly as when he had looked up out of the creek
and seen him first, the man in the gum boots and the
faded overalls of a Negro but with a heavy gold watch-
chain looping across the bib of the overalls and shortly
after they entered the room he had been conscious of
the man turning and taking something from the cluttered mantel and putting it into his mouth and later he
had seen what it was: a gold toothpick such as his own
grandfather had used: and the hat was a worn handmade
beaver such as his grandfather had paid thirty and forty
dollars apiece for, not set but raked slightly above the

face pigmented like a Negro's but with a nose high in
the bridge and even hooked a little and what looked out
through it or from behind it not black nor white either,
not arrogant at all and not even scornful: just intolerant
inflexible and composed.

Then Aleck Sander came back with his clothes, dried
now and still almost hot from the stove and he dressed,
stamping into his stiffened boots; Edmonds' boy squatting again against the wall was still eating something
from his hand and he said: 'I'll have my dinner at Mr
Edmonds'.'

The man neither protested nor acquiesced. He didn't
stir; he was not even looking at him. He just said, inflexible and calm: 'She done already dished it up now:' and
he went on past the old woman who stood aside from
the door to let him pass, into the kitchen: an oilcloth-
covered table set in the bright sunny square of a southern window where—he didn't know how he knew it
since there were no signs, traces, soiled plates to show
it—Edmonds' boy and Aleck Sander had already eaten,
and sat down and ate in his turn of what obviously was
to be Lucas' dinner—collard greens, a slice of sidemeat
fried in flour, big flat pale heavy half-cooked biscuits, a
glass of buttermilk: nigger food too, accepted and then
dismissed also because it was exactly what he had expected, it was what Negroes ate, obviously because it was
what they liked, what they chose; not (at twelve: he
would be a man grown before he experienced his first
amazed dubiety at this) that out of their long chronicle
this was all they had had a chance to learn to like except
the ones who ate out of white folks' kitchens but that
they had elected this out of all eating because this was
their palates and their metabolism; afterward, ten min-

utes later and then for the next four years he would be
trying to tell himself that it was the food which had
thrown him off. But he would know better; his initial
error, misjudgment had been there all the time, not even
needing to be abetted by the smell of the house and the
quilt in order to survive what had looked out (and not
even at him: just looked out) from the man's face; rising
at last and with the coin, the half-dollar already in his
hand going back into the other room: when he saw for
the first time because he happened to be facing it now
the gold-framed portrait-group on its gold easel and he
went to it, stooping to peer at it in its shadowy corner
where only the gold leaf gleamed, before he knew he
was going to do it. It had been retouched obviously;
from behind the round faintly prismatic glass dome as
out of a seer's crystal ball there looked back at him again
the calm intolerant face beneath the swaggering rake of
the hat, a tieless starched collar clipped to a white
starched shirt with a collarbutton shaped like a snake's
head and almost as large, the watch-chain looped now
across a broadcloth vest inside a broadcloth coat and
only the toothpick missing, and beside him the tiny doll-
like woman in another painted straw hat and a shawl;
that is it must have been the woman though it looked
like nobody he had ever seen before and then he realised
it was more than that: there was something ghastly, almost intolerably wrong about it or her: when she spoke
and he looked up, the man still standing straddled before
the fire and the woman sitting again in the rocking chair
in its old place almost in the corner and she was not
looking at him now and he knew she had never looked
at him since he re-entered yet she said:

'That's some more of Lucas' doings:' and he said,

'What?' and the man said,

'Molly dont like it because the man that made it took her headrag off:' and that was it, she had hair; it was like looking at an embalmed corpse through the hermetic glass lid of a coffin and he thought *Molly. Of course* because he remembered now what it was his uncle had told him about Lucas or about them. He said:

'Why did he take it off?'

'I told him to,' the man said. 'I didn't want no field nigger picture in the house:' and he walked toward them now, putting the fist holding the half-dollar back into his pocket and scooping the dime and the two nickels—all he had—into the palm with it, saying,

'You came from town. My uncle knows you—Lawyer Gavin Stevens.'

'I remember your mama too,' she said. 'She use to be Miss Maggie Dandridge.'

'That was my grandmother,' he said. 'My mother's name was Stevens too:' and extended the coins: and in the same second in which he knew she would have taken them he knew that only by that one irrevocable second was he forever now too late, forever beyond recall, standing with the slow hot blood as slow as minutes themselves up his neck and face, forever with his dumb hand open and on it the four shameful fragments of milled and minted dross, until at last the man had something that at least did the office of pity.

'What's that for?' the man said, not even moving, not even tilting his face downward to look at what was on his palm: for another eternity and only the hot dead moveless blood until at last it ran to rage so that at least he could bear the shame: and watched his palm turn over not flinging the coins but spurning them downward

ringing onto the bare floor, bouncing and one of the
nickels even rolling away in a long swooping curve with
a dry minute sound like the scurry of a small mouse:
and then his voice:

'Pick it up!'

And still nothing, the man didn't move, hands clasped
behind him, looking at nothing; only the rush of the hot
dead heavy blood out of which the voice spoke, address-
ing nobody: 'Pick up his money:' and he heard and saw
Aleck Sander and Edmonds' boy reach and scurry among
the shadows near the floor. 'Give it to him,' the voice
said: and saw Edmonds' boy drop his two coins into
Aleck Sander's palm and felt Aleck Sander's hand fumble
the four of them at his own dropped hand and then into
it. 'Now go on and shoot your rabbit,' the voice said.
'And stay out of that creek.'

Chapter Two

AND THEY WALKED again in the bright cold (even though it was noon now and about as warm as it would ever get today probably), back across the creek bridge and (suddenly: looking around, they had gone almost a half-mile along the creek and he didn't even remember it) the dog put a rabbit into a brier patch beside a cotton-field and yapping hysterically hoicked it out again, the small frantic tawny-colored blob looking one instant spherical and close-coupled as a croquet ball and the next one long as a snake, bursting out of the thicket ahead of the dog, the small white flare of its scut zigzagging across the skeletoned cottonrows like the sail of a toy boat on a windy pond while across the thicket Aleck Sander yelled:

'Shoot him! Shoot him!' then 'Whyn't you shoot him?' and then he turned without haste and walked steadily to the creek and drew the four coins from his pocket and threw them out into the water: and sleepless in bed that night he knew that the food had been not just the best Lucas had to offer but all he had to offer; he had gone out there this morning as the guest not of Edmonds but of old Carothers McCaslin's plantation and Lucas knew it when he didn't and so Lucas had beat him, stood straddled in front of the hearth and without even moving his clasped hands from behind his back had taken his

own seventy cents and beat him with them, and writhing
with impotent fury he was already thinking of the man
whom he had never seen but once and that only twelve
hours ago, as within the next year he was to learn every
white man in that whole section of the country had been
thinking about him for years: *We got to make him be a
nigger first. He's got to admit he's a nigger. Then maybe
we will accept him as he seems to intend to be accepted*.
Because he began at once to learn a good deal more about
Lucas. He didn't hear it: he learned it, all that anyone
who knew that part of the country could tell him about
the Negro who said 'ma'am' to women just as any white
man did and who said 'sir' and 'mister' to you if you were
white but who you knew was thinking neither and he
knew you knew it but who was not even waiting, daring
you to make the next move, because he didn't even care.
For instance, this.

It was a Saturday afternoon three years ago at the crossroads store four miles from Edmonds' place where at
some time during Saturday afternoon every tenant and
renter and freeholder white or black in the neighborhood
would at least pass and usually stop, quite often even to
buy something, the saddled trace-galled mules and horses
tied among the willows and birches and sycamores in the
trampled mud below the spring and their riders overflowing the store itself out onto the dusty banquette in
front, standing or squatting on their heels drinking
bottled sodapop and spitting tobacco and rolling without
hurry cigarettes and striking deliberate matches to
smoked-out pipes; this day there were three youngish
white men from the crew of a nearby sawmill, all a little
drunk, one of whom had a reputation for brawling and
violence, and Lucas came in in the worn black broad-

cloth suit which he wore to town and on Sundays and the
worn fine hat and the heavy watch-chain and the toothpick, and something happened, the story didn't say or
perhaps didn't even know what, perhaps the way Lucas
walked, entered speaking to no one and went to the
counter and made his purchase (it was a five-cent carton
of gingersnaps) and turned and tore the end from the
carton and removed the toothpick and put it into his
breast pocket and shook one of the gingersnaps into his
palm and put it into his mouth, or perhaps just nothing
was enough, the white man on his feet suddenly saying
something to Lucas, saying 'You goddamn biggity stiff-
necked stinking burrheaded Edmonds sonofabitch:' and
Lucas chewed the gingersnap and swallowed and the
carton already tilted again over his other hand, turned
his head quite slowly and looked at the white man a
moment and then said:

'I aint a Edmonds. I dont belong to these new folks.
I belongs to the old lot. I'm a McCaslin.'

'Keep on walking around here with that look on your
face and what you'll be is crowbait,' the white man said.
For another moment or at least a half one Lucas looked at
the white man with a calm speculative detachment; slowly
the carton in one of his hands tilted further until another
gingersnap dropped into his other palm, then lifting the
corner of his lip he sucked an upper tooth, quite loud
in the abrupt silence but with no implication whatever
of either derision or rebuttal or even disagreement, with
no implication of anything at all but almost abstractedly,
as a man eating gingersnaps in the middle of a hundred-
mile solitude would—if he did—suck a tooth, and said:

'Yes, I heard that idea before, And I notices that the
folks that brings it up aint even Edmondses:' whereupon

the white man even as he sprang up reached blindly back where on the counter behind him lay a half-dozen plow singletrees and snatched one of them up and had already started the downswing when the son of the store's proprietor, himself a youngish active man, came either around or over the counter and grasped the other so that the singletree merely flew harmlessly across the aisle and crashed against the cold stove; then another man was holding the man too.

'Get out of here, Lucas!' the proprietor's son said over his shoulder. But still Lucas didn't move, quite calm, not even scornful, not even contemptuous, not even very alert, the gaudy carton still poised in his left hand and the small cake in the right, just watching while the proprietor's son and his companion held the foaming and cursing white man. 'Get to hell out of here, you damn fool!' the proprietor's son shouted: and only then did Lucas move, without haste, turning without haste and going on toward the door, raising his right hand to his mouth so that as he went out the door they could see the steady thrust of his chewing.

Because there was the half-dollar. The actual sum was seventy cents of course and in four coins but he had long since during that first few fractions of a second transposed translated them into the one coin one integer in mass and weight out of all proportion to its mere convertible value; there were times in fact when, the capacity of his spirit for regret or perhaps just simple writhing or whatever it was at last spent for a moment and even quiescent, he would tell himself *At least I have the half-dollar, at least I have something* because now not only his mistake and its shame but its protagonist too— the man, the Negro, the room, the moment, the day

itself—had annealed vanished into the round hard symbol of the coin and he would seem to see himself lying
watching regretless and even peaceful as day by day the
coin swelled to its gigantic maximum, to hang fixed at
last forever in the black vault of his anguish like the last
dead and waneless moon and himself, his own puny
shadow gesticulant and tiny against it in frantic and vain
eclipse: frantic and vain yet indefatigable too because
he would never stop, he could never give up now who
had debased not merely his manhood but his whole race
too; each afternoon after school and all day Saturday,
unless there was a ballgame or he went hunting or there
was something else he wanted or needed to do, he would
go to his uncle's office where he would answer the telephone or run errands, all with some similitude of responsibility even if not actually of necessity; at least it
was an intimation of his willingness to carry some of his
own weight. He had begun it when he was a child, when
he could scarcely remember, out of that blind and absolute attachment to his mother's only brother which he
had never tried to reason about, and he had done it ever
since; later, at fifteen and sixteen and seventeen he would
think of the story of the boy and his pet calf which he
lifted over the pasture fence each day; years passed and
they were a grown man and a bull still being lifted over
the pasture fence each day.

He deserted his calf. It was less than three weeks to
Christmas; every afternoon after school and all day Saturday he was either in the Square or where he could see
it, watch it. It was cold for another day or two, then it
got warm, the wind softened then the bright sun hazed
over and it rained yet he still walked or stood about the
street where the store windows were already filling with

toys and Christmas goods and fireworks and colored
lights and evergreen and tinsel or behind the steamy
window of the drugstore or barbershop watched the
country faces, the two packages—the four two-for-a-
quarter cigars for Lucas and the tumbler of snuff for his
wife—in their bright Christmas paper in his pocket,
until at last he saw Edmonds and gave them to him to
deliver Christmas morning. But that merely discharged
(with doubled interest) the seventy cents; there still remained the dead monstrous heatless disc which hung
nightly in the black abyss of the rage and impotence:
*If he would just be a nigger first, just for one second, one
little infinitesimal second:* so in February he began to
save his money—the twenty-five cents his father gave
him each week as allowance and the twenty-five cents his
uncle paid him as office salary—until in May he had
enough and with his mother helping him chose the
flowered imitation silk dress and sent it by mail to Molly
Beauchamp, care of Carothers Edmonds R.F.D. and at
last he had something like ease because the rage was gone
and all he could not forget was the grief and the shame;
the disc still hung in the black vault but it was almost a
year old now and so the vault itself was not so black with
the disc paling and he could even sleep under it as even
the insomniac dozes at last under his waning and glare-
less moon. Then it was September; school would begin
in another week. He came home one afternoon and his
mother was waiting for him.

'Here's something for you,' she said. It was a gallon
bucket of fresh homemade sorghum molasses and he
knew the answer at once long before she finished speaking: 'Somebody from Mr Edmonds' place sent it to you.'

'Lucas Beauchamp,' he said, cried almost. 'How long has he been gone? Why didn't he wait for me?'

'No,' his mother said. 'He didn't bring it himself. He sent it in. A white boy brought it on a mule.'

And that was all. They were right back where they had started; it was all to do over again; it was even worse this time because this time Lucas had commanded a white hand to pick up his money and give it back to him. Then he realised that he couldn't even start over again because to take the can of molasses back and fling it into Lucas' front door would only be the coins again for Lucas again to command somebody to pick up and return, not to mention the fact that he would have to ride a Shetland pony which he had outgrown and was ashamed of except that his mother wouldn't agree yet to let him have a fullsized horse or at least the kind of full-sized horse he wanted and that his uncle had promised him, seventeen miles in order to reach the door to fling it through. This would have to be all; whatever would or could set him free was beyond not merely his reach but even his ken; he could only wait for it if it came and do without it if it didn't.

And four years later he had been free almost eighteen months and he thought it was all: old Molly dead and her and Lucas' married daughter moved with her husband to Detroit and he heard now at last by chance remote and belated hearsay that Lucas was living alone in the house, solitary kinless and intractable, apparently not only without friends even in his own race but proud of it. He had seen him three times more, on the Square in town and not always on Saturday—in fact it would be a year from the last time before he would realise that he had never seen him in town on Saturday when all the other Negroes and most of the whites too from the country came in, nor even that the occasions when he did see him were almost exactly a year apart and that the reason he saw him then was not that Lucas' presence had happened to coincide with his own chance passage through the Square but that he had coincided with Lucas' annual and necessary visits—but on weekdays like the white men who were not farmers but planters, who wore neckties and vests like the merchants and doctors and lawyers themselves, as if he refused, declined to accept even that little of the pattern not only of Negro but of country Negro behavior, and always in the worn brushed obviously once-expensive black broadcloth suit of the portrait-photograph on the gold easel and the raked fine hat and the boiled white shirt of his own grandfather's time and the tieless collar and the heavy watch-chain and the gold toothpick like the one his own grandfather had carried in his upper vest pocket: the first time in the second winter; he had spoken first though Lucas had remembered him at once; he thanked him for the molasses and Lucas had answered exactly as his grandfather himself might, only the words, the grammar any different:

'They turned out good this year. When I was making um I remembered how a boy's always got a sweet tooth for good molasses:' and went on, saying over his shoulder: 'Dont fall in no more creeks this winter:' and saw him twice more after that—the black suit, the hat, the watch-chain but the next time he didn't have the toothpick and this time Lucas looked straight at him, straight into his eyes from five feet away and passed him and he thought *He has forgotten me. He doesn't even remember me anymore* until almost the next year when his uncle

told him that Molly, the old wife, had died a year ago.
Nor did he bother, take time to wonder then how his
uncle (obviously Edmonds had told him) happened to
know about it because he was already counting rapidly
backward; he said thought with a sense of vindication,
easement, triumph almost: *She had just died then. That
was why he didn't see me. That was why he didn't have
the toothpick:* thinking with a kind of amazement: *He
was grieving. You dont have to not be a nigger in order
to grieve* and then he found that he was waiting, haunt-
ing the Square almost as he had done two years ago when
he was watching for Edmonds to give him the two Christmas presents to deliver, through the next two then three
then four months before it occurred to him that when
he had seen Lucas in town it had always been only once
each year in January or February and then for the first
time he realised why: he had come in to pay the yearly
taxes on his land. So it was late January, a bright cold
afternoon. He stood on the bank corner in the thin sun
and saw Lucas come out of the courthouse and cross the
Square directly toward him, in the black suit and the
tieless shirt and the fine old hat at its swaggering rake,
walking so erect that the coat touched him only across
the shoulders from which it hung and he could already
see the cocked slanted glint of the gold toothpick and
he could feel the muscles of his face, waiting and then
Lucas looked up and once more looked straight into his
eyes for perhaps a quarter of a minute and then away
and came straight on and then even side-stepped a little
in order to pass him and passed him and went on; nor
did he look back either, standing at the curb-edge in the
thin cold sun thinking *He didn't even fail to remember
me this time. He didn't even know me. He hasn't even*

bothered to forget me: thinking in a sort of peace even:
It's over. That was all because he was free, the man who
for three years had obsessed his life waking and sleeping
too had walked out of it. He would see him again of
course; without doubt they would pass on the street in
town like this once each year for the rest of Lucas' life
but that would be all: the one no longer the man but
only the ghost of him who had ordered the two Negro
boys to pick up his money and give it back to him; the
other only the memory of the child who had offered it
and then flung it down, carrying into manhood only the
fading tagend of that old once-frantic shame and anguish
and need not for revenge, vengeance but simply for re-
equalization, reaffirmation of his masculinity and his
white blood. And someday the one would not even be
any longer the ghost of the man who had ordered the
coins picked up and to the other the shame and anguish
would no longer be a thing remembered and recallable
but merely a breath a whisper like the bitter-sweet-sour
taste of the sheep sorrel eaten by the boy in his dead
childhood, remembered only in the instant of tasting
and forgotten before it could be placed and remembered;
he could imagine them as old men meeting, quite old, at
some point in that agony of naked inanesthetisable nerve-
ends which for lack of a better word men call being alive
at which not only their elapsed years but the half-century
of discrepancy between them would be as indistinguishable and uncountable as that many sand grains in a coal
pile and he saying to Lucas: *I was the boy who when you
gave me half of your dinner tried to pay you with some
things which people in those days called seventy cents'
worth of money and so all I could think of to save my
face was to fling it on the floor? Dont you remember?*

and Lucas: *Was that me?* or vice versa, turned around and it was Lucas saying *I was the man when you throwed your money on the floor and wouldn't pick it up I had to have two niggers pick it up and hand it back to you? Dont you remember?* and he this time: *Was that me?* Because it was over now. He had turned the other cheek and it had been accepted. He was free.

Then he came back through the Square late that Saturday afternoon (there had been a ball game on the High School field) and he heard that Lucas had killed Vinson Gowrie out at Fraser's store; word had come for the sheriff about three oclock and had been relayed on by another party-line telephone down into the opposite corner of the county where the sheriff had gone this morning on business and where a messenger might quite possibly find him some time between now and tomorrow's sunup: which would make little difference since even if the sheriff had been in his office he would probably be too late since Fraser's store was in Beat Four and if Yoknapatawpha County was the wrong place for a nigger to shoot a white man in the back then Beat Four was the last place even in Yoknapatawpha County a nigger with any judgment—or any other stranger of any color—would have chosen to shoot anybody least of all one named Gowrie before or behind either; already the last car full of the young men and some not so young whose business addresses not only on Saturday afternoons but all week too were the poolhall and the barbershop and some of whom even had some vague connection with cotton or automobiles or land- and stock-sales, who bet on prizefights and punchboards and national ball-games, had long since left the Square to hurry the fifteen miles to park along the highway in front of the con-

stable's house where the constable had taken Lucas and
the story said had handcuffed him to a bedpost and was
now sitting over him with a shotgun (and Edmonds too
of course by now; even a fool country constable would
have had sense enough to send for Edmonds only four
miles away even before hollering for the sheriff) in case
the Gowries and their connections decided not to wait
until they had buried Vinson first; of course Edmonds
would be there; if Edmonds had been in town today he
would certainly have seen him at some time during the
morning and before he went to the ballpark and since he
had not obviously Edmonds had been at home, only four
miles away; a messenger could have reached him and
Edmonds himself could have been at the constable's
house almost before the other messenger had memorised
the sheriff's telephone and the message to give him and
then rode to the nearest telephone where he could use
either: which—Edmonds (again something nagged for a
second's flash at his attention) and the constable—would
be two while the Lord Himself would have to stop to
count the Gowries and Ingrums and Workitts and if
Edmonds was busy eating supper or reading the paper or
counting his money or something the constable would
be just one even with the shotgun: but then he was free,
hardly even pausing really, walking on to the corner
where he would turn for home and not until he saw how
much of sun, how much was left of afternoon still in the
street then turned back retracing his steps for several
yards before he remembered why in the world he didn't
cut straight across the now almost empty Square to the
outside stairs leading up to the office.

Though of course there was really no reason to expect
his uncle to be in the office this late on Saturday after-

noon but once on the stairs he could at least throw that
away, happening to be wearing rubber soles today though
even then the wooden stairs creaked and rumbled unless
you trod the inside edge close to the wall: thinking how
he had never really appreciated rubber soles before, how
nothing could match them for giving you time to make
up your mind what you really wanted to do and then he
could see the office door closed now although it was still
too early for his uncle to have had the lights on but
besides the door itself had that look which only locked
doors have so even hard soles wouldn't have mattered,
unlocking the door with his key then locking it with
the thumb-latch behind him and crossed to the heavy
swivel roller chair which had been his grandfather's before his uncle's and sat down behind the littered table
which his uncle used in place of the rolltop desk of his
grandfather's old time and across which the county's legal
business had passed longer than he could remember,
since in fact his memory was memory or anyway his, and
so battered table and dogeared faded papers and the
needs and passions they represented and the measured
and bounded county too were all coeval and one, the last
of the sun coming through the mulberry tree then the
window behind him onto the table the stacked untidy
papers the inkwell the tray of paperclips and fouled
rusted penpoints and pipecleaners and the overturned
corncob pipe in its spill of ash beside the stained un-
washed coffeecup and saucer and the colored mug from
the Heidelberg *stübe* filled with twisted spills of newspaper to light the pipes with like the vase sitting on
Lucas' mantel that day and before he even knew he had
thought of it he rose taking up the cup and saucer and
crossed the room picking up the coffeepot and the kettle

too in passing and in the lavatory emptied the grounds
and rinsed the pot and cup and filled the kettle and set
it and the pot the cup and saucer back on the shelf and
returned to the chair and sat down again after really no
absence at all, still in plenty of time to watch the table
and all its familiar untidy clutter all fading toward one
anonymity of night as the sunlight died: thinking remembering how his uncle had said that all man had was
time, all that stood between him and the death he feared
and abhorred was time yet he spent half of it inventing
ways of getting the other half past: and suddenly he remembered from nowhere what it was that had been nag-
ging at his attention: Edmonds was not at home nor
even in Mississippi; he was in a hospital in New Orleans
being operated on for gallstones, the heavy chair making
a rumbling clatter on the wooden floor almost as loud
as a wagon on a wooden bridge as he rose and then stood
beside the table until the echo died away and there was
only the sound of his breathing: because he was free: and
then he moved: because his mother would know what
time baseball games finished even if she couldn't have
heard the yelling from across the edge of town and she
would know that even he could use up only so much of
twilight getting home, locking the door behind him then
down the stairs again, the Square filled with dusk now
and the first lights coming on in the drugstore (they
had never been off in the barbershop and the poolhall
since the bootblack and the porter unlocked the doors
and swept out the hair and cigarette stubs at six oclock
this morning) and the mercantile ones too so that the
rest of the county except Beat Four would have somewhere to wait until word could come in from Fraser's
store that all was okeydoke again and they could unpark

the trucks and cars and wagons and mules from the back
streets and alleys and go home and go to bed: turning the
corner this time and now the jail, looming, lightless except for the one crossbarred rectangle in the upper front
wall where on ordinary nights the nigger crapshooters
and whiskey-peddlers and razor-throwers would be yelling down to their girls and women on the street below
and where Lucas would have been these three hours now
(very likely banging on the steel door for somebody to
bring him his supper or perhaps having already had it
and now merely to complain about its quality since
without doubt he would consider that his right too along
with the rest of his lodging and keep) except that people
seemed to hold that the one sole end of the entire estab-
lishment of public office was to elect one man like Sheriff
Hampton big enough or at least with sense and character
enough to run the county and then fill the rest of the
jobs with cousins and inlaws who had failed to make a
living at everything else they ever tried. But then he
was free and besides it was probably all over by now
and even if it wasn't he knew what he was going to do
and there was plenty of time yet for that, tomorrow
would be time enough for that; all he would need to do
tonight was to give Highboy about two extra cups of
oats against tomorrow and at first he believed he was or
at least in a moment was going to be ravenously hungry
himself, sitting down at the familiar table in the familiar
room among the bright linen and silver and the water
glasses and the bowl of narcissus and gladioli and a few
roses in it too and his uncle said,

'Your friend Beauchamp seems to have done it this
time.'

'Yes,' he said. 'They're going to make a nigger out of him once in his life anyway.'

'Charles!' his mother said.—eating rapidly, eating quite a lot and talking rapidly and quite a lot too about the ballgame and waiting to get hungry any minute any second now until suddenly he knew that even the last bite had been too much, still chewing at it to get it down to where it would swallow, already getting up.

'I'm going to the picture show,' he said.

'You haven't finished,' his mother said: then she said, 'The show doesn't begin for almost an hour yet:' and then not even just to his father and uncle but to all time all A.D. of Our Lord one thousand and nine hundred and thirty and forty and fifty: 'I dont want him to go to town tonight. I dont want—' and then at last one wail one cry to the supreme: his father himself: out of that nightraddled dragonregion of fears and terrors in which women—mothers anyway—seemed from choice almost to dwell: 'Charlie—' until his uncle put his napkin down and rose too and said:

'Then here's your chance to wean him. I want him to do an errand for me anyway:' and out: on the front gallery in the dark cool and after a while his uncle said: 'Well? Go on.'

'Aint you coming?' he said. Then he said, 'But why? Why?'

'Does that matter?' his uncle said, and then said what he had already heard when he passed the barbershop going on two hours ago now: 'Not now. Not to Lucas nor anybody else of his color out there.' But he had already thought of that himself not just before his uncle said it but even before whoever it had been in front of the barbershop two hours ago did, and for that matter the rest of it too: 'In fact the true why is not what crisis he faced beyond which life would be no longer bearable until he shot a white man in the back but why of all white men he must pick a Gowrie to shoot and out of all possible places Beat Four to do it in. —Go on. But don't be late. After all a man ought to be kind even to his parents now and then.'

And sure enough one of the cars and for all he knew maybe all of them had got back to the barbershop and the poolhall so apparently Lucas was still chained and peaceful to the bedpost and the constable sitting over him (it was probably a rocking chair) with the cold shotgun and probably the constable's wife had served their supper there and Lucas with a good appetite, sharp set for his since he not only wouldn't have to pay for it but you dont shoot somebody every day in the week: and at last it seemed to be more or less authentic that the sheriff had finally got the word and sent word back that he would return to town late tonight and would fetch Lucas in early tomorrow morning and he would have to do something, pass the time somehow until the picture show was out so he might as well go to it and he crossed the Square to the courthouse yard and sat down on a bench in the dark cool empty solitude among the bitten shadows the restless unwindy vernal leaves against the starry smore of heaven where he could watch the lighted marquee in front of the picture show and perhaps the sheriff was right; he seemed able to establish enough contact with Gowries and Ingrums and Workitts and McCallums to persuade them to vote for him every eight years so maybe he knew approximately what they would do under given situations or perhaps the people in the barbershop were right and the Ingrums and Gowries and Workitts

were waiting not until they had buried Vinson tomorrow
but simply because it would be Sunday in three hours
now and they didn't want to have to hurry, bolt through
the business in order to finish it by midnight and not
violate the Sabbath: then the first of the crowd dribbled
then flowed beneath the marquee blinking into the light
and even fumbling a little for a second or even a minute
or two yet, bringing back into the shabby earth a fading
remnant of the heart's celluloid and derring dream so
he could go home now, in fact he would have to: who
knew by simple instinct when picture shows were over
just as she did when ballgames were and though she
would never really forgive him for being able to button
his own buttons and wash behind his ears at least she
accepted it and would not come after him herself but
merely send his father and by starting now ahead of the
picture show's dispersal he would have the empty street
until he got home, until he reached the corner of the
yard in fact and his uncle stepped out from beside the
hedge, hatless, smoking one of the cob pipes.

'Listen,' his uncle said. 'I talked to Hampton down at
Peddlers Field Old Town and he had already telephoned
Squire Fraser and Fraser himself went to Skipworth's
house and saw Lucas handcuffed to the bedpost and it's
all right, everything's quiet out there tonight and tomorrow morning Hampton will have Lucas locked up in the
jail—'

'I know,' he said. 'They wont lynch him until after
midnight tomorrow night, after they have buried Vinson
and got rid of Sunday:' walking on: 'It's all right with
me. Lucas didn't have to work this hard not to be a
nigger just on my account.' Because he was free: in bed:
in the cool familiar room in the cool familiar dark be-

cause he knew what he was going to do and he had forgotten after all to tell Aleck Sander to give Highboy the
extra feed against tomorrow but in the morning would
do just as well because he was going to sleep tonight because he had something about ten thousand times quicker
than just sheep to count; in fact he was going to go to
sleep so fast he probably wouldn't have time to count
more than about ten of them: with rage, an almost unbearable excruciation of outrage and fury: any white
man to shoot in the back but this one of all white men
at all: youngest of a family of six brothers one of whom
had already served a year in federal penitentiary for
armed resistance as an army deserter and another term
at the state penal farm for making whiskey, and a rami-
fication of cousins and inlaws covering a whole corner of
the county and whose total number probably even the
old grandmothers and maiden aunts couldn't have stated
offhand—a connection of brawlers and farmers and foxhunters and stock- and timber-traders who would not
even be the last anywhere to let one of its number be
killed by anyone but only among the last since it in its
turn was integrated and interlocked and intermarried
with other brawlers and foxhunters and whiskeymakers
not even into a simple clan or tribe but a race a species
which before now had made their hill stronghold good
against the county and the federal government too,
which did not even simply inhabit nor had merely cor-
rupted but had translated and transmogrified that
whole region of lonely pine hills dotted meagrely with
small tilted farms and peripatetic sawmills and contra-
band whiskey-kettles where peace officers from town
didn't even go unless they were sent for and strange
white men didn't wander far from the highway after

dark and no Negro at any time—where as a local wit
said once the only stranger ever to enter with impunity
was God and He only by daylight and on Sunday—into
a synonym for independence and violence: an idea with
physical boundaries like a quarantine for plague so that
solitary unique and alone out of all the county it was
known to the rest of the county by the number of its
survey co-ordinate—Beat Four—as in the middle twenties
people knew where Cicero Illinois was and who lived
there and what they did who neither knew nor cared
what state Chicago was in: and since this was not enough
choosing the one moment when the one man white or
black—Edmonds—out of all Yoknapatawpha County or
Mississippi or America or the world too for that matter
who would have had any inclination let alone power and
ability (and here he had to laugh even though he was
just about to go to sleep, remembering how he had even
thought at first that if Edmonds had been at home it
would have made any difference anywhere, remembering
the face the angle of the hat the figure straddled baronial
as a duke or a squire or a congressman before the fire
hands clasped behind it and not even looking down at
them but just commanding two nigger boys to pick up
the coins and give them back to him, not even needing
to remember his uncle reminding him ever since he had
got big enough to understand the words that no man
could come between another man and his destiny because even his uncle for all Harvard and Heidelberg
couldn't have pointed out the man with enough temerity
and delusion just to come between Lucas and merely
what he wanted to do) to try to stand between Lucas and
the violent fate he had courted was lying flat on his back
in a New Orleans operating room: yet that was what

Lucas had had to pick, that time that victim and that place: another Saturday afternoon and the same store where he had already had trouble with a white man at least once before: chose the first suitable convenient Saturday afternoon and with an old single action Colt pistol of a calibre and type not even made anymore which was exactly the sort of pistol Lucas would own exactly as no other still alive man in the county owned a gold toothpick lay in wait at the store—the one sure place where sooner or later on Saturday afternoon that whole end of the county would pass—until the victim appeared and shot him and nobody knew why yet and as far as he had discovered that afternoon or even when he finally left the Square that night nobody had even wondered yet since why didn't matter least of all to Lucas since he had apparently he had been working for twenty or twentyfive years with indefatigable and un- flagging concentration toward this one crowning mo- ment; followed him into the woods about one good spit from the store and shot him in the back within hearing distance of the crowd around it and was still standing over the body the fired pistol put neatly away into his hip pocket again when the first ones reached the scene where he would without doubt have been lynched im- mediately out of hand except for the same Doyle Fraser who had saved him from the singletree seven years ago and old Skipworth, the constable—a little driedup wizened stonedeaf old man not much larger than a half- grown boy with a big nickelplated pistol loose in one coat pocket and in the other a guttapercha eartrumpet on a rawhide thong around his neck like a foxhorn, who on this occasion anyway revealed an almost gratuitous hardihood and courage, getting Lucas (who made no re-

sistance whatever, merely watching this too with that
same calm detached not even scornful interest) out of the
crowd and took him to his home and chained him to
the bedpost until the sheriff could come and get him
and bring him in to town and keep him while the
Gowries and Workitts and Ingrums and the rest of their
guests and connections could get Vinson buried and
Sunday passed and so be fresh and untrammelled for the
new week and its duties and believe it or not even the
night passed, the tentative roosters at false dawn then the
interval then the loud fairy clangor of the birds and
through the east window he could see the trees against
gray light and then the sun itself high and furious above
the trees glaring at him and it was already late, this of
course must happen to him too: but then he was free
and he would feel better after breakfast and he could
always say he was going to Sunday school but then he
wouldn't have to say anything by going out the back,
strolling: across the back yard and into the lot and across
it and through the woods to the railroad to the depot
and then back to the Square then he thought of a simpler
way than that and then quit thinking about it at all,
through the front hall and across the front gallery and
down the walk to the street and it was here he would
remember later having first noticed that he had seen no
Negro except Paralee when she brought his breakfast;
by ordinary at this hour on Sunday morning he would
have seen on almost every gallery housemaids or cooks
in their fresh Sunday aprons with brooms or perhaps
talking from gallery to gallery across the contiguous
yardspaces and the children too fresh and scrubbed for
Sunday school with clutched palmsweaty nickels though
perhaps it was a little too early for that or perhaps by

mutual consent or even interdiction there would be no
Sunday school today, only church and so at some mutual
concorded moment say about halfpast eleven all the air
over Yoknapatawpha County would reverbèrate sound·
lessly like heatshimmer with one concerted adjuration
calm the hearts of these bereaved and angry men vengeance is mine saith the lord thou shalt not kill except
that this was a little late too, they should have mentioned
this to Lucas yesterday, past the jail the barred second
storey window whose interstices on an ordinary Sunday
would have been thick with dark hands and beyond
them even a glint now and then of eyewhites in the shadows and the mellow voices calling and laughing down
to the Negro girls and women passing or stopping along
the street and this was when he realised that except for
Paralee he had seen no Negro since yesterday afternoon
though it would be tomorrow before he would learn
that the ones who lived in the Hollow and Freedman-
town hadn't come to work at all since Saturday night:
nor on the Square either, not even in the barbershop
where Sunday morning was the bootblack's best day
shining shoes and brushing clothes and running errands
and drawing baths for the bachelor truckdrivers and
garage hands who lived in rented rooms and the young
men and the ones not so young who worked hard all
week in the poolhall and the sheriff really had finally
got back to town and had even torn himself away from
his Sunday to go for Lucas: listening: hearing the talk:
a dozen of them who had hurried out to Fraser's store
yesterday afternoon and returned empty-handed (and
he gathered one car full had even gone back last night,
yawning and lounging now and complaining of lack of
sleep: and that to be added to Lucas' account too) and

he had heard all this before too and had even thought
of it himself before that:

'I wonder if Hampton took a shovel .with him. That's
all he's going to need.'

'They'll lend him a shovel out there.'

'Yes—if there's anything to bury. They have gasoline
even in Beat Four.'

'I thought old Skipworth was going to take care of
that.'

'Sure. But that's Beat Four. They'll do what Skipworth
tells them as long as he's got the nigger. But he's going
to turn him over to Hampton. That's when it'll happen.
Hope Hampton might be sheriff in Yoknapatawpha
County but he's just another man in Beat Four.'

'No. They wont do nothing today. They're burying
Vinson this afternoon and to burn a nigger right while
the funeral's going on wouldn't be respectful to Vinson.'

'That's so. It'll probably be tonight.'

'On Sunday night?'

'Is that the Gowries' fault? Lucas ought to thought of
that before he picked out Saturday to kill Vinson on.'

'I don't know about that. Hope Hampton's going to
be a hard man to take a prisoner away from too.'

'A nigger murderer? Who in this county or state
either is going to help him protect a nigger that shoots
white men in the back?'

'Or the South either.'

'Yes. Or the South either.' He had heard it all before:
outside again now: only his uncle might decide to come
to town before time to go for the noon mail at the postoffice and if his uncle didn't see him then he really could
tell his mother he didn't know where he was and of
course he thought first of the empty office but if he went

there that's exactly where his uncle would come too: because—and he remembered again that he had forgot to
give Highboy the extra feed this morning too but it was
too late now and besides he was going to carry feed with
him anyway—he knew exactly what he was going to do:
the sheriff had left town about nine oclock; the constable's house was fifteen miles away on a gravel road
not too good but the sheriff should certainly go there and
be back with Lucas by noon even if he stopped to make
a few votes while there; long before that time he would
go home and saddle Highboy and tie a sack of feed behind the saddle and turn him in a straight line in the
opposite direction from Fraser's store and ride in that
one undeviable direction for twelve hours which would
be about midnight tonight and feed Highboy and rest
him until daylight or even longer if he decided to and
then ride the twelve hours back which would be eighteen actually or maybe even twenty-four or even thirty-
six but at least all over finished done, no more fury and
outrage to have to lie in bed with like trying to put
yourself to sleep counting sheep and he turned the corner
and went along the opposite side of the street and under
the shed in front of the closed blacksmith shop, the heavy
double wooden doors not locked with a hasp or latch
but with a padlocked chain passed through an augerhole
in each one so that the slack of the chain created an
insag almost like an alcove; standing in it nobody could
have seen him from either up the street or down it nor
even passing along it (which would not be his mother
anyway today) unless they stopped to look and now the
bells began ringing in mellow unhurried discordant
strophe and antistrophe from steeple to pigeonswirled
steeple across the town, streets and Square one sudden

decorous flow of men in their dark suits and women in
silks and parasols and girls and young men two and two,
flowing and decorous beneath that mellow uproar into
that musical clamor: gone, Square and street empty
again though still the bells rang on for a while yet, sky-
dwellers, groundless denizens of the topless air too high
too far insentient to the crawling earth then ceasing
stroke by hasteless stroke from the subterrene shudder
of organs and the cool frantic monotone of the settled
pigeons. Two years ago his uncle had told him that there
was nothing wrong with cursing; on the contrary it was
not only useful but substituteless but like everything
else valuable it was precious only because the supply was
limited and if you wasted it on nothing on its urgent
need you might find yourself bankrupt so he said *What
the hell am I doing here* then answered himself the obvious answer: not to see Lucas, he had seen Lucas but
so that Lucas could see him again if he so wished, to
look back at him not just from the edge of mere unique-
less death but from the gasoline-roar of apotheosis. Because he was free. Lucas was no longer his responsibility,
he was no longer Lucas' keeper; Lucas himself had discharged him.

Then suddenly the empty street was full of men. Yet
there were not many of them, not two dozen, some suddenly and quietly from nowhere. Yet they seemed to fill
it, block it, render it suddenly interdict as though not
that nobody could pass them, pass through it, use it as
a street but that nobody would dare, would even ap-
proach near enough to essay the gambit as people
stay well away from a sign saying High Voltage or Ex-
plosive. He knew, recognised them all; some of them
he had even seen and listened to in the barbershop two

hours ago—the young men or men under forty, bachelors, the homeless who had the Saturday and Sunday
baths in the barbershop—truckdrivers and garagehands,
the oiler from the cotton gin, a sodajerker from the drugstore and the ones who could be seen all week long in
or around the poolhall who did nothing at all that anyone knew, who owned automobiles and spent money
nobody really knew exactly how they earned on week-
ends in Memphis or New Orleans brothels—the men
who his uncle said were in every little Southern town,
who never really led mobs nor even instigated them but
were always the nucleus of them because of their mass
availability. Then he saw the car; he recognised it too
even in the distance without knowing or for that matter
stopping to wonder how, himself moving out of his con-
cealing doorway into the street and then across it to the
edge of the crowd which made no sound but just stood
there blocking the sidewalk beside the jail fence and
overflowing into the street while the car came up not fast
but quite deliberately, almost decorously as a car should
move on Sunday morning, and drew in to the curb in
front of the jail and stopped. A deputy was driving it.
He made no move to get out. Then the rear door opened
and the sheriff emerged—a big, a tremendous man with
no fat and little hard pale eyes in a cold almost bland
pleasant face who without even glancing at them turned
and held the door open. Then Lucas got out, slowly
and stiffly, exactly like a man who has spent the night
chained to a bedpost, fumbling a little and bumping or
at least raking his head against the top of the door so
that as he emerged his crushed hat tumbled from his
head onto the pavement almost under his feet. And that
was the first time he had ever seen Lucas without the hat

on and in the same second he realised that with the
possible exception of Edmonds they there in the street
watching him were probably the only white people in
the county who had ever seen him uncovered: watching
as, still bent over as he had emerged from the car, Lucas
began to reach stiffly for the hat. But already in one vast
yet astonishingly supple stoop the sheriff had picked it
up and handed it back to Lucas who still bent over
seemed to fumble at the hat too. Yet almost at once the
hat was creased back into its old shape and now Lucas
was standing up, erect except for his head, his face as
he brushed the hat back and forth against the sleeve of
his forearm rapid and light and deft as you stroke a razor.
Then his head, his face went back and up too and in a
motion not quite sweeping he set the hat back on his
head at the old angle which the hat itself seemed to
assume as if he had flung it up, and erect now in the
black suit crumpled too from whatever night he had
spent (there was a long grimed smear down one entire
side from shoulder to ankle as if he had been lying on
an unswept floor a long time in one position without
being able to change it) Lucas looked at them for the
first time and he thought *Now. He will see me now* and
then he thought *He saw me. And that's all* and then he
thought *He hasn't seen anybody* because the face was not
even looking at them but just toward them, arrogant
and calm and with no more defiance in it than fear: detached, impersonal, almost musing, intractable and composed, the eyes blinking a little in the sunlight even
after the sound, an indraw of breath went up from somewhere in the crowd and a single voice said:

'Knock it off again, Hope. Take his head too this
time.'

'You boys get out of here,' the sheriff said. 'Go back to the barbershop:' turning, saying to Lucas: 'All right. Come on.' And that was all, the face for another moment looking not at them but just toward them, the sheriff already walking toward the jail door when Lucas turned at last to follow him and by hurrying a little he could even get Highboy saddled and be out of the lot before his mother began to send Aleck Sander to look for him to come and eat dinner. Then he saw Lucas stop and turn and he was wrong because Lucas even knew where he was in the crowd before he turned, looking straight at him before he got turned around even, speaking to him:

'You, young man,' Lucas said. 'Tell your uncle I wants to see him:' then turned again and walked on after the sheriff, still a little stiffly in the smeared black suit, the hat arrogant and pale in the sunlight, the voice in the crowd saying:

'Lawyer hell. He wont even need an undertaker when them Gowries get through with him tonight:' walking on past the sheriff who himself had stopped now and was looking back at them, saying in his mild cold bland heatless voice:

'I told you folks once to get out of here. I aint going to tell you again.'

Chapter Three

So IF HE HAD GONE straight home from the barbershop this morning and saddled Highboy when he first thought of it he would be ten hours away by now, probably fifty miles.

There were no bells now. What people on the street now would have been going to the less formal more intimate evening prayer-meeting, walking decorously across the shadow-bitten darkness from streetlamp to streetlamp; so in keeping with the Sabbath's still suspension that he and his uncle would have been passing them steadily, recognising them yards ahead without knowing or even pausing to speculate on when or how or why they had done so—not by silhouette nor even the voice needed: the presence, the aura perhaps; perhaps merely the juxtaposition: this living entity at this point at this moment on this day, as is all you need to recognise the people with, among whom you have lived all your life—stepping off the concrete onto the bordering grass to pass them, speaking (his uncle) to them by name, perhaps exchanging a phrase, a sentence then on, onto the concrete again.

But tonight the street was empty. The very houses themselves looked close and watchful and tense as though the people who lived in them, who on this soft May night (those who had not gone to church) would have been sitting on the dark galleries for a little while after supper in rocking chairs or porchswings, talking quietly among themselves or perhaps talking from gallery to gallery when the houses were close enough. But tonight they passed only one man and he was not walking but standing just inside the front gate to a small neat shoebox of a house built last year between two other houses already close enough together to hear one another's toilets flush (his uncle had explained that: 'When you were born and raised and lived all your life where you cant hear anything but owls at night and roosters at dawn and on damp days when sound carries your nearest neighbor chopping wood two miles away, you like to live where you can hear and smell people on either side of you every time they flush a drain or open a can of salmon or of soup.'), himself darker than shadow and certainly stiller—a countryman who had moved to town a year ago and now owned a small shabby side street grocery whose customers were mostly Negroes, whom they had not even seen until they were almost on him though he had already recognised them or at least his uncle some distance away and was waiting for them, already speaking to his uncle before they came abreast of him:

'Little early, aint you, Lawyer? Them Beat Four folks have got to milk and then chop wood to cook breakfast tomorrow with before they can eat supper and get in to town.'

'Maybe they'll decide to stay at home on a Sunday night,' his uncle said pleasantly, passing on: whereupon the man said almost exactly what the man in the barbershop had said this morning (and he remembered his uncle saying once how little of vocabulary man really

needed to get comfortably and even efficiently through
his life, how not only in the individual but within his
whole type and race and kind a few simple clichés served
his few simple passions and needs and lusts):

'Sho now. It aint their fault it's Sunday. That sonofabitch ought to thought of that before he taken to killing
white men on a Saturday afternoon.' Then he called
after them as they went on, raising his voice: 'My wife
aint feeling good tonight, and besides I dont want to
stand around up there just looking at the front of that
jail. But tell um to holler if they need help.'

'I expect they know already they can depend on you,
Mr Lilley,' his uncle said. They went on. 'You see?' his
uncle said. 'He has nothing against what he calls niggers.
If you ask him, he will probably tell you he likes them
even better than some white folks he knows and he will
believe it. They are probably constantly beating him out
of a few cents here and there in his store and probably
even picking up things—packages of chewing gum or
bluing or a banana or a can of sardines or a pair of shoe-
laces or a bottle of hair-straightener—under their coats
and aprons and he knows it; he probably even gives them
things free of charge—the bones and spoiled meat out of
his butcher's icebox and spoiled candy and lard. All he
requires is that they act like niggers. Which is exactly
what Lucas is doing: blew his top and murdered a white
man—which Mr Lilley is probably convinced all Negroes want to do—and now the white people will take
him out and burn him, all regular and in order and
themselves acting exactly as he is convinced Lucas would
wish them to act: like white folks; both of them observ-
ing implicitly the rules: the nigger acting like a nigger
and the white folks acting like white folks and no real

hard feelings on either side (since Mr Lilley is not a
Gowrie) once the fury is over; in fact Mr Lilley would
probably be one of the first to contribute cash money
toward Lucas' funeral and the support of his widow and
children if he had them. Which proves again how no
man can cause more grief than that one clinging blindly
to the vices of his ancestors.'

Now they could see the Square, empty too—the am-
phitheatric lightless stores, the slender white pencil of
the Confederate monument against the mass of the courthouse looming in columned upsoar to the dim quadruple
face of the clock lighted each by a single faint bulb with
a quality as intransigeant against those four fixed me-
chanical shouts of adjuration and warning as the glow
of a firefly. Then the jail and at that moment, with a
flash and glare and wheel of lights and a roar of engine at
once puny against the vast night and the empty town yet
insolent too, a car rushed from nowhere and circled the
Square; a voice, a young man's voice squalled from it—
no words, not even a shout: a squall significant and
meaningless—and the car rushed on around the Square,
completing the circle back to nowhere and died away.
They turned in at the jail.

It was of brick, square, proportioned, with four brick
columns in shallow basrelief across the front and even a
brick cornice under the eaves because it was old, built
in a time when people took time to build even jails with
grace and care and he remembered how his uncle had
said once that not courthouses nor even churches but
jails were the true records of a county's, a community's
history, since not only the cryptic forgotten initials and
words and even phrases cries of defiance and indictment
scratched into the walls but the very bricks and stones

themselves held, not in solution but in suspension, intact
and biding and potent and indestructible, the agonies
and shames and griefs with which hearts long since un-
marked and unremembered dust had strained and perhaps burst. Which was certainly true of this one because
it and one of the churches were the oldest buildings in
the town, the courthouse and everything else on or in the
Square having been burned to rubble by Federal occu-
pation forces after a battle in 1864. Because scratched
into one of the panes of the fanlight beside the door was
a young girl's single name, written by her own hand into
the glass with a diamond in that same year and sometimes two or three times a year he would go up onto the
gallery to look at it, it cryptic now in reverse, not for a
sense of the past but to realise again the eternality, the
deathlessness and changelessness of youth—the name of
one of the daughters of the jailer of that time (and his
uncle who had for everything an explanation not in facts
but long since beyond dry statistics into something far
more moving because it was truth: which moved the
heart and had nothing whatever to do with what mere
provable information said, had told him this too: how
this part of Mississippi was new then, as a town a settlement a community less than fifty years old, and all the
men who had come into it less long ago almost than even
the oldest's lifetime were working together to secure it,
doing the base jobs along with the splendid ones not for
pay or politics but to shape a land for their posterity, so
that a man could be the jailer then or the innkeeper or
farrier or vegetable peddler yet still be what the lawyer
and planter and doctor and parson called a gentleman)
who stood at that window that afternoon and watched
the battered remnant of a Confederate brigade retreat

through the town, meeting suddenly across that space the eyes of the ragged unshaven lieutenant who led one of the broken companies, scratching into the glass not his name also, not only because a young girl of that time would never have done that but because she didn't know his name then, let alone that six months later he would be her husband.

In fact it still looked like a residence with its balustraded wooden gallery stretching across the front of the lower floor. But above that the brick wall was windowless except for the single tall crossbarred rectangle and he thought again of the Sunday nights which seemed now to belong to a time as dead as Nineveh when from suppertime until the jailer turned the lights out and yelled up the stairs for them to shut up, the dark limber hands would lie in the grimed interstices while the mellow untroubled repentless voices would shout down to the women in the aprons of cooks or nurses and the girls in their flash cheap clothes from the mail order houses or the other young men who had not been caught yet or had been caught and freed yesterday, gathered along the street. But not tonight and even the room behind it was dark though it was not yet eight oclock and he could see, imagine them not huddled perhaps but certainly all together, within elbow's touch whether they were actually touching or not and certainly quiet, not laughing tonight nor talking either, sitting in the dark and watching the top of the stairs because this would not be the first time when to mobs of white men not only all black cats were gray but they didn't always bother to count them either.

And the front door was open, standing wide to the street which he had never seen before even in summer

although the ground floor was the jailer's living quarters,
and tilted in a chair against the back wall so that he
faced the door in full sight of the street, was a man who
was not the jailer nor even one of the sheriff's deputies
either. Because he had recognised him too: Will Legate,
who lived on a small farm two miles from town and was
one of the best woodsmen, the finest shot and the best
deer-hunter in the county, sitting in the tilted chair
holding the colored comic section of today's Memphis
paper, with leaning against the wall beside him not the
hand-worn rifle with which he had killed more deer (and
even running rabbits with it) than even he remembered
but a double barrelled shotgun, who apparently without
even lowering or moving the paper had already seen and
recognised them even before they turned in at the gate
and was now watching them steadily as they came up
the walk and mounted the steps and crossed the gallery
and entered: at which moment the jailer himself emerged
from a door to the right—a snuffy untidy potbellied man
with a harried concerned outraged face, wearing a heavy
pistol holstered onto a cartridge belt around his waist
which looked as uncomfortable and out of place as a silk
hat or a fifth-century iron slavecollar, who shut the door
behind him, already crying at his uncle:

'He wont even shut and lock the front door! Just setting there with that durn funny paper waiting for anybody that wants to to walk right in!'

'I'm doing what Mr Hampton told me to,' Legate
said in his pleasant equable voice.

'Does Hampton think that funny paper's going to
stop them folks from Beat Four?' the jailer cried.

'I don't think he's worrying about Beat Four yet,'

Legate said still pleasantly and equably. 'This here's just for local consumption now.'

His uncle glanced at Legate. 'It seems to have worked. We saw the car—or one of them—make one trip around the Square as we came up. I suppose it's been by here too.'

'Oh, once or twice,' Legate said. 'Maybe three times. I really aint paid much mind.'

'And I hope to hell it keeps on working,' the jailer said. 'Because you sure aint going to stop anybody with just that one britch-loader.'

'Sure,' Legate said. 'I don't expect to stop them. If enough folks get their minds made up and keep them made up, aint anything likely to stop them from what they think they want to do. But then, I got you and that pistol to help me.'

'Me?' the jailer cried. 'Me get in the way of them Gowries and Ingrums for seventy-five dollars a month? Just for one nigger? And if you aint a fool, you wont neither.'

'Oh I got to,' Legate said in his easy pleasant voice. 'I got to resist. Mr Hampton's paying me five dollars for it.' Then to his uncle: 'I reckon you want to see him.'

'Yes,' his uncle said. 'If it's all right with Mr Tubbs.'

The jailer stared at his uncle, irate and harried. 'So you got to get mixed up in it too. You can't let well enough alone neither.' He turned abruptly. 'Come on:' and led the way through the door beside which Legate's chair was tilted, into the back hall where the stairway rose to the upper floor, snapping on the light switch at the foot of the stairs and began to mount them, his uncle then he following while he watched the hunch and sag of the holster at the jailer's hip. Suddenly the jailer seemed about to stop; even his uncle thought so, stopping too but the jailer went on, speaking over his shoulder: 'Dont mind me. I'm going to do the best I can; I taken an oath of office too.' His voice rose a little, still calm, just louder: 'But dont think nobody's going to make me admit I like it. I got a wife and two children; what good am I going to be to them if I get myself killed protecting a goddamn stinking nigger?' His voice rose again; it was not calm now: 'And how am I going to live with myself if I let a passel of nogood sonabitches take a prisoner away from me?' Now he stopped and turned on the step above them, higher than both, his face once more harried and frantic, his voice frantic and outraged: 'Better for everybody if them folks had took him as soon as they laid hands on him yesterday——'

'But they didn't,' his uncle said. 'I dont think they will. And if they do, it wont really matter. They either will or they wont and if they dont it will be all right and if they do we will do the best we can, you and Mr Hampton and Legate and the rest of us, what we have to do, what we can do. So we dont need to worry about it. You see?'

'Yes,' the jailer said. Then he turned and went on, unsnapping his keyring from his belt under the pistol belt, to the heavy oak door which closed off the top of the stairs (It was one solid handhewn piece over two inches thick, locked with a heavy modern padlock in a handwrought iron bar through two iron slots which like the heavy risette-shaped hinges were handwrought too, hammered out over a hundred years ago in the blacksmith shop across the street where he had stood yesterday; one day last summer a stranger, a city man, an architect who reminded him somehow of his uncle, hatless and tieless, in tennis shoes and a pair of worn flannel trousers and what was left of a case of champagne in a convertible-top car which must have cost three thousand dollars, driving not through town but into it, not hurting anyone but just driving the car up onto the pavement and across it through a plate glass window, quite drunk, quite cheerful, with less than fifty cents in cash in his pocket but all sorts of identification cards and a check folder whose stubs showed a balance in a New York bank of over six thousand dollars, who insisted on being put in jail even though the marshal and the owner of the window both were just trying to persuade him to go to the hotel and sleep it off so he could write a check for the window and the wall: until the marshal finally put him in jail where he went to sleep at once like a baby and the garage sent for the car and the next morning the jailer telephoned the marshal at five oclock to come and get the man out because he had waked the whole household up talking from his cell across to the niggers in the bullpen. So the marshal came and made him leave and then he wanted to go out with the street gang to work and they wouldn't let him do that and his car was ready too but he still wouldn't leave, at the hotel that night and two nights later his uncle even brought him to supper, where he and his uncle talked for three hours about Europe and Paris and Vienna and he and his mother listening too though his father had excused himself: and still there two days after that, still trying from his uncle and the mayor and the board of aldermen and at last the board of supervisors themselves to buy the whole door or if they wouldn't sell that, at least the bar and slots and the hinges.) and unlocked it and swung it back.

But already they had passed out of the world of man,

men: people who worked and had homes and raised
families and tried to make a little more money than they
perhaps deserved by fair means of course or at least by
legal, to spend a little on fun and still save something
against old age. Because even as the oak door swung
back there seemed to rush out and down at him the stale
breath of all human degradation and shame—a smell of
creosote and excrement and stale vomit and incorrigi-
bility and defiance and repudiation like something
palpable against the thrust and lift of their bodies as
they mounted the last steps and into a passage which was
actually a part of the main room, the bullpen, cut off from
the rest of the room by a wall of wire mesh like a
chicken run or a dog-kennel, inside which in tiered
bunks against the farther wall lay five Negroes, motionless, their eyes closed but no sound of snoring, no sound
of any sort, lying there immobile orderly and composed
under the dusty glare of the single shadeless bulb as if
they had been embalmed, the jailer stopping again, his
own hands gripped into the mesh while he glared at the
motionless shapes. 'Look at them,' the jailer said in that
voice too loud, too thin, just under hysteria: 'Peaceful
as lambs but aint a damned one of them asleep. And I
dont blame them, with a mob of white men boiling in
here at midnight with pistols and cans of gasoline.—
Come on,' he said and turned and went on. Just beyond
there was a door in the mesh, not padlocked but just
hooked with a hasp and staple such as you might see on
a dog-kennel or a corn crib but the jailer passed it.

'You put him in the cell, did you?' his uncle said.

'Hampton's orders,' the jailer said over his shoulder.
'I dont know what the next white man that figgers he

cant rest good until he kills somebody is going to think about it. I taken all the blankets off the cot though.'

'Maybe because he wont be here long enough to have to go to sleep?' his uncle said.

'Ha ha,' the jailer said in that strained high harsh voice without mirth: 'Ha ha ha ha:' and following behind his uncle he thought how of all human pursuits murder has the most deadly need of privacy; how man will go to almost any lengths to preserve the solitude in which he evacuates or makes love but he will go to any length for that in which he takes life, even to homicide, yet by no act can he more completely and irrevocably destroy it: a modern steel barred door this time with a built-in lock as large as a woman's handbag which the jailer unlocked with another key on the ring and then turned, the sound of his feet almost as rapid as running back down the corridor until the sound of the oak door at the head of the stairs cut them off, and beyond it the cell lighted by another single dim dusty flyspecked bulb behind a wire screen cupped to the ceiling, not much larger than a broom closet and in fact just wide enough for the double bunk against the wall, from both beds of which not just the blankets but the mattresses too had been stripped, he and his uncle entering and still all he saw yet was the first thing he had seen: the hat and the black coat hanging neatly from a nail in the wall: and he would remember afterward how he thought in a gasp, a surge of relief: *They've already got him. He's gone. It's too late. It's already over now.* Because he didn't know what he had expected, except that it was not this: a careful spread of newspaper covering neatly the naked springs of the lower cot and another section as carefully placed on the upper one so it would shield his eyes from the

light and Lucas himself lying on the spread papers,
asleep, on his back, his head pillowed on one of his shoes
and his hands folded on his breast, quite peacefully or as
peacefully as old people sleep, his mouth open and
breathing in faint shallow jerky gasps; and he stood in
an almost unbearable surge not merely of outrage but of
rage, looking down at the face which for the first time,
defenceless at last for a moment, revealed its age, and the
lax gnarled old man's hands which only yesterday had
sent a bullet into the back of another human being,
lying still and peaceful on the bosom of the old-fashioned
collarless boiled white shirt closed at the neck with the
oxidising brass button shaped like an arrow and almost
as large as the head of a small snake, thinking: *He's just
a nigger after all for all his high nose and his stiff neck
and his gold watch-chain and refusing to mean mister to
anybody even when he says it. Only a nigger could kill a
man, let alone shoot him in the back, and then sleep like
a baby as soon as he found something flat enough to lie
down on;* still looking at him when without moving
otherwise Lucas closed his mouth and his eyelids opened,
the eyes staring up for another second, then still without
the head moving at all the eyeballs turned until Lucas
was looking straight at his uncle but still not moving:
just lying there looking at him.

'Well, old man,' his uncle said. 'You played hell at
last.' Then Lucas moved. He sat up stiffly and swung
his legs stiffly over the edge of the cot, picking one of
them up by the knee between his hands and swinging
it around as you open or close a sagging gate, groaning,
grunting not just frankly and unabashed and aloud but
comfortably, as the old grunt and groan with some long
familiar minor stiffness so used and accustomed as to be

no longer even an ache and which if they were ever
actually cured of it, they would be bereft and lost; he
listening and watching still in that rage and now amazement too at the murderer not merely in the shadow of
the gallows but of a lynch-mob, not only taking time to
groan over a stiffness in his back but doing it as if he
had all the long rest of a natural life in which to be
checked each time he moved by the old familiar catch.

'Looks like it,' Lucas said. 'That's why I sent for you.
What you going to do with me?'

'Me?' his uncle said. 'Nothing. My name aint Gowrie.
It aint even Beat Four.'

Moving stiffly again Lucas bent and peered about his
feet, then he reached under the cot and drew out the
other shoe and sat up again and began to turn creakily
and stiffly to look behind him when his uncle reached
and took the first shoe from the cot and dropped it beside the other. But Lucas didn't put them on. Instead
he sat again, immobile, his hands on his knees, blinking.
Then with one hand he made a gesture which completely
dismissed Gowries, mob, vengeance, holocaust and all.
'I'll worry about that when they walks in here,' he said.
'I mean the law. Aint you the county lawyer?'

'Oh,' his uncle said. 'It's the District Attorney that'll
hang you or send you to Parchman—not me.'

Lucas was still blinking, not rapidly: just steadily. He
watched him. And suddenly he realised that Lucas was
not looking at his uncle at all and apparently had not
been for three or four seconds.

'I see,' Lucas said. 'Then you can take my case.'

'Take your case? Defend you before the judge?'

'I'm gonter pay you,' Lucas said. 'You dont need to
worry.'

'I dont defend murderers who shoot people in the back,' his uncle said.

Again Lucas made the gesture with one of the dark gnarled hands. 'Let's forgit the trial. We aint come to it yet.' And now he saw that Lucas was watching his uncle, his head lowered so that he was watching his uncle upward from beneath through the grizzled tufts of his eyebrows—a look shrewd secret and intent. Then Lucas said: 'I wants to hire somebody—' and stopped. And watching him, he thought remembered an old lady, dead now, a spinster, a neighbor who wore a dyed transformation and had always on a pantry shelf a big bowl of homemade teacakes for all the children on the street, who one summer (he couldn't have been over seven or eight then) taught all of them to play Five Hundred: sitting at the card table on her screened side gallery on hot summer mornings and she would wet her fingers and take a card from her hand and lay it on the table, her hand not still poised over it of course but just lying nearby until the next player revealed exposed by some movement or gesture of triumph or exultation or maybe by just simple increased hard breathing his intention to trump or overplay it, whereupon she would say quickly: 'Wait. I picked up the wrong one' and take up the card and put it back into her hand and play another one. That was exactly what Lucas had done. He had sat still before but now he was absolutely immobile. He didn't even seem to be breathing.

'Hire somebody?' his uncle said. 'You've got a lawyer. I had already taken your case before I came in here. I'm going to tell you what to do as soon as you have told me what happened.'

'No,' Lucas said. 'I wants to hire somebody. It dont have to be a lawyer.'

Now it was his uncle who stared at Lucas. 'To do what?'

He watched them. Now it was no childhood's game of stakeless Five Hundred. It was more like the poker games he had overlooked. 'Are you or aint you going to take the job?' Lucas said.

'So you aint going to tell me what you want me to do until after I have agreed to do it,' his uncle said. 'All right,' his uncle said. 'Now I'm going to tell you what to do. Just exactly what happened out there yesterday?'

'So you dont want the job,' Lucas said. 'You aint said yes or no yet.'

'No!' his uncle said, harsh, too loud, catching himself but already speaking again before he had brought his voice back down to a sort of furious explicit calm: 'Because you aint got any job to offer anybody. You're in jail, depending on the grace of God to keep those damned Gowries from dragging you out of here and hanging you to the first lamp post they come to. Why they ever let you get to town in the first place I still dont understand——'

'Nemmine that now,' Lucas said. 'What I needs is——'

'Nemmine that!' his uncle said. 'Tell the Gowries to never mind it when they bust in here tonight. Tell Beat Four to just forget it——' He stopped; again with an effort you could almost see he brought his voice back to that furious patience. He drew a deep breath and expelled it. 'Now. Tell me exactly what happened yesterday.'

For another moment Lucas didn't answer, sitting on the bunk, his hands on his knees, intractable and com-

posed, no longer looking at his uncle, working his mouth
faintly as if he were tasting something. He said: 'They
was two folks, partners in a sawmill. Leastways they was
buying the lumber as the sawmill cut it——'

'Who were they?' his uncle said.

'Vinson Gowrie was one of um.'

His uncle stared at Lucas for a long moment. But his
voice was quite calm now. 'Lucas,' he said, 'has it ever
occurred to you that if you just said mister to white
people and said it like you meant it, you might not be
sitting here now?'

'So I'm to commence now,' Lucas said. 'I can start off
by saying mister to the folks that drags me out of here
and builds a fire under me.'

'Nothing's going to happen to you—until you go before the judge,' his uncle said. 'Dont you know that even
Beat Four dont take liberties with Mr Hampton—at
least not here in town?'

'Shurf Hampton's home in bed now.'

'But Mr Will Legate's sitting down stairs with a shotgun.'

'I aint 'quainted with no Will Legate.'

'The deer-hunter? The man that can hit a running
rabbit with a thirty-thirty rifle?'

'Hah,' Lucas said. 'Them Gowries aint deer. They
might be cattymounts and panthers but they aint deer.'

'All right,' his uncle said. 'Then I'll stay here if you'll
feel better. Now. Go on. Vinson Gowrie and another
man were buying lumber together. What other man?'

'Vinson Gowrie's the only one that's public yet.'

'And he got public by being shot in broad daylight in
the back,' his uncle said. 'Well, that's one way to do it.—
All right,' his uncle said. 'Who was the other man?'

Lucas didn't answer. He didn't move; he might not even have heard, sitting peaceful and inattentive, not even really waiting: just sitting there while his uncle watched him. Then his uncle said:

'All right. What were they doing with it?'

'They was yarding it up as the mill cut it, gonter sell it all at once when the sawing was finished. Only the other man was hauling it away at night, coming in late after dark with a truck and picking up a load and hauling it over to Glasgow or Hollymount and selling it and putting the money in his pocket.'

'How do you know?'

'I seen um. Watched um.' Nor did he doubt this for a moment because he remembered Ephraim, Paralee's father before he died, an old man, a widower who would pass most of the day dozing and waking in a rocking chair on Paralee's gallery in summer and in front of the fire in winter and at night would walk the roads, not going anywhere, just moving, at times five and six miles from town before he would return at dawn to doze and wake all day in the chair again.

'All right,' his uncle said. 'Then what?'

'That's all,' Lucas said. 'He was just stealing a load of lumber every night or so.'

His uncle stared at Lucas for perhaps ten seconds. He said in a voice of calm, almost hushed amazement: 'So you took your pistol and went to straighten it out. You, a nigger, took a pistol and went to rectify a wrong between two white men. What did you expect? What else did you expect?'

'Nemmine expecting,' Lucas said. 'I wants——'

'You went to the store,' his uncle said, 'only you happened to find Vinson Gowrie first and followed him into the woods and told him his partner was robbing him and naturally he cursed you and called you a liar whether it was true or not, naturally he would have to do that; maybe he even knocked you down and walked on and you shot him in the back——'

'Never nobody knocked me down,' Lucas said.

'So much the worse,' his uncle said. 'So much the worse for you. It's not even self-defense. You just shot him in the back. And then you stood there over him with the fired pistol in your pocket and let the white folks come up and grab you. And if it hadn't been for that little shrunk-up rheumatic constable who had no business being there in the first place and in the second place had no business whatever, at the rate of a dollar a prisoner every time he delivered a subpoena or served a warrant, having guts enough to hold off that whole damn Beat Four for eighteen hours until Hope Hampton saw fit or remembered or got around to bringing you in to jail—— holding off that whole countryside that you nor all the friends you could drum up in a hundred years——'

'I aint got friends,' Lucas said with stern and inflexible pride, and then something else though his uncle was already talking:

'You're damned right you haven't. And if you ever had that pistol shot would have blown them to kingdom come too—— What?' his uncle said. 'What did you say?'

'I said I pays my own way,' Lucas said.

'I see,' his uncle said. 'You dont use friends; you pay cash. Yes. I see. Now you listen to me. You'll go before the grand jury tomorrow. They'll indict you. Then if you like I'll have Mr Hampton move you to Mottstown or even further away than that, until court convenes next month. Then you'll plead guilty; I'll persuade the

District Attorney to let you do that because you're an old
man and you never were in trouble before; I mean as far
as the judge and the District Attorney will know since
they dont live within fifty miles of Yoknapatawpha
County. Then they wont hang you; they'll send you to
the penitentiary; you probably wont live long enough
to be paroled but at least the Gowries cant get to you
there. Do you want me to stay in here with you tonight?'

'I reckon not,' Lucas said. 'They kept me up all last
night and I'm gonter try to get some sleep. If you stay
here you'll talk till morning.'

'Right,' his uncle said harshly, then to him: 'Come on:'
already moving toward the door. Then his uncle stopped.
'Is there anything you want?'

'You might send me some tobacco,' Lucas said. 'If them
Gowries leaves me time to smoke it.'

'Tomorrow,' his uncle said. 'I dont want to keep you
awake tonight:' and went on, he following, his uncle
letting him pass first through the door so that he stepped
aside in his turn and stood looking back into the cell
while his uncle came through the door and drew it after
him, the heavy steel plunger crashing into its steel groove
with a thick oily sound of irrefutable finality like that
ultimate cosmolined doom itself when as his uncle said
man's machines had at last effaced and obliterated him
from the earth and, purposeless now to themselves with
nothing left to destroy, closed the last carborundum-
grooved door upon their own progenitorless apotheosis
behind one clockless lock responsive only to the last
stroke of eternity, his uncle going on, his feet ringing
and echoing down the corridor and then the sharp rattle
of his knuckles on the oak door while he and Lucas still
looked at one another through the steel bars, Lucas

standing too now in the middle of the floor beneath the
light and looking at him with whatever it was in his face
so that he thought for a second that Lucas had spoken
aloud. But he hadn't, he was making no sound: just looking at him with that mute patient urgency until the
jailer's feet thumped nearer and nearer on the stairs and
the slotted bar on the door rasped back.

And the jailer locked the bar again and they passed
Legate still with his funny paper in the tilted chair
beside the shotgun facing the open door, then outside,
down the walk to the gate and the street, following
through the gate where his uncle had already turned
toward home: stopping, thinking *a nigger a murderer
who shoots white people in the back and aint even sorry*.

He said: 'I imagine I'll find Skeets McGowan loafing
somewhere on the Square. He's got a key to the drugstore. I'll take Lucas some tobacco tonight.' His uncle
stopped.

'It can wait till morning,' his uncle said.

'Yes,' he said, feeling his uncle watching him, not even
wondering what he would do if his uncle said no, not
even waiting really, just standing there.

'All right,' his uncle said. 'Dont be too long.' So he
could have moved then. But still he didn't.

'I thought you said nothing would happen tonight.'

'I still dont think it will,' his uncle said. 'But you cant
tell. People like the Gowries dont attach a great deal of
importance to death or dying. But they do put a lot of
stock in the dead and how they died—particularly their
own. If you get the tobacco, let Tubbs carry it up to him
and you come on home.'

So he didn't have to say even yes this time, his uncle
turning first then he turned and walked toward the

Square, walking on until the sound of his uncle's feet
had ceased, then standing until his uncle's black silhouette had changed to the white gleam of his linen suit and
then that faded beyond the last arclight and if he had
gone on home and got Highboy as soon as he recognised
the sheriff's car this morning that would be eight hours
and almost forty miles, turning then and walking back
toward the gate with Legate's eyes watching him, already
recognising him across the top of the funny paper even
before he reached the gate and if he just went straight on
now he could follow the lane behind the hedge and
across into the lot and saddle Highboy and go out by
the pasture gate and turn his back on Jefferson and nigger murderers and all and let Highboy go as fast as he
wanted to go and as far as he wanted to go even when
he had blown himself at last and agreed to walk, just so
his tail was still turned to Jefferson and nigger murderers: through the gate and up the walk and across the
gallery and again the jailer came quickly through the
door at the right, his expression already giving way to
the one of harried outrage.

'Again,' the jailer said. 'Dont you never get enough?'
'I forgot something,' he said.
'Let it wait till morning,' the jailer said.
'Let him get it now,' Legate said in his equable drawl.
'If he leaves it there till morning it might get trompled
on.' So the jailer turned; again they mounted the stairs,
again the jailer unlocked the bar across the oak door.
'Never mind the other one,' he said. 'I can attend to it
through the bars:' and didn't wait, the door closed behind him, he heard the bar slide back into the slot but
still all he had to do was just to rap on it, hearing the
jailer's feet going away back down the stairs but even

then all he had to do was just to yell loud and bang on
the floor and Legate anyway would hear him, thinking
*Maybe he will remind me of that goddamn plate of col-
lards and sidemeat or maybe he'll even tell me I'm all
he's got, all that's left and that will be enough*——walking fast, then the steel door and Lucas had not moved,
still standing in the middle of the cell beneath the light,
watching the door when he came up to it and stopped
and said in a voice as harsh as his uncle's had ever been:
    'All right. What do you want me to do?'
    'Go out there and look at him,' Lucas said.
    'Go out where and look at who?' he said. But he under-
stood all right. It seemed to him that he had known all
the time what it would be; he thought with a kind of
relief *So that's all it is* even while his automatic voice was
screeching with outraged disbelief: 'Me? *Me?*' It was like
something you have dreaded and feared and dodged for
years until it seemed like all your life, then despite everything it happened to you and all it was was just pain, all
it did was hurt and so it was all over, all finished, all right.
    'I'll pay you,' Lucas said.
So he wasn't listening, not even to his own voice in
amazed incredulous outrage: 'Me go out there and dig up
that grave?' He wasn't even thinking anymore *So this is
what that plate of meat and greens is going to cost me.*
Because he had already passed that long ago when that
something—whatever it was—had held him here five
minutes ago looking back across the vast, the almost
insuperable chasm between him and the old Negro murderer and saw, heard Lucas saying something to him not
because he was himself, Charles Mallison junior, nor
because he had eaten the plate of greens and warmed
himself at the fire, but because he alone of all the white

people Lucas would have a chance to speak to between now and the moment when he might be dragged out of the cell and down the steps at the end of a rope, would hear the mute unhoping urgency of the eyes. He said:

'Come here.' Lucas did so, approaching, taking hold of two of the bars as a child stands inside a fence. Nor did he remember doing so but looking down he saw his own hands holding to two of the bars, the two pairs of hands, the black ones and the white ones, grasping the bars while they faced one another above them. 'All right,' he said. 'Why?'

'Go and look at him,' Lucas said. 'If it's too late when you get back, I'll sign you a paper now saying I owes you whatever you think it's worth.'

But still he wasn't listening; he knew it: only to himself: 'I'm to go seventeen miles out there in the dark——'

'Nine,' Lucas said. 'The Gowries buries at Caledonia Chapel. You takes the first right hand up into the hills just beyond the Nine-Mile branch bridge. You can be there in a half hour in your uncle's automobile.'

'——I'm to risk having the Gowries catch me digging up that grave. I aim to know why. I dont even know what I'll be looking for. Why?'

'My pistol is a fawty-one Colt,' Lucas said. Which it would be; the only thing he hadn't actually known was the calibre—that weapon workable and efficient and well cared for yet as archaic peculiar and unique as the gold toothpick, which had probably (without doubt) been old Carothers McCaslin's pride a half century ago.

'All right,' he said. 'Then what?'

'He wasn't shot with no fawty-one Colt.'

'What was he shot with?'

But Lucas didn't answer that, standing there on his

side of the steel door, his hands light-clasped and motionless around the two bars, immobile save for the faint
movement of his breathing. Nor had he expected Lucas
to and he knew that Lucas would never answer that, say
any more, any further to any white man, and he knew
why, as he knew why Lucas had waited to tell him, a
child, about the pistol when he would have told neither
his uncle nor the sheriff who would have been the one
to open the grave and look at the body; he was surprised
that Lucas had come as near as he had to telling his uncle
about it and he realised, appreciated again that quality
in his uncle which brought people to tell him things they
would tell nobody else, even tempting Negroes to tell
him what their nature forbade them telling white men:
remembering old Ephraim and his mother's ring that
summer five years ago—a cheap thing with an imitation
stone; two of them in fact, identical, which his mother
and her room-mate at Sweetbriar Virginia had saved
their allowances and bought and exchanged to wear until
death as young girls will, and the room-mate grown and
living in California with a daughter of her own at Sweetbriar now and she and his mother had not seen one
another in years and possibly never would again yet his
mother still kept the ring: then one day it disappeared;
he remembered how he would wake late at night and see
lights burning downstairs and he would know she was
still searching for it: and all this time old Ephraim was
sitting in his home-made rocking chair on Paralee's front
gallery until one day Ephraim told him that for half a
dollar he would find the ring and he gave Ephraim the
half dollar and that afternoon he left for a week at a
Scout camp and returned and found his mother in the
kitchen where she had spread newspapers on the table

and emptied the stone crock she and Paralee kept the
cornmeal in onto it and she and Paralee were combing
through the meal with forks and for the first time in a
week he remembered the ring and went back to Paralee's
house and there was Ephriam sitting in the chair on the
gallery and Ephraim said, 'Hit's under the hawg-trough
at your pa's farm:' nor did Ephriam need to tell him
how then because he had already remembered by then:
Mrs Downs: an old white woman who lived alone in a
small filthy shoebox of a house that smelled like a foxden
on the edge of town in a settlement of Negro houses, in
and out of which Negroes came and went steadily all day
long and without doubt most of the night: who (this not
from Paralee who seemed always to not know or at least
to have no time at the moment to talk about it, but from
Aleck Sander) didn't merely tell fortunes and cure hexes
but found things: which was where the half dollar had
gone and he believed at once and so implicitly that the
ring was now found that he dismissed that phase at once
and forever and it was only the thing's secondary and
corollary which moved his interest, saying to Ephraim:
'You've known all this week where it was and you didn't
even tell them?' and Ephraim looked at him a while,
rocking steadily and placidly and sucking at his cold
ashfilled pipe with each rock like the sound of a small
asthmatic cylinder: 'I mought have told your maw. But
she would need help. So I waited for you. Young folks
and womens, they aint cluttered. They can listen. But a
middle-year man like your paw and your uncle, they cant
listen. They aint got time. They're too busy with facks.
In fact, you mought bear this in yo mind; someday you
mought need it. If you ever needs to get anything done
outside the common run, dont waste yo time on the men-

folks; get the womens and children to working at it.' And
he remembered his father's not rage so much as outrage,
his almost furious repudiation, his transferrence of the
whole thing into a realm of assailed embattled moral
principle, and even his uncle who until now had had no
more trouble than he believing things that all other
grown people doubted for the sole reason that they were
unreasonable, while his mother went serenely and stub-
bornly about her preparations to go out to the farm
which she hadn't visited in over a year and even his
father hadn't seen it since months before the ring was
missing and even his uncle refused to drive the car so
his father hired a man from the garage and he and his
mother went out to the farm and with the help of the
overseer found under the trough where the hogs were
fed, the ring. Only this was no obscure valueless little
ring exchanged twenty years ago between two young
girls but the death by shameful violence of a man who
would die not because he was a murderer but because his
skin was black. Yet this was all Lucas was going to tell
him and he knew it was all; he thought in a kind of
raging fury: *Believe? Believe what?* because Lucas was
not even asking him to believe anything; he was not even
asking a favor, making no last desperate plea to his
humanity and pity but was even going to pay him provided the price was not too high, to go alone seventeen
miles (no, nine: he remembered at least that he had
heard that now) in the dark and risk being caught violat-
ing the grave of a member of a clan of men already at the
pitch to commit the absolute of furious and bloody outrage, without even telling him why. Yet he tried it again,
as he knew Lucas not only knew he was going to but
knew that he knew what answer he would get:

'What gun was he shot with, Lucas?' and got exactly what even Lucas knew he had expected:

'I'm gonter pay you,' Lucas said. 'Name yo price at anything in reason and I will pay it.'

He drew a long breath and expelled it while they faced each other through the bars, the bleared old man's eyes watching him, inscrutable and secret. They were not even urgent now and he thought peacefully *He's not only beat me, he never for one second had any doubt of it*. He said: 'All right. Just for me to look at him wouldn't do any good, even if I could tell about the bullet. So you see what that means. I've got to dig him up, get him out of that hole before the Gowries catch me, and in to town where Mr Hampton can send to Memphis for an expert that can tell about bullets.' He looked at Lucas, at the old man holding gently to the bars inside the cell and not even looking at him anymore. He drew a long breath again. 'But the main thing is to get him up out of the ground where somebody can look at him before the . . . . .' He looked at Lucas. 'I'll have to get out there and dig him up and get back to town before midnight or one oclock and maybe even midnight will be too late. I dont see how I can do it. I cant do it.'

'I'll try to wait,' Lucas said.

Chapter Four

THERE WAS A WEATHERED battered second-hand-looking pickup truck parked at the curb in front of the house when he reached home. It was now well past eight oclock; it was a good deal more than a possibility that there remained less than four hours for his uncle to go to the sheriff's house and convince him and then find a J.P. or whoever they would have to find and wake and then convince too to open the grave (in lieu of permission from the Gowries, which for any reason whatever, worst of all to save a nigger from being burned over a bonfire, the President of the United States himself let alone a country sheriff would never get) and then go out to Caledonia church and dig up the body and get back to town with it in time. Yet this of all nights would be one when a farmer whose stray cow or mule or hog had been impounded by a neighbor who insisted on collecting a dollar pound fee before he would release it, must come in to see his uncle, to sit for an hour in his uncle's study saying yes or no or I reckon not while his uncle talked about crops or politics, one of which his uncle knew nothing about and the other the farmer didn't, until the man would get around to telling what he came for.

But he couldn't stand on ceremony now. He had been walking pretty fast since he left the jail but he was trotting now, catacorner across the lawn, onto the gallery

and across it into the hall past the library where his
father would still be sitting under one reading lamp with
the Memphis paper's Sunday crossword puzzle page and
his mother under the other one with the new Book-of-
the-Month book, and on back to what his mother used
to try to call Gavin's study but which Paralee and Aleck
Sander had long since renamed the office so that everyone
now called it that. The door was closed; he could hear
the murmur of the man's voice beyond it during the
second in which without even stopping he rapped twice
and at the same time opened the door and entered,
already saying:

'Good evening, sir. Excuse me. Uncle Gavin——'

Because the voice was his uncle's; seated opposite his
uncle beyond the desk, instead of a man with a shaved
sunburned neck in neat tieless Sunday shirt and pants,
was a woman in a plain cotton print dress and one of the
round faintly dusty-looking black hats set squarely on the
top of her head such as his grandmother had used to wear
and then he recognised her even before he saw the watch
—small gold in a hunting case suspended by a gold
brooch on her flat bosom almost like and in almost
exactly the same position as the heart sewn on the breast
of the canvas fencing vest—because since his grandmother's death no other woman in his acquaintance wore
or even owned one and in fact he should have recognised
the pickup truck: Miss Habersham, whose name was now
the oldest which remained in the county. There had
been three once: Doctor Habersham and a tavern keeper
named Holston and a Huguenot younger son named
Grenier who had ridden horseback into the county before its boundaries had ever been surveyed and located
and named, when Jefferson was a Chickasaw trading post

with a Chickasaw word to designate it out of the trackless
wilderness of canebrake and forest of that time but all
gone now, vanished except the one even from the
county's spoken recollection: Holston merely the name
of the hotel on the Square and few in the county to know
or care where the word came from, and the last of the
blood of Louis Grenier the *elegante*, the *dilettante*, the
Paris-educated architect who had practised a little of law
but had spent most of his time as a planter and painter
(and more amateur as a raiser of food and cotton than
with canvas and brush) now warmed the bones of an
equable cheerful middleaged man with the mind and
face of a child who lived in a half-shed half-den he built
himself of discarded boards and pieces of flattened stove-
pipe and tin cans on the bank of the river twenty miles
away, who didn't know his age and couldn't write even
the Lonnie Grinnup which he now called himself and
didn't even know that the land he squatted on was the
last lost scrap of the thousands of acres which his ancestor
had been master of and only Miss Habersham remained: a
kinless spinster of seventy living in the columned colonial
house on the edge of town which had not been painted
since her father died and had neither water nor electricity
in it, with two Negro servants (and here again something
nagged for an instant at his mind his attention but already in the same second gone, not even dismissed: just
gone) in a cabin in the back yard, who (the wife) did the
cooking while Miss Habersham and the man raised
chickens and vegetables and peddled them about town
from the pickup truck. Until two years ago they had
used a plump aged white horse (it was said to be twenty
years old when he first remembered it, with a skin beneath the burnished white hairs as clean and pink as a

baby's) and a buggy. Then they had a good season or
something and Miss Habersham bought the pickup truck
second hand and every morning winter and summer they
would be seen about the streets from house to house,
Miss Habersham at the wheel in cotton stockings and
the round black hat which she had been wearing for at
least forty years and the clean print dresses which you
could see in the Sears Roebuck catalogues for two dollars
and ninety-eight cents with the neat small gold watch
pinned to the flat unmammary front and the shoes and
the gloves which his mother said were made to her
measure in a New York shop and cost thirty and forty
dollars a pair for the one and fifteen and twenty for the
other, while the Negro man trotted his vast belly in and
out of the houses with a basket of bright greens or eggs
in one hand and the plucked naked carcass of a chicken
in the other;—recognised, remembered, even (his attention) nagged at and already dismissed because there
wasn't time, saying rapidly:

'Good evening, Miss Habersham. Excuse me. I've got
to speak to Uncle Gavin:' then again to his uncle: 'Uncle
Gavin——'

'So is Miss Habersham,' his uncle said quick and immediate, in a tone a voice which in ordinary times he
would have recognised at once; at an ordinary time he
might even have comprehended the implication of what
his uncle had said. But not now. He didn't actually hear
it. He wasn't listening. In fact he really didn't have time
to talk himself, saying rapid yet calm too, merely urgent
and even that only to his uncle because he had already
forgotten Miss Habersham, even her presence:

'I've got to speak to you:' and only then stopped not
because he had finished, he hadn't even begun yet, but

because for the first time he was hearing his uncle who
hadn't even paused, sitting half sideways in the chair,
one arm thrown over the back and the other hand holding the burning cob pipe on the table in front of him,
still speaking in that voice like the idle flicking of a
small limber switch:

'So you took it up to him yourself. Or maybe you
didn't even bother with tobacco. And he told you a tale.
I hope it was a good one.'

And that was all. He could go now, in fact should. For
that matter he should never have stopped on his way
through the hall or even come into the house at all but
on around it where he could have called Aleck Sander
on his way to the stable; Lucas had told him that thirty
minutes ago in the jail when even he had come almost
to the point and even under the very shadow of the
Gowries had in the end known better than to try to tell
his uncle or any other white man. Yet still he didn't
move. He had forgotten Miss Habersham. He had dismissed her; he had said 'Excuse me' and so evanished
her not only from the room but the moment too as the
magician with one word or gesture disappears the palm
tree or the rabbit or the bowl of roses and only they
remained, the three of them: he at the door and still
holding it, half in the room which he had never actually
entered and shouldn't have come even that far and half
already back out of it in the hall where he should never
have wasted time passing to begin with, and his uncle half
sprawled behind the table littered with papers too and
another of the German beermugs filled with paper spills
and probably a dozen of the corncob pipes in various
stages of char, and half a mile away the old kinless friendless opinionated arrogant hardheaded intractable inde-

pendent (insolent too) Negro man alone in the cell where the first familiar voice he would hear would probably be old one-armed Nub Gowrie's in the hall below saying, 'Git out of the way, Will Legate. We've come for that nigger,' while outside the quiet lamplit room the vast millrace of time roared not toward midnight but dragging midnight with it, not to hurl midnight into wreckage but to hurl the wreckage of midnight down upon them in one poised skyblotting yawn: and he knew now that the irrevocable moment was not when he said 'All right' to Lucas through the steel door of the cell but when he would step back into the hall and close this one behind him. So he tried again, still calm, not even rapid now, not even urgent: just specious explicit and reasonable:

'Suppose it wasn't his pistol that killed him.'

'Of course,' his uncle said. 'That's exactly what I would claim myself if I were Lucas—or any other Negro murderer for that matter or any ignorant white murderer either for the matter of that. He probably even told you what he fired his pistol at. What was it? a rabbit, or maybe a tin can or a mark on a tree just to see if it really was loaded, really would go off. But let that pass. Grant it for the moment: then what? What do you suggest? No; what did Lucas tell you to do?'

And he even answered that: 'Couldn't Mr Hampton dig him up and see?'

'On what grounds? Lucas was caught within two minutes after the shot, standing over the body with a recently-fired pistol in his pocket. He never denied having fired it; in fact he refused to make any statement at all, even to me, his lawyer—the lawyer he himself sent for. And how risk it? I'd just as soon go out there and shoot

another one of his sons as to tell Nub Gowrie I wanted
to dig his boy's body up out of the ground it had been
consecrated and prayed into. And if I went that far, I'd
heap rather tell him I just wanted to exhume it to dig the
gold out of its teeth than to tell him the reason was to
save a nigger from being lynched.'

'But suppose——' he said.

'Listen to me,' his uncle said with a sort of weary yet
indomitable patience: 'Try to listen. Lucas is locked behind a proof steel door. He's got the best protection
Hampton or anybody else in this county can possibly
give him. As Will Legate said, there are enough people
in this county to pass him and Tubbs and even that door
if they really want to. But I dont believe there are that
many people in this county who really want to hang
Lucas to a telephone pole and set fire to him with gasoline.'

And now too. But he still tried. 'But just suppose——'
he said again and now he heard for the third time almost
exactly what he had heard twice in twelve hours, and he
marvelled again at the paucity, the really almost stand-
ardised meagreness not of individual vocabularies but of
Vocabulary itself, by means of which even man can live
in vast droves and herds even in concrete warrens in
comparative amity: even his uncle too:

'Suppose it then. Lucas should have thought of that
before he shot a white man in the back.' And it was only
later that he would realise his uncle was speaking to
Miss Habersham too now; at the moment he was neither
rediscovering her presence in the room nor even discovering it; he did not even remember that she had
already long since ceased to exist, turning, closing the
door upon the significantless speciosity of his uncle's

voice: 'I've told him what to do. If anything was going
to happen, they would have done it out there, at home,
in their own back yard; they would never have let Mr
Hampton get to town with him. In fact, I still dont understand why they did. But whether it was luck or mis-
management or old Mr Gowrie is failing with age, the
result is good; he's all right now and I'm going to persuade him to plead guilty to manslaughter; he's old and
I think the District Attorney will accept it. He'll go to
the penitentiary and perhaps in a few years if he
lives——' and closed the door, who had heard it all
before and would no more, out of the room which he
had never completely entered anyway and shouldn't have
stopped at all, releasing the knob for the first time since
he had put his hand on it and thinking with the frantic
niggling patience of a man in a burning house trying to
gather up a broken string of beads: *Now I'll have to walk
all the way back to the jail to ask Lucas where it is:*
realising how Lucas probability doubts and everything
else to the contrary he actually had expected his uncle
and the sheriff would take charge and make the expedi-
tion, not because he thought they would believe him but
simply because he simply could not conceive of himself
and Aleck Sander being left with it: until he remembered that Lucas had already taken care of that too, fore-
seen that too; remembering not with relief but rather with
a new burst of rage and fury beyond even his own concept
of his capacity how Lucas had not only told him what he
wanted but exactly where it was and even how to get
there and only then as afterthought asked him if he
would:—hearing the crackle of the paper on his father's
lap beyond the library door and smelling the cigar burning in the ashtray at his hand and then he saw the blue

wisp of its smoke float slowly out the open door as his
father must have picked it up in some synonymous hiatus
or throe and puffed it once: and (remembering) even by
what means to get out there and back and he thought of
himself opening the door again and saying to his uncle:
Forget Lucas. Just lend me your car and then walking
into the library and saying to his father who would have
their car keys in his pocket until he would remember
when he undressed to leave them where his mother
could find them tomorrow: *Let me have the keys, Pop. I
want to run out to the country and dig up a grave;* he
even remembered Miss Habersham's pickup truck in
front of the house (not Miss Habersham; he never
thought of her again. He just remembered a motor vehicle sitting empty and apparently unwatched on the
street not fifty yards away); the key might be, probably
was, still in the switch and the Gowrie who caught him
robbing his son's or brother's or cousin's grave might as
well catch a car-thief too.

Because (quitting abandoning emerging from scattering with one sweep that confetti-swirl of raging facetiae)
he realised that he had never doubted getting out there
and even getting the body up. He could see himself
reaching the church, the graveyard without effort nor
even any great elapse of time; he could see himself
singlehanded even having the body up and out still with
no effort, no pant and strain of muscles and lungs nor
laceration of the shrinking sensibilities. It was only then
that the whole wrecked and tumbling midnight which
peer and pant though he would he couldn't see past and
beyond, would come crashing down on him. So (moving:
he had not stopped since the first second's fraction while
he closed the office door) he flung himself bodily with

one heave into a kind of deadly reasonableness of en-
raged calculation, a calm sagacious and desperate ration-
ality not of pros and cons because there were no pros:
the reason he was going out there was that somebody had
to and nobody else would and the reason somebody had
to was that not even Sheriff Hampton (vide Will Legate
and the shotgun stationed in the lower hall of the jail
like on a lighted stage where anybody approaching would
have to see him or them before they even reached the
gate) were completely convinced that the Gowries and
their kin and friends would not try to take Lucas out of
the jail tonight and so if they were all in town tonight
trying to lynch Lucas there wouldn't be anybody hanging around out there to catch him digging up the grave
and if that was a concrete fact then its obverse would be
concrete too: if they were not in town after Lucas tonight then any one of the fifty or a hundred men and
boys in the immediate connection by blood or just fox-
hunting and whiskeymaking and pine lumbertrading
might stumble on him and Aleck Sander: and that too,
that again: he must go on a horse for the same reason:
that nobody else would except a sixteen-year-old boy who
owned nothing to go on but a horse and he must even
choose here: either to go alone on the horse in half the
time and spend three times the time getting the body up
alone because alone he would not only have to do all the
digging but the watching and listening too, or take Aleck
Sander with him (he and Aleck Sander had travelled that
way before on Highboy for even more than ten miles—a
big rawboned gelding who had taken five bars even
under a hundred and seventy-five pounds and a good
slow canter even with two up and a long jolting driving
trot as fast as the canter except that not even Aleck

Sander could stand it very long behind the saddle and
then a shuffling nameless halfrun halfwalk which he
could hold for miles under both of them, Aleck Sander
behind him for the first mile at the canter then trotting
beside the horse holding to the off stirrup for the next
one) and so get the body up in a third of the time at the
risk of having Aleck Sander keeping Lucas company
when the Gowries came with the gasoline: and suddenly
he found himself escaped back into the confetti exactly
as you put off having to step finally into the cold water,
thinking seeing hearing himself trying to explain that to
Lucas too:

We have to use the horse. We cant help it: and Lucas:
You could have axed him for the car: and he:

*He would have refused. Dont you understand? He
wouldn't only have refused, he would have locked me up
where I couldn't even have walked out there, let alone
had a horse:* and Lucas:

*All right, all right. I aint criticising you. After all, it
aint you them Gowries is fixing to set afire:*—moving
down the hall to the back door: and he was wrong; not
when he had said All right to Lucas through the steel
bars nor when he had stepped back into the hall and
closed the office door behind him, but here was the irrevocable moment after which there would be no return;
he could stop here and never pass it, let the wreckage of
midnight crash harmless and impotent against these walls
because they were strong, they would endure; they were
home, taller than wreckage, stronger than fear;—not
even stopping, not even curious to ask himself if perhaps
he dared not stop, letting the screen door quietly to
behind him and down the steps into the vast furious
vortex of the soft May night and walking fast now across

the yard toward the dark cabin where Paralee and Aleck
Sander were no more asleep than all the other Negroes
within a mile of town would sleep tonight, not even in
bed but sitting quietly in the dark behind the closed
doors and shuttered windows waiting for what sound
what murmur of fury and death to breathe the spring
dark: and stopped and whistled the signal he and Aleck
Sander had been using to one another ever since they
learned to whistle, counting off the seconds until the
moment should come to repeat it, thinking how if he
were Aleck Sander he wouldn't come out of the house to
anybody's whistle tonight either when suddenly with no
sound and certainly no light behind to reveal him by
Aleck Sander stood out from the shadows, walking,
already quite near in the moonless dark, a little taller
than he though there was only a few months' difference
between them: and came up, not even looking at him
but past, over his head, toward the Square as if looking
could make a lofting trajectory like a baseball, over the
trees and the streets and the houses, to drop seeing into
the Square—not the homes in the shady yards and the
peaceful meals and the resting and the sleep which were
the end and the reward, but the Square: the edifices
created and ordained for trade and government and judgment and incarceration where strove and battled the
passions of men for which the rest and the little death of
sleep were the end and the escape and the reward.

'So they aint come for old Lucas yet,' Aleck Sander
said.

'Is that what your people think about it too?' he said.

'And so would you,' Aleck Sander said. 'It's the ones
like Lucas makes trouble for everybody.'

'Then maybe you better go to the office and sit with
Uncle Gavin instead of coming with me.'

'Going where with you?' Aleck Sander said. And he
told him, harsh and bald, in four words:

'Dig up Vinson Gowrie.' Aleck Sander didn't move,
still looking past and over his head toward the Square.
'Lucas said it wasn't his gun that killed him.'

Still not moving Aleck Sander began to laugh, not
loud and with no mirth: just laughing; he said exactly
what his uncle had said hardly a minute ago: 'So would
I,' Aleck Sander said. He said: 'Me? Go out there and
dig that dead white man up? Is Mr Gavin already in the
office or do I just sit there until he comes?'

'Lucas is going to pay you,' he said. 'He told me that
even before he told me what it was.'

Aleck Sander laughed, without mirth or scorn or anything else: with no more in the sound of it than there is
anything in the sound of breathing but just breathing.
'I aint rich,' he said. 'I dont need money.'

'At least you'll saddle Highboy while I hunt for a
flashlight, wont you?' he said. 'You're not too proud
about Lucas to do that, are you?'

'Certainly,' Aleck Sander said, turning.

'And get the pick and shovel. And the long tie-rope.
I'll need that too.'

'Certainly,' Aleck Sander said. He paused, half turned.
'How you going to tote a pick and shovel both on Highboy when he dont even like to see a riding switch in
your hand?'

'I dont know,' he said and Aleck Sander went on and
he turned back toward the house and at first he thought
it was his uncle coming rapidly around the house from
the front, not because he believed that his uncle might

have suspected and anticipated what he was about because he did not, his uncle had dismissed that too immediately and thoroughly not only from conception but from possibility too, but because he no longer remembered anyone else available for it to have been and even after he saw it was a woman he assumed it was his mother, even after he should have recognised the hat, right up to the instant when Miss Habersham called his name and his first impulse was to step quickly and quietly around the corner of the garage, from where he could reach the lot fence still unseen and climb it and go on to the stable and so go out the pasture gate without passing the house again at all, flashlight or not but it was already too late: calling his name: 'Charles:' in that tense urgent whisper then came rapidly up and stopped facing him, speaking in that tense rapid murmur:

'What did he tell you?' and now he knew what it was that had nudged at his attention back in his uncle's office when he had recognised her and then in the next second flashed away: old Molly, Lucas' wife, who had been the daughter of one of old Doctor Habersham's, Miss Habersham's grandfather's, slaves, she and Miss Habersham the same age, born in the same week and both suckled at Molly's mother's breast and grown up together almost inextricably like sisters, like twins, sleeping in the same room, the white girl in the bed, the Negro girl on a cot at the foot of it almost until Molly and Lucas married, and Miss Habersham had stood up in the Negro church as godmother to Molly's first child.

'He said it wasn't his pistol,' he said.

'So he didn't do it,' she said, rapid still and with something even more than urgency in her voice now.

'I dont know,' he said.

'Nonsense,' she said. 'If it wasn't his pistol——'

'I dont know,' he said.

'You must know. You saw him—talked to him——'

'I dont know,' he said. He said it calmly, quietly, with a kind of incredulous astonishment as though he had only now realised what he had promised, intended: 'I just dont know. I still dont know. I'm just going out there ......' He stopped, his voice died. There was an instant a second in which he even remembered he should have been wishing he could recall it, the last unfinished sentence. Though it was probably already too late and she had already done herself what little finishing the sentence needed and at any moment now she would cry, protest, ejaculate and bring the whole house down on him. Then in the same second he stopped remembering it. She said:

'Of course:' immediate murmurous and calm; he thought for another half of a second that she hadn't understood at all and then in the other half forgot that too, the two of them facing each other indistinguishable in the darkness across the tense and rapid murmur: and then he heard his own voice speaking in the same tone and pitch, the two of them not conspiratorial exactly but rather like two people who have irrevocably accepted a gambit they are not at all certain they can cope with: only that they will resist it: 'We dont even know it wasn't his pistol. He just said it wasn't.'

'Yes.'

'He didn't say whose it was nor whether or not he fired it. He didn't even tell you he didn't fire it. He just said it wasn't his pistol.'

'Yes.'

'And your uncle told you there in his study that that's

just exactly what he would say, all he could say.' He didn't answer that. It wasn't a question. Nor did she give him time. 'All right,' she said. 'Now what? To find out if it wasn't his pistol—find out whatever it was he meant? Go out there and what?'

He told her, as badly as he had told Aleck Sander, explicit and succinct: 'Look at him:' not even pausing to think how here he should certainly have anticipated at least a gasp. 'Go out there and dig him up and bring him to town where somebody that knows bullet holes can look at the bullet hole in him——'

'Yes,' Miss Habersham said. 'Of course. Naturally he wouldn't tell your uncle. He's a Negro and your uncle's a man:' and now Miss Habersham in her turn repeating and paraphrasing and he thought how it was not really a paucity a meagreness of vocabulary, it was in the first place because the deliberate violent blotting out obliteration of a human life was itself so simple and so final that the verbiage which surrounded it enclosed it insulated it intact into the chronicle of man had of necessity to be simple and uncomplex too, repetitive, almost monotonous even; and in the second place, vaster than that, adumbrating that, because what Miss Habersham paraphrased was simple truth, not even fact and so there was not needed a great deal of diversification and originality to express it because truth was universal, it had to be universal to be truth and so there didn't need to be a great deal of it just to keep running something no bigger than one earth and so anybody could know truth; all they had to do was just to pause, just to stop, just to wait: 'Lucas knew it would take a child—or an old woman like me: someone not concerned with probability, with evidence. Men like your uncle and Mr Hampton have

had to be men too long, busy too long.——Yes?' she said.
'Bring him in to town where someone who knows can
look at the bullet hole. And suppose they look at it and
find out it was Lucas' pistol?' And he didn't answer that
at all, nor had she waited again, saying, already turning:
'We'll need a pick and shovel. I've got a flashlight in
the truck——'

'We?' he said.

She stopped; she said almost patiently: 'It's fifteen
miles out there——'

'Ten,' he said.

'——a grave is six feet deep. It's after eight now and
you may have only until midnight to get back to town in
time——' and something else but he didn't even hear it.
He wasn't even listening. He had said this himself to
Lucas only fifteen minutes ago but it was only now that
he understood what he himself had said. It was only after
hearing someone else say it that he comprehended not
the enormity of his intention but the simple inert un-
wieldy impossible physical vastness of what he faced;
he said quietly, with hopeless indomitable amazement:

'We cant possibly do it.'

'No,' Miss Habersham said. 'Well?'

'Ma'am?' he said. 'What did you say?'

'I said you haven't even got a car.'

'We were going on the horse.'

Now she said, 'We?'

'Me and Aleck Sander.'

'Then we'll have three,' she said. 'Get your pick and
shovel. They'll begin to wonder in the house why they
haven't heard my truck start.' She moved again.

'Yessum,' he said. 'Drive on down the lane to the pasture gate. We'll meet you there.'

He didn't wait either. He heard the truck start as he climbed the lot fence; presently he could see Highboy's blaze in the black yawn of the stable hallway; Aleck Sander jerked the buckled girth-strap home through the keeper as he came up. He unsnapped the tie-rope from the bit-ring before he remembered and snapped it back and untied the other end from the wall-ring and looped it and the reins up over Highboy's head and led him out of the hallway and got up.

'Here,' Aleck Sander said reaching up the pick and shovel but Highboy had already begun to dance even before he could have seen them as he always did even at a hedge switch and he set him back hard and steadied him as Aleck Sander said 'Stand still!' and gave Highboy a loud slap on the rump, passing up the pick and shovel and he steadied them across the saddle-bow and managed to hold Highboy back on his heels for another second, long enough to free his foot from the near stirrup for Aleck Sander to get his foot into it, Highboy moving then in a long almost buck-jump as Aleck Sander swung up behind and still trying to run until he steadied him again with one hand, the pick and shovel jouncing on the saddle, and turned him across the pasture toward the gate. 'Hand me them damn shovels and picks,' Aleck Sander said. 'Did you get the flashlight?'

'What do you care?' he said. Aleck Sander reached his spare hand around him and took the pick and shovel; again for a second Highboy could actually see them but this time he had both hands free for the snaffle and the curb too. 'You aint going anywhere to need a flashlight. You just said so.'

They had almost reached the gate. He could see the dark blob of the halted truck against the pale road beyond it; that is, he could believe he saw it because he knew it was there. But Aleck Sander actually saw it: who seemed able to see in the dark almost like an animal. Carrying the pick and shovel, Aleck Sander had no free hand, nevertheless he had one with which he reached suddenly again and caught the reins outside his own hands and jerked Highboy almost back to a squat and said in a hissing whisper: 'What's that?'

'It's Miss Eunice Habersham's truck,' he said. 'She's going with us. Turn him loose, confound it!' wrenching the reins from Aleck Sander, who released them quickly enough now, saying,

'She's gonter take the truck:' and not even dropping the pick and shovel but flinging them clattering and clanging against the gate and slipping down himself and just in time because now Highboy stood erect on his hind feet until he struck him hard between the ears with the looped tie-rope.

'Open the gate,' he said.

'We wont need the horse,' Aleck Sander said. 'Unsaddle and bridle him here. We'll put um up when we get back.'

Which was what Miss Habersham said; through the gate now and Highboy still sidling and beating his hooves while Aleck Sander put the pick and shovel into the back of the truck as though he expected Aleck Sander to throw them at him this time, and Miss Habersham's voice from the dark cab of the truck:

'He sounds like a good horse. Has he got a four-footed gait too?'

'Yessum,' he said. 'Nome,' he said. 'I'll take the horse too. The nearest house is a mile from the church but somebody might still hear a car. We'll leave the truck at the bottom of the hill when we cross the branch.' Then he answered that too before she had time to say it: 'We'll need the horse to bring him back down to the truck.'

'Heh,' Aleck Sander said. It wasn't laughing. But then nobody thought it was. 'How do you reckon that horse is going to tote what you dug up when he dont even want to tote what you going to do the digging with?' But he had already thought of that too, remembering his grandfather telling of the old days when deer and bear and wild turkey could be hunted in Yoknapatawpha County within twelve miles of Jefferson, of the hunters: Major de Spain who had been his grandfather's cousin and old General Compson and Uncle Ike McCaslin, Carothers Edmonds' great-uncle, still alive at ninety, and Boon Hogganbeck whose mother's mother had been a Chickasaw woman and the Negro Sam Fathers whose father had been a Chickasaw chief, and Major de Spain's one-eyed hunting mule Alice who wasn't afraid even of the smell of bear and he thought how if you really were the sum of your ancestry it was too bad the ancestors who had evolved him into a secret resurrector of country graveyards hadn't thought to equip him with a descendant of that unspookable one-eyed mule to transport his subjects on.

'I dont know,' he said.

'Maybe he'll learn by the time we get back to the truck,' Miss Habersham said. 'Can Aleck Sander drive?'

'Yessum,' Aleck Sander said.

Highboy was still edgy; held down he would merely have lathered himself to no end so since it was cool tonight for the first mile he actually kept in sight of the truck's tail-light. Then he slowed, the light fled diminishing on and vanished beyond a curve and he settled High-

boy into the shambling halfrun halfwalk which no show
judge would ever pass but which covered ground; nine
miles of it to be covered and he thought with a kind of
ghastly amusement that at last he would have time to
think, thinking how it was too late to think now, not one
of the three of them dared think now, if they had done but
one thing tonight it was at least to put all thought ratio-
cination contemplation forever behind them; five miles
from town and he would cross (probably Miss Habersham and Aleck Sander in the truck already had) the
invisible surveyor's line which was the boundary of Beat
Four: the notorious, the fabulous almost and certainly
least of all did any of them dare think now, thinking
how it was never difficult for an outlander to do two
things at once which Beat Four wouldn't like since Beat
Four already in advance didn't like most of the things
which people from town (and from most of the rest of
the county too for that matter) did: but that it remained
for them, a white youth of sixteen and a Negro one of
the same and an old white spinster of seventy to elect
and do at the same time the two things out of all man's
vast reservoir of invention and capability that Beat Four
would repudiate and retaliate on most violently: to violate the grave of one of its progeny in order to save a
nigger murderer from its vengeance.

But at least they would have some warning (not speculating on who the warning could help since they who
would be warned were already six and seven miles from
the jail and still moving away from it as fast as he dared
push the horse) because if Beat Four were coming in
tonight he should begin to pass them soon (or they pass
him)—the battered mud-stained cars, the empty trucks
for hauling cattle and lumber, and the saddled horses

and mules. Yet so far he had passed nothing whatever since he left town; the road lay pale and empty before and behind him too; the lightless houses and cabins squatted or loomed beside it, the dark land stretched away into the darkness strong with the smell of plowed earth and now and then the heavy scent of flowering orchards lying across the road for him to ride through like stagnant skeins of smoke so maybe they were making better time than even he had hoped and before he could stop it he had thought *Maybe we can, maybe we will after all;*—before he could leap and spring and smother and blot it from thinking not because he couldn't really believe they possibly could and not because you dont dare think whole even to yourself the entirety of a dear hope or wish let alone a desperate one else you yourself have doomed it but because thinking it into words even only to himself was like the struck match which doesn't dispel the dark but only exposes its terror—one weak flash and glare revealing for a second the empty road's the dark and empty land's irrevocable immitigable negation.

Because—almost there now; Aleck Sander and Miss Habersham had already arrived probably a good thirty minutes ago and he took a second to hope Aleck Sander had had forethought enough to drive the truck off the road where anybody passing would not see it, then in the same second he knew that of course Aleck Sander had done that and it was not Aleck Sander he had ever doubted but himself for even for one second doubting Aleck Sander—he had not seen one Negro since leaving town, with whom at this hour on Sunday night in May the road should have been constant as beads almost—the men and young women and girls and even a few old men and women and even children before it got too late, but

mostly the men the young bachelors who since last Monday at daylight had braced into the shearing earth the
lurch and heave of plows behind straining and surging
mules then at noon Saturday had washed and shaved and
put on the clean Sunday shirts and pants and all Saturday night had walked the dusty roads and all day Sunday
and all Sunday night would still walk them until barely
time to reach home and change back into the overalls
and the brogans and catch and gear up the mules and
forty-eight hours even bedless save for the brief time
there was a woman in it be back in the field again the
plow's point set into the new furrow when Monday's
sun rose: but not now, not tonight: where in town except for Paralee and Aleck Sander he had seen none
either for twenty-four hours but he had expected that,
they were acting exactly as Negroes and whites both
would have expected Negroes to act at such a time; they
were still there, they had not fled, you just didn't see
them—a sense a feeling of their constant presence and
nearness: black men and women and children breathing
and waiting inside their barred and shuttered houses, not
crouching cringing shrinking, not in anger and not quite
in fear: just waiting, biding since theirs was an armament
which the white man could not match nor—if he but
knew it—even cope with: patience; just keeping out of
sight and out of the way,—but not here, no sense feeling
here of a massed adjacence, a dark human presence biding and unseen; this land was a desert and a witness, this
empty road its postulate (it would be some time yet before he would realise how far he had come: a provincial
Mississippian, a child who when the sun set this same day
had appeared to be—and even himself believed, provided he had thought about it at all—still a swaddled

unwitting infant in the long tradition of his native land
—or for that matter a witless foetus itself struggling—if
he was aware that there had been any throes—blind and
insentient and not even yet awaked in the simple painless convulsion of emergence) of the deliberate turning
as with one back of the whole dark people on which the
very economy of the land itself was founded, not in heat
or anger nor even regret but in one irremediable invincible inflexible repudiation, upon not a racial outrage
but a human shame.

Now he was there; Highboy tightened and even began
to drive a little, even after nine miles, smelling water
and now he could see distinguish the bridge or at least
the gap of lighter darkness where the road spanned the
impenetrable blackness of the willows banding the
branch and then Aleck Sander stood out from the bridge
rail; Highboy snorted at him then he recognised him too,
without surprise, not even remembering how he had
wondered once if Aleck Sander would have forethought
to hide the truck, not even remembering that he had
expected no less, not stopping, checking Highboy back
to a walk across the bridge then giving him his head to
turn from the road beyond the bridge and drop in stiff
fore-legged jolts down toward the water invisible for a
moment longer then he too could see the reflected wim-
pling where it caught the sky: until Highboy stopped
and snorted again then heaved suddenly up and back,
almost unseating him.

'He smell quicksand,' Aleck Sander said. 'Let him
wait till he gets home, anyway. I'd rather be doing something else than what I am too.'

But he took Highboy a little further down the bank
where he might get down to the water but again he only

feinted at it so he pulled away and back onto the road
and freed the stirrup for Aleck Sander, Highboy again
already in motion when Aleck Sander swung up. 'Here,'
Aleck Sander said but he had already swung Highboy
off the gravel and into the narrow dirt road turning sharp
toward the black loom of the ridge and beginning almost
at once its long slant up into the hills though even before
it began to rise the strong constant smell of pines was
coming down on them with no wind behind it yet firm
and hard as a hand almost, palpable against the moving
body as water would have been. The slant steepened
under the horse and even carrying double he essayed to
run at it as was his habit at any slope, gathering and
surging out until he checked him sharply back and even
then he had to hold him hard-wristed in a strong lurching
uneven walk until the first level of the plateau flattened
and even as Aleck Sander said 'Here' again Miss Habersham stood out of the obscurity at the roadside carrying
the pick and shovel. Aleck Sander slid down as Highboy
stopped. He followed.

'Stay on,' Miss Habersham said. 'I've got the tools and
the flashlight.'

'It's a half mile yet,' he said. 'Up hill. This aint a side-
saddle but maybe you could sit sideways. Where's the
truck?' he said to Aleck Sander.

'Behind them bushes,' Aleck Sander said. 'We aint
holding a parade. Leastways I aint.'

'No no,' Miss Habersham said. 'I can walk.'

'We'll save time,' he said. 'It must be after ten now.
He's gentle. That was just when Aleck Sander threw the
pick and shovel——'

'Of course,' Miss Habersham said. She handed the
tools to Aleck Sander and approached the horse.

'I'm sorry it aint——' he said.

'Pah,' she said and took the reins from him and before he could even brace his hand for her foot she put it in the stirrup and went up as light and fast as either he or Aleck Sander could have done, onto the horse astride so that he had just time to avert his face, feeling her looking down in the darkness at his turned head. 'Pah,' she said again. 'I'm seventy years old. Besides, we'll worry about my skirt after we are done with this:'—moving Highboy herself before he had hardly time to take hold of the bit, back into the road when Aleck Sander said:

'Hush.' They stopped, immobile in the long constant invisible flow of pine. 'Mule coming down the hill,' Aleck Sander said.

He began to turn the horse at once. 'I dont hear anything,' Miss Habersham said. 'Are you sure?'

'Yessum,' he said, turning Highboy back off the road: 'Aleck Sander's sure.' And standing at Highboy's head among the trees and undergrowth, his other hand lying on the horse's nostrils in case he decided to nicker at the other animal, he heard it too—the horse or mule coming steadily down the road from the crest. It was unshod probably; actually the only sound he really heard was the creak of leather and he wondered (without doubting for one second that he had) how Aleck Sander had heard it at all the two minutes and more it had taken the animal to reach them. Then he could see it or that is where it was passing them—a blob, a movement, a darker shadow than shadow against the pale dirt of the road, going on down the hill, the soft steady shuffle and screak of leather dying away, then gone. But they waited a moment more.

'What was that he was toting on the saddle in front of him?' Aleck Sander said.

'I couldn't even see whether it was a man on it or not,' he said.

'I couldn't see anything,' Miss Habersham said. He led the horse back into the road. 'Suppose——' she said.

'Aleck Sander will hear it in time,' he said. So once more Highboy surged strong and steady at the steepening pitch, he carrying the shovel and clutching the leather under Miss Habersham's thin hard calf on one side and Aleck Sander with the pick on the other, mounting, really moving quite fast through the strong heady vivid living smell of the pines which did something to the lungs, the breathing as (he imagined: he had never tasted it. He could have—the sip from the communion cup didn't count because it was not only a sip but sour consecrated and sharp: the deathless blood of our Lord not to be tasted, moving not downward toward the stomach but upward and outward into the Allknowledge between good and evil and the choice and the repudiation and the acceptance forever—at the table at Thanksgiving and Christmas but he had never wanted to.) wine did to the stomach. They were quite high now, the ridged land opening and tumbling away invisible in the dark yet with the sense, the sensation of height and space; by day he could have seen them, ridge on pine-dense ridge rolling away to the east and the north in similitude of the actual mountains in Carolina and before that in Scotland where his ancestors had come from but he hadn't seen yet, his breath coming a little short now and he could not only hear but feel too the hard short blasts from Highboy's lungs as he was actually trying to run at this slope too even carrying a rider and dragging two, Miss

Habersham steadying him, holding him down until they came out onto the true crest and Aleck Sander said once more 'Here' and Miss Habersham turned the horse out of the road because he could still see nothing until they were off the road and only then he distinguished the clearing not because it was a clearing but because in a thin distillation of starlight there stood, canted a little where the earth had sunk, the narrow slab of a marble headstone. And he could hardly see the church (weathered, unpainted, of wood and not much larger than a single room) at all even when he led Highboy around behind it and tied the reins to a sapling and unsnapped the tie-rope from the bit and went back to where Miss Habersham and Aleck Sander were waiting.

'It'll be the only fresh one,' he said. 'Lucas said there hasn't been a burying here since last winter.'

'Yes,' Miss Habersham said. 'The flowers too. Aleck Sander's already found it.' But to make sure (he thought quietly, he didn't know to whom: *I'm going to make a heap more mistakes but dont let this be one of them.*) he hooded the flashlight in his wadded handkerchief so that one thin rapid pencil touched for a second the raw mound with its meagre scattering of wreaths and bouquets and even single blooms and then for another second the headstone adjacent to it, long enough to read the engraved name: *Amanda Workitt wife of N. B. Forrest Gowrie 1878 1926* then snapped it off and again the darkness came in and the strong scent of the pines and they stood for a moment beside the raw mound, doing nothing at all. 'I hate this,' Miss Habersham said.

'You aint the one,' Aleck Sander said. 'It's just a half a mile back to the truck. Down hill too.'

She moved; she was first. 'Move the flowers,' she said. 'Carefully. Can you see?'

'Yessum,' Aleck Sander said. 'Aint many. Looks like they throwed them at it too.'

'But we wont,' Miss Habersham said. 'Move them carefully.' And it must be nearing eleven now; they would not possibly have time; Aleck Sander was right: the thing to do was to go back to the truck and drive away, back to town and through town and on, not to stop, not even to have time to think for having to keep on driving, steering, keeping the truck going in order to keep on moving, never to come back; but then they had never had time, they had known that before they ever left Jefferson and he thought for an instant how if Aleck Sander really had meant it when he said he would not come and if he would have come alone in that case and then (quickly) he wouldn't think about that at all, Aleck Sander using the shovel for the first shift while he used the pick though the dirt was still so loose they didn't really need the pick (and if it hadn't been still loose they couldn't have done it at all even by daylight); two shovels would have done and faster too but it was too late for that now until suddenly Aleck Sander handed him the shovel and climbed out of the hole and vanished and (not even using the flashlight) with that same sense beyond sight and hearing both which had realised that what Highboy smelled at the branch was quicksand and which had discovered the horse or the mule coming down the hill a good minute before either he or Miss Habersham could begin to hear it, returned with a short light board so that both of them had shovels now and he could hear the *chuck!* and then the faint swish as Aleck Sander thrust the board into the dirt and then flung the load up and outward, expelling his breath, saying 'Hah!' each time—a sound furious raging and restrained, going faster and faster until the ejaculation was almost as rapid as the beat of someone running: 'Hah! . . . Hah! . . . Hah!' so that he said over his shoulder:

'Take it easy. We're doing all right:' straightened his own back for a moment to mop his sweating face and seeing as always Miss Habersham in motionless silhouette on the sky above him in the straight cotton dress and the round hat on the exact top of her head such as few people had seen in fifty years and probably no one at any time looking up out of a halfway rifled grave: more than halfway because spading again he heard the sudden thud of wood on wood, then Aleck Sander said sharply:

'Go on. Get out of here and gimme room:' and flung the board up and out and took, jerked the shovel from his hands and he climbed out of the pit and even as he stooped groping Miss Habersham handed him the coiled tie-rope.

'The flashlight too,' he said and she handed him that and he stood too while the strong hard immobile flow of the pines bleached the sweat from his body until his wet shirt felt cold on his flesh and invisible below him in the pit the shovel rasped and scraped on wood, and stooping and hooding the light again he flashed it downward upon the unpainted lid of the pine box and switched it off.

'All right,' he said. 'That's enough. Get out:' and Aleck Sander with the last shovel of dirt released the shovel too, flinging the whole thing arcing out of the pit like a javelin and followed it in one motion, and carrying the rope and the light he dropped into the pit and only then remembered he would need a hammer, crowbar—something to open the lid with and the only thing of that nature would be what Miss Habersham might happen to have in the truck a half-mile away and the walk back uphill, stooping to feel, examine the catch or whatever it was to be forced when he discovered that the lid was not fastened at all: so that straddling it, balancing himself on one foot he managed to open the lid up and back and prop it with one elbow while he shook the rope out and found the end and snapped on the flashlight and pointed it down and then said, 'Wait.' He said, 'Wait.' He was still saying 'Wait' when he finally heard Miss Habersham speaking in a hissing whisper:

'Charles . . . . . Charles.'

'This aint Vinson Gowrie,' he said. 'This man's name is Montgomery. He's some kind of a shoestring timber-buyer from over in Crossman County.'

Chapter Five

THEY HAD TO FILL THE HOLE back up of course and besides he had the horse. But even then it was a good while until daylight when he left Highboy with Aleck Sander at the pasture gate and tried remembered to tiptoe into the house but at once his mother her hair loose and in her nightdress wailed from right beside the front door: 'Where have you been?' then followed him to his uncle's door and then while his uncle was putting some clothes on: 'You? Digging up a grave?' and he with a sort of weary indefatigable patience, just about worn out himself now from riding and digging then turning around and undigging and then riding again, somehow managing to stay that one jump ahead of what he had really never hoped to beat anyway:

'Aleck Sander and Miss Habersham helped:' which if anything seemed to be worse though she was still not loud: just amazed and inexpugnable until his uncle came out fully dressed even to his necktie but not shaved and said,

'Now Maggie, do you want to wake Charley?' then following them back to the front door and this time she said—and he thought again how you could never really beat them because of their fluidity which was not just a capacity for mobility but a willingness to abandon with the substanceless promptitude of wind or air itself not

only position but principle too; you didn't have to marshal your forces because you already had them: superior
artillery, weight, right justice and precedent and usage
and everything else and made your attack and cleared
the field, swept all before you—or so you thought until
you discovered that the enemy had not retreated at all
but had already abandoned the field and had not merely
abandoned the field but had usurped your very battlecry
in the process; you believed you had captured a citadel
and instead found you had merely entered an untenable
position and then found the unimpaired and even un-
marked battle set up again in your unprotected and un-
suspecting rear—she said:

'But he's got to sleep! He hasn't even been to bed!' so
that he actually stopped until his uncle said, hissed at
him:

'Come on. What's the matter with you? Dont you know
she's tougher than you and me both just as old Habersham was tougher than you and Aleck Sander put to-
together; you might have gone out there without her to
drag you by the hand but Aleck Sander wouldn't and
I'm still not so sure you would when you came right
down to it.' So he moved on too beside his uncle toward
where Miss Habersham sat in the truck behind his
uncle's parked car (it had been in the garage at nine
oclock last night; later when he had time he would remember to ask his uncle just where his mother had sent
him to look for him). 'I take that back,' his uncle said.
'Forget it. Out of the mouths of babes and sucklings and
old ladies——' he paraphrased. 'Quite true, as a lot of
truth often is, only a man just dont like to have it flung
in his teeth at three oclock in the morning. And dont
even forget your mother, which of course you cant; she

has already long since seen to that. Just remember that they can stand anything, accept any fact (it's only men who burk at facts) provided they dont have to face it; can assimilate it with their heads turned away and one hand extended behind them as the politician accepts the bribe. Look at her: who will spend a long contented happy life never abating one jot of her refusal to forgive you for being able to button your own pants.'

And still a good while until daylight when his uncle stopped the car at the sheriff's gate and led the way up the short walk and onto the rented gallery. (Since he couldn't succeed himself, although now in his third term the elapsed time covering Sheriff Hampton's tenure was actually almost twice as long as the twelve years of his service. He was a countryman, a farmer and son of farmers when he was first elected and now owned himself the farm and house where he had been born, living in the rented one in town during his term of office then returning to the farm which was his actual home at each expiration, to live there until he could run for—and be elected—sheriff again.)

'I hope he's not a heavy sleeper,' Miss Habersham said.

'He aint asleep,' his uncle said. 'He's cooking breakfast.'

'Cooking breakfast?' Miss Habersham said: and then he knew that, for all her flat back and the hat which had never shifted from the exact top of her head as though she kept it balanced there not by any pins but simply by the rigid unflagging poise of her neck as Negro women carry a whole family wash, she was about worn out with strain and lack of sleep too.

'He's a country man,' his uncle said. 'Any food he eats after daylight in the morning is dinner. Mrs. Hampton's in Memphis with their daughter waiting for the baby and the only woman who'll cook a man's breakfast at half-past three a. m. is his wife. No hired town cook's going to do it. She comes at a decent hour about eight oclock and washes the dishes.' His uncle didn't knock. He started to open the door then stopped and looked back past both of them to where Aleck Sander stood at the bottom of the front steps. 'And dont you think you're going to get out of it just because your mama dont vote,' he told Aleck Sander. 'You come on too.'

Then his uncle opened the door and at once they smelled the coffee and the frying hogmeat, walking on linoleum toward a faint light at the rear of the hall then across a linoleum-floored diningroom in rented Grand Rapids mission into the kitchen, into the hard cheerful blast of a woodstove where the sheriff stood over a sputtering skillet in his undershirt and pants and socks, his braces dangling and his hair mussed and tousled with sleep like that of a ten-year-old boy, a battercake turner in one hand and a cuptowel in the other. The sheriff had already turned his vast face toward the door before they entered it and he watched the little hard pale eyes flick from his uncle to Miss Habersham to himself and then to Aleck Sander and even then it was not the eyes which widened so much for that second but rather the little hard black pupils which had tightened in that one flick to pinpoints. But the sheriff said nothing yet, just looking at his uncle now and now even the little hard pupils seemed to expand again as when an expulsion of breath untightens the chest and while the three of them stood quietly and steadily watching the sheriff his uncle told it, rapid and condensed and succinct, from the moment in the jail last night when his uncle had realised that

Lucas had started to tell—or rather ask—him something, to the one when he had entered his uncle's room ten minutes ago and waked him up, and stopped and again they watched the little hard eyes go flick. flick. slick. across their three faces then back to his uncle again, staring at his uncle for almost a quarter of a minute without even blinking. Then the sheriff said:

'You wouldn't come here at four oclock in the morning with a tale like that if it wasn't so.'

'You aint listening just to two sixteen-year-old children,' his uncle said. 'I remind you that Miss Habersham was there.'

'You dont have to,' the sheriff said. 'I haven't forgot it. I dont think I ever will.' Then the sheriff turned. A gigantic man and in the fifties too, you wouldn't think he could move fast and he didn't really seem to yet he had taken another skillet from a nail in the wall behind the stove and was already turning toward the table (where for the first time he noticed, saw the side of smoked meat) before he seemed to have moved at all, picking up a butcher knife from beside the meat before his uncle could even begin to speak:

'Have we got time for that? You've got to drive sixty miles to Harrisburg to the District Attorney; you'll have to take Miss Habersham and these boys with you for witnesses to try and persuade him to originate a petition for the exhumation of Vinson Gowrie's body——'

The sheriff wiped the handle of the knife rapidly with the cuptowel. 'I thought you told me Vinson Gowrie aint in that grave.'

'Officially he is,' his uncle said. 'By the county records he is. And if you, living right here and knowing Miss Habersham and me all your political life, had to ask me

twice, what do you think Jim Halladay is going to do?—
Then you've got to drive sixty miles back here with your
witnesses and the petition and get Judge Maycox to issue
an order——'

The sheriff dropped the cuptowel onto the table.
'Have I?' he said mildly, almost inattentively: so that his
uncle stopped perfectly still watching him as the sheriff
turned from the table, the knife in his hand.

'Oh,' his uncle said.

'I've thought of something else too,' the sheriff said.
'I'm surprised you aint. Or maybe you have.'

His uncle stared at the sheriff. Then Aleck Sander—
he was behind them all, not yet quite through the diningroom door into the kitchen—said in a voice as mild and
impersonal as though he were reading off a slogan catch-
phrase advertising some object he didn't own and never
expected to want:

'It mought not a been a mule. It mought have been a
horse.'

'Maybe you've thought of it now,' the sheriff said.

'Oh,' his uncle said. He said: 'Yes.' But Miss Habersham was already talking. She had given Aleck Sander
one quick hard look but now she was looking at the
sheriff again as quick and as hard.

'So do I,' she said. 'And I think we deserve better than
secrecy.'

'I do too, Miss Eunice,' the sheriff said. 'Except that
the one that needs considering right now aint in this
room.'

'Oh,' Miss Habersham said. She said 'Yes' too. She
said, 'Of course:' already moving, meeting the sheriff
halfway between the table and the door and taking the
knife from him and going on to the table when he passed

her and came on toward the door, his uncle then he then
Aleck Sander moving out of the way as the sheriff went
on into the diningroom and across it into the dark hall,
shutting the door behind him: and then he was wondering why the sheriff hadn't finished dressing when he got
up; a man who didn't mind or had to or anyway did get
up at half-past three in the morning to cook himself
some breakfast would hardly mind getting up five minutes earlier and have time to put his shirt and shoes on
too then Miss Habersham spoke and he remembered
her; a lady's presence of course was why he had gone to
put on the shirt and shoes without even waiting to eat
the breakfast and Miss Habersham spoke and he jerked,
without moving heaved up out of sleep, having been
asleep for seconds maybe even minutes on his feet as a
horse sleeps but Miss Habersham was still only turning
the side of meat onto its edge to cut the first slice. She
said: 'Cant he telephone to Harrisburg and have the
District Attorney telephone back to Judge Maycox?'

'That's what he doing now,' Aleck Sander said. 'Telephoning.'

'Maybe you'd better go to the hall where you can
overhear good what he's saying,' his uncle told Aleck
Sander. Then his uncle looked at Miss Habersham again;
he too watched her slicing rapid slice after slice of the
bacon as fast and even almost as a machine could have
done it. 'Mr Hampton says we wont need any papers.
We can attend to it ourselves without bothering Judge
Maycox——'

Miss Habersham released the knife. She didn't lay it
down, she just opened her hand and in the same motion
picked up the cuptowel and was wiping her hands as
she turned from the table, crossing the kitchen toward

them faster, a good deal faster than even the sheriff had moved. 'Then what are we wasting time here for?' she said. 'For him to put on his necktie and coat?'

His uncle stepped quickly in front of her. 'We cant do anything in the dark,' he said. 'We must wait for daylight.'

'We didn't,' Miss Habersham said. Then she stopped; it was either that or walk over his uncle though his uncle didn't touch her, just standing between her and the door until she had to stop at least for the second for his uncle to get out of the way: and he looked at her too, straight, thin, almost shapeless in the straight cotton dress beneath the round exactitude of the hat and he thought *She's too old for this* and then corrected it: *No a woman a lady shouldn't have to do this* and then remembered last night when he had left the office and walked across the back yard and whistled for Aleck Sander and he knew he had believed—and he still believed it—that he would have gone alone even if Aleck Sander had stuck to his refusal but it was only after Miss Habersham came around the house and spoke to him that he knew he was going to go through with it and he remembered again what old Ephraim had told him after they found the ring under the hog trough: *If you got something outside the common run that's got to be done and cant wait, dont waste your time on the menfolks; they works on what your uncle calls the rules and the cases. Get the womens and the children at it; they works on the circumstances.* Then the hall door opened. He heard the sheriff cross the diningroom to the kitchen door. But the sheriff didn't enter the kitchen, stopping in the door, standing in it even after Miss Habersham said in a harsh, almost savage voice:

'Well?' and he hadn't put on his shoes nor even picked up the dangling galluses and he didn't seem to have heard Miss Habersham at all: just standing looming bulging in the door looking at Miss Habersham—not at the hat, not at her eyes nor even her face: just at her— as you might look at a string of letters in Russian or Chinese which someone you believed had just told you spelled your name, saying at last in a musing baffled voice:

'No:' then turning his head to look at him and saying, 'It aint you neither:' then turning his head further until he was looking at Aleck Sander while Aleck Sander slid his eyes up at the sheriff then slid them away again then slid them up again. 'You,' the sheriff said. 'You're the one. You went out there in the dark and helped dig up a dead man. Not only that, a dead white man that the rest of the white folks claimed another nigger had murdered. Why? Was it because Miss Habersham made you?'

'Never nobody made me,' Aleck Sander said. 'I didn't even know I was going. I had done already told Chick I didn't aim to. Only when we got to the truck everybody seemed to just take it for granted I wasn't going to do nothing else but go and before I knowed it I wasn't.'

'Mr Hampton,' Miss Habersham said. Now the sheriff looked at her. He even heard her now.

'Haven't you finished slicing that meat yet?' he said. 'Give me the knife then.' He took her by the arm, turning her back to the table. 'Aint you done enough rushing and stewing around tonight to last you a while? It'll be daylight in fifteen minutes and folks dont start lynchings in daylight. They might finish one by daylight if they had a little trouble or bad luck and got behind with it. But they dont start them by daylight because then they would have to see one another's faces. How many can eat more than two eggs?'

They left Aleck Sander with his breakfast at the kitchen table and carried theirs into the diningroom, he and his uncle and Miss Habersham carrying the platter of fried eggs and meat and the pan of biscuits baked last night and warmed again in the oven until they were almost like toast and the coffeepot in which the unstrained grounds and the water had been boiling together until the sheriff had thought to remove the pot from the hot part of the stove; four of them although the sheriff had set five places and they had barely sat down when the sheriff raised his head listening though he himself heard nothing, then rose and went into the dark hall and toward the rear of the house and then he heard the sound of the back door and presently the sheriff came back with Will Legate though minus the shotgun, and he turned his head enough to look out the window behind him and sure enough it was daylight.

The sheriff served the plates while his uncle and Legate passed theirs and the sheriff's cup to Miss Habersham at the coffeepot. Then at once he seemed to have been hearing for a long time the sheriff from a great distance saying '. . . boy . . . boy . . .' then 'Wake him up, Gavin. Let him eat his breakfast before he goes to sleep:' and he jerked, it was still only daylight, Miss Habersham was still pouring coffee into the same cup and he began to eat, chewing and even swallowing, rising and falling as though to the motion of the chewing along the deep soft bottomless mire of sleep, into then

out of the voices buzzing of old finished things no longer
concern of his: the sheriff's:

'Do you know Jake Montgomery, from over in Crossman County? Been in and out of town here for the last
six months or so?' then Legate's:

'Sure. A kind of jackleg timber buyer now. Used to
run a place he called a restaurant just across the Tennessee line out of Memphis, though I never heard of
nobody trying to buy nothing that had to be chewed in
it, until a man went and got killed in it one night two-
three years ago. They never did know just how much
Jake did or didn't have to do with it but the Tennessee
police run him back across the Mississippi line just on
principle. Since then I reckon he's been laying around
his pa's farm over beyond Glasgow. Maybe he's waiting
until he figgers folks have forgot about that other business and he can set up again in another place on a highway with a hole under the floor big enough to hide a
case of whiskey in.'

'What was he doing around here?' the sheriff said: then
Legate:

'Buying timber, aint he? Aint him and Vinson
Gowrie . . . . .' Then Legate said with the barest inflection, '*Was?*' and then with no inflection at all: 'What
is he doing?' and he this time, his own voice indifferent
along the soft deep edge of sleep, too indifferent to
bother if it were aloud or not:

'He aint doing anything now.'

But it was better afterward, out of the stale warm
house again into the air, the morning, the sun in one
soft high level golden wash in the highest tips of the
trees, gilding the motionless obese uprush of the town
water tank in spiderlegged elongate against the blue,

the four of them in his uncle's car once more while the
sheriff stood leaned above the driver's window, dressed
now even to a bright orange-and-yellow necktie, saying
to his uncle:

'You run Miss Eunice home so she can get some sleep.
I'll pick you up at your house in say an hour——'

Miss Habersham in the front seat with his uncle said
'Pah.' That was all. She didn't curse. She didn't need
to. It was far more definite and final than just cursing.
She leaned forward to look past his uncle at the sheriff.
'Get in your car and go to the jail or wherever you'll go
to get somebody to do the digging this time. We had to
fill it up again because we knew you wouldn't believe
it even yet unless you saw it there yourself. Go on,' she
said. 'We'll meet you out there. Go on,' she said.

But the sheriff didn't move. He could hear him breathing, vast subterrene and deliberate, like sighing almost.
'Of course I dont know about you,' the sheriff said. 'A
lady without nothing but a couple thousand chickens to
feed and nurse and water and a vegetable farm hardly
five acres big to run, might not have nothing to do all
day. But these boys anyway have got to go to school.
Leastways I never heard about any rule in the School
Board to give holidays for digging up corpses.'

And that even stopped her. But she didn't sit back
yet. She still leaned forward where she could look past
his uncle at the sheriff and he thought again *She's too
old for this, to have to do this:* only if she hadn't then
he and Aleck Sander, what she and his uncle and the
sheriff all three and his mother and father and Paralee
too would have called children, would have had to do
it—not would have done it but would have had to do
it to preserve not even justice and decency but inno-
cence: and he thought of man who apparently had to

kill man not for motive or reason but simply for the sake the need the compulsion of having to kill man, inventing creating his motive and reason afterward so that he could still stand up among man as a rational creature: whoever had had to kill Vinson Gowrie had then to dig him up dead and slay another to put in his vacated grave so that whoever had to kill him could rest; and Vinson Gowrie's kin and neighbors who would have to kill Lucas or someone or anyone, it would not really matter who, so that they could lie down and breathe quiet and even grieve quiet and so rest. The sheriff's voice was mild, almost gentle even: 'You go home. You and these boys have done fine. Likely you saved a life. Now you go home and let us attend to the rest of it. That wont be any place for a lady out there.'

But Miss Habersham was just stopped, nor even that for long: 'It wasn't for a man either last night.'

'Wait, Hope,' his uncle said. Then his uncle turned to Miss Habersham. 'Your job's in town here,' he said. 'Dont you know that?' Now Miss Habersham watched his uncle. But she still hadn't sat back in the seat, giving no ground to anyone yet; watching, it was as though she had not at all exchanged one opponent for another but without pause or falter had accepted them both, asking no quarter, crying no odds. 'Will Legate's a farmer,' his uncle said. 'Besides being up all night. He's got to go home and see to his own business for a little while.'

'Hasn't Mr Hampton got other deputies?' Miss Habersham said. 'What are they for?'

'They're just men with guns,' his uncle said. 'Legate himself told Chick and me last night that if enough men made up their minds and kept them made up, they would pass him and Mr Tubbs both in time. But if a woman, a lady, a white lady . . . . .' His uncle stopped, ceased; they stared at each other; watching them he thought again of his uncle and Lucas in the cell last night (it was last night, of course; it seemed like years now); again except for the fact that his uncle and Miss Habersham were actually looking into each other's physical eyes instead of bending each upon the other that absolute concentration of all the senses in the sum of which mere clumsy fallible perception weighed little more than the ability to read Sanskrit would, he might have been watching the last two stayers in a poker-pot. '. . . . just to sit there, in sight, where the first one that passes can have the word spread long before Beat Four can even get the truck cranked up to start to town . . . . . while we go out there and finish it for good, for ever——'

Miss Habersham leaned slowly back until her back came against the seat. She said: 'So I'm to sit there on that staircase with my skirts spread or maybe better with my back against the balustrade and one foot propped against the wall of Mrs Tubbs' kitchen while you men who never had time yesterday to ask that old nigger a few questions and so all he had last night was a boy, a child——' His uncle said nothing. The sheriff leaned above the window breathing vast subterranean sighs, not breathing hard but just as a big man seems to have to breathe. Miss Habersham said: 'Drive me home first. I've got some mending to do. I aint going to sit there all morning doing nothing so that Mrs Tubbs will think she has to talk to me. Drive me home first. I realised an hour ago what a rush and hurry you and Mr Hampton are in but you can spare the time for that. Aleck Sander can bring my truck to the jail on his way to school and leave it in front of the gate.'

'Yessum,' his uncle said.

Chapter Six

So THEY DROVE Miss Habersham home, out to the edge
of town and through the shaggy untended cedar grove
to the paintless columned portico where she got out and
went into the house and apparently on through it without even stopping because at once they could hear her
somewhere in the back yelling at someone—the old
Negro man probably who was Molly's brother and Lucas'
brother-in-law—in her strong voice strained and a little
high from sleeplessness and fatigue, then she came out
again carrying a big cardboard box full of what looked
like unironed laundry and long limp webs and ropes of
stockings and got back into the car and they drove back
to the Square through the fresh quiet morning streets:
the old big decaying wooden houses of Jefferson's long-
ago foundation set like Miss Habersham's deep in shaggy
untended lawns of old trees and rootbound scented and
flowering shrubs whose very names most people under
fifty no longer knew and which even when children
lived in them seemed still to be spellbound by the shades
of women, old women still spinsters and widows waiting
even seventy-five years later for the slow telegraph to
bring them news of Tennessee and Virginia and Pennsylvania battles, which no longer even faced the street but
peered at it over the day-after-tomorrow shoulders of the
neat small new one-storey houses designed in Florida

and California set with matching garages in their neat
plots of clipped grass and tedious flowerbeds, three and
four of them now, a subdivision now in what twenty-five
years ago had been considered a little small for one
decent front lawn, where the prosperous young married
couples lived with two children each and (as soon as they
could afford it) an automobile each and the memberships
in the country club/and the bridge clubs and the junior
rotary and chamber of commerce and the patented elec-
tric gadgets for cooking and freezing and cleaning and
the neat trim colored maids in frilled caps to run them
and talk to one another over the telephone from house
to house while the wives in sandals and pants and painted
toenails puffed lipstick-stained cigarettes over shopping
bags in the chain groceries and drugstores.

Or would have been and should have been; Sunday
and they might have passed, accepted a day with no one
to plug and unplug the humming sweepers and turn the
buttons on the stoves as a day off a vacation or maybe an
occasion like a baptising or a picnic or a big funeral but
this was Monday, a new day and a new week, rest and
the need to fill time and conquer boredom was over,
children fresh for school and husband and father for
store or office or to stand around the Western Union
desk where the hourly cotton reports came in; breakfast
must be forward and the pandemoniac bustle of exodus
yet still no Negro had they seen—the young ones with
straightened hair and makeup in the bright trig tomorrow's clothes from the mailorder houses who would not
even put on the Harper's Bazaar caps and aprons until
they were inside the white kitchens and the older ones
in the ankle-length homemade calico and gingham who
wore the long plain homemade aprons all the time so

that they were no longer a symbol but a garment, not
even the men who should have been mowing the lawns
and clipping the hedges; not even (crossing the Square
now) the street department crews who should have been
flushing the pavement with hoses and sweeping up the
discarded Sunday papers and empty cigarette packs;
across the Square and on to the jail where his uncle got
out too and went up the walk with Miss Habersham and
up the steps and through the still-open door where he
could still see Legate's empty chair still propped against
the wall and he heaved himself bodily again out of the
long soft timeless rushing black of sleep to find as usual
that no time had passed, his uncle still putting his hat
back on and turning to come back down the walk to the
car. Then they stopped at home, Aleck Sander already
out of the car and gone around the side of the house
and vanished and he said,

'No.'

'Yes,' his uncle said. 'You've got to go to school. Or
better still, to bed and to sleep. —Yes,' his uncle said
suddenly: 'and Aleck Sander too. He must stay at home
today too. Because this mustn't be talked about, not
one word about it until we have finished it. You understand that.'

But he wasn't listening, he and his uncle were not even
talking about the same thing, not even when he said
'No' again and his uncle out of the car and already turning toward the house stopped and looked back at him
and then stood looking at him for a good long moment
and then said,

'We are going at this a little hindpart-before, aint we?
I'm the one who should be asking you if I can go.' Because he was thinking about his mother, not just remem-

bered about her because he had done that as soon as
they crossed the Square five minutes ago and the simplest
thing would have been to get out of his uncle's car there
and go and get in the sheriff's car and simply stay in it
until they were ready to go back out to the church and
he had probably thought about it at the time and would
even have done it probably if he hadn't been so worn out
and anticlimaxed and dull for sleep and he knew he
couldn't cope with her this time even if he had been completely fresh; the very fact that he had already done it
twice in eleven hours, once by secrecy and once by sheer
surprise and rapidity of movement and of mass, but
doomed him completer now to defeat and rout: musing
on his uncle's naïve and childlike rationalising about
school and bed when faced with that fluid and implacable attack, when once more his uncle read his mind,
standing beside the car and looking down at him for
another moment with compassion and no hope even
though he was a bachelor of fifty thirty-five years free of
woman's dominion, his uncle too knowing remembering
how she would use the excuses of his education and his
physical exhaustion only less quicker than she would
have discarded them; who would listen no more to rational reasons for his staying at home than for—civic
duty or simple justice or humanity or to save a life or
even the peace of his own immortal soul—his going. His
uncle said:

'All right. Come on. I'll talk to her.'

He moved, getting out; he said suddenly and quietly,
in amazement not at despair of hope but at how much
hopelessness you could really stand: 'You're just my
uncle.'

'I'm worse than that,' his uncle said. 'I'm just a man.'

Then his uncle read his mind again: 'All right. I'll try to talk to Paralee too. The same condition obtains there; motherhood doesn't seem to have any pigment in its skin.'

And his uncle too was probably thinking how you not only couldn't beat them, you couldn't even find the battlefield in time to admit defeat before they had moved it again; he remembered, it was two years ago now, he had finally made the high school football team or that is he had won or been chosen for one of the positions to make an out-of-town trip because the regular player had been injured in practice or fallen behind in his grades or maybe his mother either wouldn't let him go, something, he had forgotten exactly what because he had been too busy all that Thursday and Friday racking his brains in vain to think how to tell his mother he was going to Mottstown to play on the regular team, right up to the last minute when he had to tell her something and so did: badly: and weathered it since his father happened to be present (though he really hadn't calculated it that way—not that he wouldn't have if he hadn't been too worried and perplexed with a blending of anger and shame and shame at being angry and ashamed ((crying at her at one point: 'Is it the team's fault that I'm the only child you've got?')) to think of it) and left that Friday afternoon with the team feeling as he imagined a soldier might feel wrenching out of his mother's restraining arms to go fight a battle for some shameful cause; she would grieve for him of course if he fell and she would even look on his face again if he didn't but there would be always ineradicable between them the ancient green and perennial adumbration: so that all that Friday night trying to go to sleep in a strange bed and all the

next forenoon too waiting for the game to start he
thought better for the team if he had not come since he
probably had too much on his mind to be worth anything to it: until the first whistle blew and on and afterward until bottom-most beneath the piled mass of both
teams, the ball clutched to his chest and his mouth and
nostrils both full of the splashed dried whitewash marking the goal line he heard and recognised above all the
others that one voice shrill triumphant and bloodthirsty
and picked up at last and the wind thumped back into
him he saw her foremost in the crowd not sitting in the
grandstand but among the ones trotting and even running up and down the sideline following each play, then
in the car that evening on the way back to Jefferson,
himself in the front seat beside the hired driver and his
mother and three of the other players in the back and
her voice as proud and serene and pitiless as his own
could have been: 'Does your arm still hurt?'—entering
the hall and only then discovering that he had expected
to find her still just inside the front door still in the
loose hair and the nightdress and himself walking back
even after three hours into the unbroken uninterrupted
wail. But instead it was his father already roaring who
came out of the diningroom and still at it even with his
uncle yelling back almost into his face:

'Charley. Charley. Dammit, will you wait?' and only
then his mother fully dressed, brisk busy and composed,
coming up the hall from the back, the kitchen, saying to
his father without even raising her voice:

'Charley. Go back and finish your breakfast. Paralee
isn't feeling well this morning and she doesn't want to
be all day getting dinner ready:' then to him—the fond
constant familiar face which he had known all his life

and therefore could neither have described it so that a
stranger could recognise it nor recognise it himself from
anyone's description but only brisk calm and even a little
inattentive now, the wail a wail only because of the
ancient used habit of its verbiage: 'You haven't washed
your face:' nor even pausing to see if he followed, on up
the stairs and into the bathroom, even turning on the
tap and putting the soap into his hands and standing
with the towel open and waiting, the familiar face wearing the familiar expression of amazement and protest and
anxiety and invincible repudiation which it had worn
all his life each time he had done anything removing
him one more step from infancy, from childhood: when
his uncle had given him the Shetland pony someone had
taught to take eighteen- and twenty-four-inch jumps and
when his father had given him the first actual powder-
shooting gun and the afternoon when the groom delivered Highboy in the truck and he got up for the first
time and Highboy stood on his hind legs and her scream
and the groom's calm voice saying, 'Hit him hard over
the head when he does that. You dont want him falling
over backward on you' but the muscles merely falling
into the old expression through inattention and long
usage as her voice had merely chosen by inattention and
usage the long-worn verbiage of wailing because there
was something else in it now—the same thing which had
been there in the car that afternoon when she said,
'Your arm doesn't hurt at all now does it?' and on the
other afternoon when his father came home and found
him jumping Highboy over the concrete watertrough in
the lot, his mother leaning on the fence watching and his
father's fury of relief and anger and his mother's calm
voice this time: 'Why not? The trough isn't near as tall

as that flimsy fence-thing you bought him that isn't even nailed together:' so that even dull for sleep he recognised it and turned his face and hands dripping and cried at her in amazed and incredulous outrage: 'You aint going too! You cant go!' then even dull for sleep realising the fatuous naïveté of anyone using cant to her on any subject and so playing his last desperate card: 'If you go, then I wont! You hear me? I wont go!'

'Dry your face and comb your hair,' she said. 'Then come on down and drink your coffee.'

That too. Paralee was all right too apparently because his uncle was at the telephone in the hall when he entered the diningroom, his father already roaring again before he had even sat down:

'Dammit, why didn't you tell me last night? Dont you ever again——'

'Because you wouldn't have believed him either,' his uncle said coming in from the hall. 'You wouldn't have listened either. It took an old woman and two children for that, to believe truth for no other reason than that it was truth, told by an old man in a fix deserving pity and belief, to someone capable of the pity even when none of them really believed him. Which you didn't at first,' his uncle said to him. 'When did you really begin to believe him? When you opened the coffin, wasn't it? I want to know, you see. Maybe I'm not too old to learn either. When was it?'

'I dont know,' he said. Because he didn't know. It seemed to him that he had known all the time. Then it seemed to him that he had never really believed Lucas. Then it seemed to him that it had never happened at all, heaving himself once more with no movement up out of the long deep slough of sleep but at least to some elapse of time now, he had gained that much anyway, maybe enough to be safe on for a while like the tablets night truck drivers took not as big hardly as a shirt button yet in which were concentrated enough wakefulness to reach the next town because his mother was in the room now brisk and calm, setting the cup of coffee down in front of him in a way that if Paralee had done it she would have said that Paralee had slopped it at him: which, the coffee, was why neither his father nor his uncle had even looked at her, his father on the contrary exclaiming,

'Coffee? What the devil is this? I thought the agreement was when you finally consented for Gavin to buy that horse that he would neither ask for nor even accept a spoonful of coffee until he was eighteen years old:' and his mother not even listening, with the same hand and in the same manner half shoving and half popping the cream pitcher then the sugar bowl into his reach and already turning back toward the kitchen, her voice not really hurried and impatient: just brisk:

'Drink it now. We're already late:' and now they looked at her for the first time: dressed, even to her hat, with in the crook of her other arm the straw basket out of which she had darned his and his father's and his uncle's socks and stockings ever since he could remember, though his uncle at first saw only the hat and for a moment seemed to join him in the same horrified surprise he had felt in the bathroom.

'Maggie!' his uncle said. 'You cant! Charley——'

'I dont intend to,' his mother said, not even stopping. 'This time you men will have to do the digging. I'm going to the jail:' already in the kitchen now and only her voice coming back: 'I'm not going to let Miss Haber-

sham sit there by herself with the whole county gawking
at her. As soon as I help Paralee plan dinner we'll——'
but not dying fading: ceasing, quitting: since she had
dismissed them though his father still tried once more:

'He's got to go to school.'

But even his uncle didn't listen. 'You can drive Miss
Eunice's truck, cant you?' his uncle said. 'There wont
be a Negro school today for Aleck Sander to be going to
so he can leave it at the jail. And even if there was I
doubt if Paralee's going to let him cross the front yard
inside the next week.' Then his uncle seemed even to
have heard his father or at least decided to answer him:
'Nor any white school either for that matter if this boy
hadn't listened to Lucas, which I wouldn't, and to Miss
Habersham, which I didn't. Well?' his uncle said. 'Can
you stay awake that long? You can get a nap once we are
on the road.'

'Yes sir,' he said. So he drank the coffee which the soap
and water and hard toweling had unfogged him enough
to know he didn't like and didn't want but not enough
for him to choose what simple thing to do about it: that
is not drink it: tasting sipping then adding more sugar
to it until each—coffee and sugar—ceased to be either
and became a sickish quinine sweet amalgam of the worst
of both until his uncle said,

'Dammit, stop that,' and got up and went to the kitchen
and returned with a saucepan of heated milk and a soup
bowl and dumped the coffee into the bowl and poured
the hot milk into it and said, 'Go on. Forget about it.
Just drink it.' So he did, from the bowl in both hands
like water from a gourd, hardly tasting it and still his
father flung a little back in his chair looking at him and
talking, asking him just how scared Aleck Sander was

and if he wasn't even scareder than Aleck Sander only
his vanity wouldn't allow him to show it before a darky
and to tell the truth now, neither of them would have
touched the grave in the dark even enough to lift the
flowers off of it if Miss Habersham hadn't driven them
at it: his uncle interrupting:

'Aleck Sander even told you then that the grave had
already been disturbed by someone in a hurry, didn't
he?'

'Yes sir,' he said and his uncle said:

'Do you know what I'm thinking now?'

'No sir,' he said.

'I'm being glad Aleck Sander couldn't completely
penetrate darkness and call out the name of the man
who came down the hill carrying something in front of
him on the mule.' And he remembered that: the three
of them all thinking it but not one of them saying it:
just standing invisible to one another above the pit's
invisible inky yawn.

'Fill it up,' Miss Habersham said. They did, the (five
times now) loosened dirt going down much faster than
it came up though it seemed forever in the thin starlight filled with the constant sound of the windless pines
like one vast abateless hum not of amazement but of
attention, watching, curiosity; amoral, detached, not in-
volved and missing nothing. 'Put the flowers back,' Miss
Habersham said.

'It'll take time,' he said.

'Put them back,' Miss Habersham said. So they did.

'I'll get the horse,' he said. 'You and Aleck Sander——'

'We'll all go,' Miss Habersham said. So they gathered
up the tools and the rope (nor did they use the flashlight
again) and Aleck Sander said 'Wait' and found by touch

the board he had used for a shovel and carried that until
he could push it back under the church and he untied
Highboy and held the stirrup but Miss Habersham said,
'No. We'll lead him. Aleck Sander can walk exactly
behind me and you walk exactly behind Aleck Sander
and lead the horse.'

'We could go faster——' he said again and they couldn't
see her face: only the thin straight shape, the shadow,
the hat which on anyone else wouldn't even have looked
like a hat but on her as on his grandmother looked exactly right, like exactly nothing else, her voice not loud,
not much louder than breathing, as if she were not even
moving her lips, not to anyone, just murmuring:

'It's the best I know to do. I dont know anything else
to do.'

'Maybe we all ought to walk in the middle,' he said,
loud, too loud, twice louder than he had intended or
even thought; it should carry for miles especially over
a whole countryside already hopelessly waked and alerted
by the sleepless sibilant what Paralee probably and old
Ephraim certainly and Lucas too would call 'miration'
of the pines. She was looking at him now. He could
feel it.

'I'll never be able to explain to your mother but Aleck
Sander hasn't got any business here at all,' she said.
'Youall walk exactly behind me and let the horse come
last:' and turned and went on though what good that
would do he didn't know because in his understanding
the very word 'ambush' meant 'from the flank, the side':
back in single file that way down the hill to where Aleck
Sander had driven the truck into the bushes: and he
thought *If I were him this is where it would be* and so
did she; she said, 'Wait.'

'How can you keep on standing in front of us if we dont stay together?' he said. And this time she didn't even say This is all I can think of to do but just stood there so that Aleck Sander walked past her and on into the bushes and started the truck and backed it out and swung it to point down the hill, the engine running but no lights yet and she said, 'Tie the reins up and let him go. Wont he come home?'

'I hope so,' he said. He got up.

'Then tie him to a tree,' she said. 'We will come back and get him as soon as we have seen your uncle and Mr Hampton——'

'Then we can all watch him ride down the road with maybe a horse or the mule in front of him too,' Aleck Sander said. He raced the engine then let it idle again. 'Come on, get in. He's either here watching us or he aint and if he aint we're all right and if he is he's done waited too late now when he let us get back to the truck.'

'Then you ride right behind the truck,' she said. 'We'll go slow——'

'Nome,' Aleck Sander said; he leaned out. 'Get started; we're going to have to wait for you anyway when we get to town.'

So—he needed no urging—he let Highboy down the hill, only holding his head up; the truck's lights came on and it moved and once on the flat even in the short space to the highroad Highboy was already trying to run but he checked him back and up onto the highroad, the lights of the truck fanning up and out as it came down onto the flat then he slacked the curb, Highboy beginning to run, clashing the snaffle as always, thinking as always that one more champing regurg would get it forward enough to get his teeth on it, running now when

the truck lights swung up onto the highroad too, his feet
in eight hollow beats on the bridge and he leaned into the
dark hard wind and let him go, the truck lights not even
in sight during the full half-mile until he slowed him
into the long reaching hard road-gait and almost a mile
then before the truck overtook and then passed and the
ruby tail-lamp drew on and away and then was gone but
at least he was out of the pines, free of that looming
down-watching sibilance uncaring and missing nothing
saying to the whole circumambience: Look. Look: but
then they were still saying it somewhere and they had
certainly been saying it long enough for all Beat Four,
Gowries and Ingrums and Workitts and Frasers and all
to have heard it by this time so he wouldn't think about
that and so he stopped thinking about it now, all in the
same flash in which he had remembered it, swallowing
the last swallow from the bowl and setting it down as
his father more or less plunged up from the table, clattering his chairlegs back across the floor, saying:

'Maybe I better go to work. Somebody'll have to earn
a little bread around here while the rest of you are playing cops and robbers:' and went out and apparently the
coffee had done something to what he called his thinking processes or anyway the processes of what people
called thinking because now he knew the why for his
father too—the rage which was relief after the event
which had to express itself some way and chose anger
not because he would have forbidden him to go but
because he had had no chance to, the pseudo-scornful
humorous impugnment of his and Aleck Sander's courage which blinked not even as much at a rifled grave in
the dark as it did at Miss Habersham's will,—in fact the
whole heavyhanded aspersion of the whole thing by re-

ducing it to the terms of a kind of kindergarten witch-
hunt: which was probably merely the masculine form
of refusing also to believe that he was what his uncle
called big enough to button his pants and so he dismissed
his father, hearing his mother about to emerge from the
kitchen and pushing his chair back and getting up himself when suddenly he was thinking how coffee was
already a good deal more than he had known but nobody had warned him that it produced illusions like
cocaine or opium: seeing watching his father's noise and
uproar flick and vanish away like blown smoke or mist,
not merely revealing but exposing the man who had
begot him looking back at him from beyond the bridge-
less abyss of that begetting not with just pride but with
envy too; it was his uncle's abnegant and rhetorical self-
lacerating which was the phony one and his father was
gnawing the true bitter irremediable bone of all which
was dismatchment with time, being born too soon or
late to have been himself sixteen and gallop a horse ten
miles in the dark to save an old nigger's insolent and
friendless neck.

But at least he was awake. The coffee had accomplished
that anyway. He still needed to doze only now he
couldn't; the desire to sleep was there but it was wakefulness now he would have to combat and abate. It was
after eight now; one of the county schoolbusses passed
as he prepared to drive Miss Habersham's truck away
from the curb and the street would be full of children
too fresh for Monday morning with books and paper
bags of recess-time lunches and behind the schoolbus
was a string of cars and trucks stained with country mud
and dust so constant and unbroken that his uncle and
his mother would already have reached the jail before

he ever managed to cut into it because Monday was
stock-auction day at the sales barns behind the Square
and he could see them, the empty cars and trucks rank on
dense rank along the courthouse curb like shoats at a
feed-trough and the men with their stock-trader walking-
sticks not even stopping but gone straight across the
Square and along the alley to the sales barns to chew
tobacco and unlighted cigars from pen to pen amid the
ammonia-reek of manure and liniment and the bawling
of calves and the stamp and sneeze of horses and mules
and the secondhand wagons and plow gear and guns and
harness and watches and only the women (what few of
them that is since stock-sale day unlike Saturday was a
man's time) remained about the Square and the stores
so that the Square itself would be empty except for the
parked cars and trucks until the men would come back
for an hour at noon to meet them at the cafes and
restaurants.

Whereupon this time he jerked himself, no reflex now,
not even out of sleep but illusion, who had carried hyp-
nosis right out of the house with him even into the
bright strong sun of day, even driving the pickup truck
which before last night he would not even have recognised yet which since last night had become as inexpugnable a part of his memory and experience and breathing
as hiss of shovelled dirt or the scrape of a metal blade
on a pine box would ever be, through a mirage-vacuum
in which not simply last night had not happened but
there had been no Saturday either, remembering now
as if he had only this moment seen it that there had
been no children in the schoolbus but only grown people
and in the stream of cars and trucks following it and
now following him where he had finally cut in, a few of

which even on stock-auction Monday (on Saturday half of the flat open beds would have been jammed and packed with them, men women and children in the cheap meagre finery in which they came to town) should have carried Negroes, there had not been one dark face.

Nor one school-bound child on the street although he had heard without listening enough of his uncle at the telephone to know that the superintendent had called whether to have school today or not and his uncle had told him yes, and in sight of the Square now he could see already three more of the yellow busses supposed and intended to bring the county children in to school but which their owner-contractor-operators translated on Saturdays and holidays into pay-passenger transport and then the Square itself, the parked cars and trucks as always as should be but the Square itself anything but empty: no exodus of men toward the stock pens nor women into the stores so that as he drove the pickup into the curb behind his uncle's car he could see already where visible and sense where not a moil and mass of movement, one dense pulse and hum filling the Square as when the crowd overflows the carnival midway or the football field, flowing into the street and already massed along the side opposite to the jail until the head of it had already passed the blacksmith's where he had stood yesterday trying to be invisible as if they were waiting for a parade to pass (and almost in the middle of the street so that the still unbroken stream of cars and trucks had to detour around them a clump of a dozen or so more like the group in a reviewing stand in whose center in its turn he recognized the badged official cap of the town marshal who at this hour on this day would have been in front of the schoolhouse holding up traffic for children

to cross the street and he did not have to remember that
the marshal's name was Ingrum, a Beat Four Ingrum
come to town as the apostate sons of Beat Four occa-
sionally did to marry a town girl and become barbers and
bailiffs and nightwatchmen as petty Germanic prince-
lings would come down out of their Brandenburg hills
to marry the heiresses to European thrones)—the men
and the women and not one child, the weathered country faces and sunburned necks and backs of hands, the
clean faded tieless earthcolored shirts and pants and
print cotton dresses thronging the Square and the street
as though the stores themselves were closed and locked,
not even staring yet at the blank front of the jail and
the single barred window which had been empty and
silent too for going on forty-eight hours now but just
gathering, condensing, not expectant nor in anticipation
nor even attentive yet but merely in that preliminary
settling down like the before-curtain in a theatre: and he
thought that was it: holiday: which meant a day for
children yet here turned upside down: and suddenly he
realised that he had been completely wrong; it was not
Saturday which had never happened but only last night
which to them had not happened yet, that not only they
didn't know about last night but there was nobody, not
even Hampton, who could have told them because they
would have refused to believe him; whereupon something like a skim or a veil like that which crosses a
chicken's eye and which he had not even known was
there went flick! from his own and he saw them for the
first time—the same weathered still almost inattentive
faces and the same faded clean cotton shirts and pants
and dresses but no crowd now waiting for the curtain
to rise on a stage's illusion but rather the one in the

courtroom waiting for the sheriff's officer to cry Oyez Oyez Oyez This honorable court; not even impatient because the moment had not even come yet to sit in judgment not on Lucas Beauchamp, they had already condemned him but on Beat Four, come not to see what they called justice done nor even retribution exacted but to see that Beat Four should not fail its white man's high estate.

So that he had stopped the truck was out and had already started to run when he stopped himself: something of dignity something of pride remembering last night when he had instigated and in a way led and anyway accompanied the stroke which not one of the responsible elders but had failed even to recognise its value, let alone its need, and something of caution too remembering how his uncle had said almost nothing was enough to put a mob in motion so perhaps even a child running toward the jail would have been enough: then he remembered again the faces myriad yet curiously identical in their lack of individual identity, their complete relinquishment of individual identity into one We not even impatient, not even hurryable, almost gala in its complete obliviousness of its own menace, not to be stampeded by a hundred running children: and then in the same flash the obverse: not to be halted or deflected by a hundred times a hundred of them, and having realised its sheer hopelessness when it was still only an intention and then its physical imponderability when it entered accomplishment he now recognised the enormity of what he had blindly meddled with and that his first instinctive impulse—to run home and fling saddle and bridle on the horse and ride as the crow flies into the last stagger of exhaustion and then sleep and then return after it was all over—had been the right one (who now simply because he happened not to be an orphan had not even that escape) because it seemed to him now that he was responsible for having brought into the light and glare of day something shocking and shameful out of the whole white foundation of the county which he himself must partake of too since he too was bred of it, which otherwise might have flared and blazed merely out of Beat Four and then vanished back into its darkness or at least invisibility with the fading embers of Lucas' crucifixion.

But it was too late now, he couldn't even repudiate, relinquish, run: the jail door still open and opposite it now he could see Miss Habersham sitting in the chair Legate had sat in, the cardboard box on the floor at her feet and a garment of some sort across her lap; she was still wearing the hat and he could see the steady motion of her hand and elbow and it seemed to him he could even see the flash and flick of the needle in her hand though he knew he could not at this distance; but his uncle was in the way so he had to move further along the walk but at that moment his uncle turned and came out the door and recrossed the veranda and then he could see her too in the second chair beside Miss Habersham; a car drew up to the curb behind him and stopped and now without haste she chose a sock from the basket and slipped the darningegg into it; she even had the needle already threaded stuck in the front of her dress and now he could distinguish the flash and glint of it and maybe that was because he knew so well the motion, the narrow familiar suppleness of the hand which he had watched all his life but at least no man could have disputed him that it was his sock.

'Who's that?' the sheriff said behind him. He turned.
The sheriff sat behind the wheel of his car, his neck and
shoulders bowed and hunched so he could peer out
below the top of the window-frame. The engine was
still running and he saw in the back of the car the
handles of two shovels and the pick too which they would
not need and on the back seat quiet and motionless save
for the steady glint and blink of their eyewhites, two
Negroes in blue jumpers and the soiled black-ringed
convict pants which the street gangs wore.

'Who would it be?' his uncle said behind him too but
he didn't turn this time nor did he even listen further
because three men came suddenly out of the street and
stopped beside the car and as he watched five or six more
came up and in another moment the whole crowd would
begin to flow across the street; already a passing car had
braked suddenly (and then the following one behind it)
at first to keep from running over them and then for
its occupants to lean out looking at the sheriff's car
where the first man to reach it had already stooped to
peer into it, his brown farmer's hands grasping the edge
of the open window, his brown weathered face thrust
into the car curious divinant and abashless while behind
him his massed duplicates in their felt hats and sweat-
stained panamas listened.

'What you up to, Hope?' the man said. 'Dont you
know the Grand Jury'll get you, wasting county money
this way? Aint you heard about that new lynch law the
Yankees passed? the folks that lynches the nigger is supposed to dig the grave?'

'Maybe he's taking them shovels out there for Nub
Gowrie and them boys of his to practice with,' the second
said.

'Then it's a good thing Hope's taking shovel hands too,' the third said. 'If he's depending on anybody named Gowrie to dig a hole or do anything else that might bring up a sweat, he'll sure need them.'

'Or maybe they aint shovel hands,' the fourth said. 'Maybe it's them the Gowries are going to practice on.' Yet even though one guffawed they were not laughing, more than a dozen now crowded around the car to take one quick allcomprehensive glance into the back of it where the two Negroes sat immobile as carved wood staring straight ahead at nothing and no movement even of breathing other than an infinitesimal widening and closing of the whites around their eyeballs, then looking at the sheriff again with almost exactly the expression he had seen on the faces waiting for the spinning tapes behind a slotmachine's glass to stop.

'I reckon that'll do,' the sheriff said. He thrust his head and one vast arm out the window and with the arm pushed the nearest ones back and away from the car as effortlessly as he would have opened a curtain, raising his voice but not much: 'Willy.' The marshal came up; he could already hear him:

'Gangway, boys. Lemme see what the high sheriff's got on his mind this morning.'

'Why dont you get these folks out of the street so them cars can get to town?' the sheriff said. 'Maybe they want to stand around and look at the jail too.'

'You bet,' the marshal said. He turned, shoving his hands at the nearest ones, not touching them, as if he were putting into motion a herd of cattle. 'Now boys,' he said.

They didn't move, looking past the marshal still at the sheriff, not at all defiant, not really daring anyone: just tolerant, goodhumored. debonair almost.

'Why, Sheriff,' a voice said, then another:

'It's a free street, aint it, Sheriff? You town folks wont mind us just standing on it long as we spend our money with you, will you?'

'But not to block off the other folks trying to get to town to spend a little,' the sheriff said. 'Move on now. Get them out of the street, Willy.'

'Come on, boys,' the marshal said. 'There's other folks besides you wants to get up where they can watch them bricks.' They moved then but still without haste, the marshal herding them back across the street like a woman driving a flock of hens across a pen, she to control merely the direction not the speed and not too much of that, the fowls moving ahead of her flapping apron not recalcitrant, just unpredictable, fearless of her and not yet even alarmed; the halted car and the ones behind it moved too, slowly, dragging at creeping pace their loads of craned faces; he could hear the marshal shouting at the drivers: 'Get on. Get on. There's cars behind you——'

The sheriff was looking at his uncle again. 'Where's the other one?'

'The other what?' his uncle said.

'The other detective. The one that can see in the dark.'

'Aleck Sander,' his uncle said. 'You want him too?'

'No,' the sheriff said. 'I just missed him. I was just surprised to find one human in this county with taste and judgment enough to stay at home today. You ready? Let's get started.'

'Right,' his uncle said. The sheriff was notorious as a driver who used up a car a year as a heavy-handed sweeper wears out brooms: not by speed but by simple friction; now the car actually shot away from the curb and almost before he could watch it, was gone. His uncle went to theirs and opened the door. 'Jump in,' his uncle said.

Then he said it; at least this much was simple: 'I'm not going.'

His uncle paused and now he saw watching him the quizzical saturnine face, the quizzical eyes which given a little time didn't miss much; had in fact as long as he had known them never missed anything until last night.

'Ah,' his uncle said. 'Miss Habersham is of course a lady but this other female is yours.'

'Look at them,' he said, not moving, barely moving his lips even. 'Across the street. On the Square too and nobody but Willy Ingrum and that damn cap——'

'Didn't you hear them talking to Hampton?' his uncle said.

'I heard them,' he said. 'They were not even laughing at their own jokes. They were laughing at him.'

'They were not even taunting him,' his uncle said. 'They were not even jeering at him. They were just watching him. Watching him and Beat Four, to see what would happen. These people just came to town to see what either or both of them are going to do.'

'No,' he said. 'More than that.'

'All right,' his uncle said, quite soberly too now. 'Granted. Then what?'

'Suppose——' But his uncle interrupted:

'Suppose Beat Four comes in and picks up your mother's and Miss Habersham's chairs and carries them out into the yard where they'll be out of the way? Lucas aint in that cell. He's in Mr Hampton's house, probably sitting in the kitchen right now eating his breakfast. What did you think Will Legate was doing coming in by the back door within fifteen minutes of when we got there and told Mr Hampton? Aleck Sander even heard him telephoning.'

'Then what's Mr Hampton in such a hurry for?' he said: and his uncle's voice was quite sober now: but just sober, that was all:

'Because the best way to stop having to suppose or deny either is for us to get out there and do what we have to do and get back here. Jump in the car.'

Chapter Seven

THEY NEVER SAW the sheriff's car again until they
reached the church. Nor for him was the reason sleep
who in spite of the coffee might have expected that and
in fact had. Up to the moment when at the wheel of the
pickup he had got near enough to see the Square and
then the mass of people lining the opposite side of the
street in front of the jail he had expected that as soon
as he and his uncle were on the road back to the church,
coffee or no coffee he would not even be once more fight-
ing sleep but on the contrary would relinquish and accept it and so in the nine miles of gravel and the one of
climbing dirt regain at least a half-hour of the eight he
had lost last night and—it seemed to him now—the three
or four times that many he had spent trying to quit
thinking about Lucas Beauchamp the night before.

And when they reached town a little before three this
morning nobody could have persuaded him that by this
time, almost nine oclock, he would not have made back
at least five and a half hours of sleep even if not the full
six, remembering how he—and without doubt Miss
Habersham and Aleck Sander too—had believed that as
soon as they and his uncle entered the sheriff's house
that would be all of it; they would enter the front door
and lay into the sheriff's broad competent ordained palm
as you drop your hat on the hall table in passing, the

whole night's nightmare of doubt and indecision and sleeplessness and strain and fatigue and shock and amazement and (he admitted it) some of fear too. But it hadn't happened and he knew now that he had never really expected it to; the idea had ever entered their heads only because they had been worn out, spent not so much from sleeplessness and fatigue and strain as exhausted by shock and amazement and anticlimax; he had not even needed the massed faces watching the blank brick front of the jail nor the ones which had crossed the street and even blocked it while they crowded around the sheriff's car, to read and then dismiss its interior with that one mutual concordant glance comprehensive abashless trustless and undeniable as the busy parent pauses for an instant to check over and anticipate the intentions of a loved though not too reliable child. If he needed anything he certainly had that—the faces the voices not even taunting and not even jeering: just perspicuant jocular and without pity—poised under the first relaxation of succumbence like a pin in the mattress so he was as wide awake as his uncle even who had slept all night or at least most of it, free of town now and going fast now, passing within the first mile the last of the cars and trucks and then no more of them because all who would come to town today would by this time be inside that last rapidly contracting mile—the whole white part of the county taking advantage of the good weather and the good allweather roads which were their roads because their taxes and votes and the votes of their kin and connections who could bring pressure on the congressmen who had the giving away of the funds had built them, to get quickly into the town which was theirs too since it existed only by their sufferance and support to contain their jail and their courthouse, to crowd and jam and block its streets too if they saw fit: patient biding and unpitying, neither to be hurried nor checked nor dispersed nor denied since theirs was the murdered and the murderer too; theirs the affronter and the principle affronted: the white man and the bereavement of his vacancy, theirs the right not just to mere justice but vengeance too to allot or withhold.

They were going quite fast now, faster than he could ever remember his uncle driving, out the long road where he had ridden last night on the horse but in daylight now, morning's bland ineffable May; now he could see the white bursts of dogwood in the hedgerows marking the old section-line surveys or standing like nuns in the cloistral patches and bands of greening woods and the pink and white of peach and pear and the pinkwhite of the first apple trees in the orchards which last night he had only smelled: and always beyond and around them the enduring land—the fields geometric with furrows where corn had been planted when the first doves began to call in late March and April, and cotton when the first whippoorwills cried at night around the beginning of May a week ago: but empty, vacant of any movement and any life—the farmhouses from which no smoke rose because breakfast was long over by now and no dinner to be cooked where none would be home to eat it, the paintless Negro cabins where on Monday morning in the dust of the grassless treeless yards halfnaked children should have been crawling and scrabbling after broken cultivator wheels and wornout automobile tires and empty snuff-bottles and tin cans and in the back yards smoke-blackened iron pots should have been bubbling over wood fires beside the sagging fences of vegetable

patches and chickenruns which by nightfall would be
gaudy with drying overalls and aprons and towels and
unionsuits: but not this morning, not now; the wheels
and the giant-doughnuts of chewed rubber and the
bottles and cans lying scattered and deserted in the dust
since that moment Saturday afternoon when the first
voice shouted from inside the house, and in the back
yards the pots sitting empty and cold among last Monday's ashes among the empty clotheslines and as the car
flashed past the blank and vacant doors he would catch
one faint gleam of fire on hearth and no more see but
only sense among the shadows the still white roll of eyes;
but most of all, the empty fields themselves in each of
which on this day at this hour on the second Monday in
May there should have been fixed in monotonous repeti-
tion the land's living symbol—a formal group of ritual
almost mystic significance identical and monotonous as
milestones tying the county-seat to the county's ultimate
rim as milestones would: the beast the plow and the man
integrated in one foundationed into the frozen wave of
their furrow tremendous with effort yet at the same time
vacant of progress, ponderable immovable and immobile
like groups of wrestling statuary set against the land's
immensity—until suddenly (they were eight miles from
town; already the blue-green lift of the hills was in sight)
he said with an incredulous an almost shocked amazement who except for Paralee and Aleck Sander and Lucas
had not seen one in going on forty-eight hours:

'There's a nigger.'

'Yes,' his uncle said. 'Today is the ninth of May. This
county's got half of a hundred and forty-two thousand
acres to plant yet. Somebody's got to stay home and
work:'—the car rushing boring up so that across the

field's edge and the perhaps fifty yards separating them
he and the Negro behind the plow looked eye to eye into
each other's face before the Negro looked away—the face
black and gleamed with sweat and passionate with effort,
tense concentrated and composed, the car flashing past
and on while he leaned first out the open window to look
back then turned in the seat to see back through the rear
window, watching them still in their rapid unblurred
diminishment—the man and the mule and the wooden
plow which coupled them furious and solitary, fixed and
without progress in the earth, leaning terrifically against
nothing.

They could see the hills now; they were almost there—
the long lift of the first pine ridge standing across half
the horizon and beyond it a sense a feel of others, the
mass of them seeming not so much to stand rush abruptly up out of the plateau as to hang suspended over it
as his uncle had told him the Scottish highlands did
except for this sharpness and color; that was two years
ago, maybe three and his uncle had said, 'Which is why
the people who chose by preference to live on them on
little patches which wouldn't make eight bushels of corn
or fifty pounds of lint cotton an acre even if they were
not too steep for a mule to pull a plow across (but then
they dont want to make the cotton anyway, only the corn
and not too much of that because it really doesn't take a
great deal of corn to run a still as big as one man and his
sons want to fool with) are people named Gowrie and
McCallum and Fraser and Ingrum that used to be Ingra-
ham and Workitt that used to be Urquhart only the one
that brought it to America and then Mississippi couldn't
spell it either, who love brawling and fear God and believe in Hell——' and it was as though his uncle had

read his mind, holding the speedometer needle at fifty-five into the last mile of gravel (already the road was beginning to slant down toward the willow-and-cypress bottom of the Nine-Mile branch) speaking, that is volunteering to speak for the first time since they left town:

'Gowrie and Fraser and Workitt and Ingrum. And in the valleys along the rivers, the broad rich easy land where a man can raise something he can sell openly in daylight, the people named Littlejohn and Greenleaf and Armstead and Millingham and Bookwright——' and stopped, the car dropping on down the slope, increasing speed by its own weight; now he could see the bridge where Aleck Sander had waited for him in the dark and below which Highboy had smelled quicksand.

'We turn off just beyond it,' he said.

'I know,' his uncle said. '—And the ones named Sambo, they live in both, they elect both because they can stand either because they can stand anything.' The bridge was quite near now, the white railing of the entrance yawned rushing at them. 'Not all white people can endure slavery and apparently no man can stand freedom. (Which incidentally—the premise that man really wants peace and freedom—is the trouble with our relations with Europe right now, whose people not only dont know what peace is but—except for Anglo Saxons —actively fear and distrust personal liberty; we are hoping without really any hope that our atom bomb will be enough to defend an idea as obsolete as Noah's Ark.); with one mutual instantaneous accord he forces his liberty into the hands of the first demagogue who rises into view: lacking that he himself destroys and obliterates it from his sight and ken and even remembrance with the frantic unanimity of a neighborhood stamping out a

grass-fire. But the people named Sambo survived the one
and who knows? they may even endure the other. —And
who knows——'

Then a gleam of sand, a flash and glint of water; the
white rail streamed past in one roar and rush and rattle
of planking and they were across. *He'll have to slow down
now* he thought but his uncle didn't, merely declutching,
the car rolling on its own momentum which carried it
still too fast through a slewing skidding turn into the
dirt road and on for fifty yards bouncing among the ruts
until the last of flat land died headlong into the first
gentle slant, its momentum still carrying the car in high
speed gear yet up the incline until then after he saw the
tracks where Aleck Sander had driven the pickup off the
road into the bushes and where he had stood ready with
his hand poised over Highboy's nostrils while the horse
or the mule, whichever it was, had come down the hill
with the burden in front of the rider which even Aleck
Sander with his eyes like an owl or mink or whatever
else hunts at night, had failed to descry (and he remembered again not just his uncle at the table this morning
but himself standing in the yard last night during that
moment after Aleck Sander walked away and before he
recognised Miss Habersham when he actually believed
he was coming out alone to do what must be done and
he told himself now as he had at the table: *I wont think
about that.*); almost there now, practically were there in
fact: what remained of space intervened not even to be
measured in miles.

Though that little at a crawl, the car whining in second
gear now against the motionless uprush of the main ridge
and the strong constant resinous downflow of the pines
where the dogwood looked indeed like nuns now in the

long green corridors, up and onto the last crest, the
plateau and now he seemed to see his whole native land,
his home—the dirt, the earth which had bred his bones
and those of his fathers for six generations and was still
shaping him into not just a man but a specific man, not
with just a man's passions and aspirations and beliefs
but the specific passions and hopes and convictions and
ways of thinking and acting of a specific kind and even
race: and even more: even among a kind and race specific and unique (according to the lights of most, certainly of all of them who had thronged into town this
morning to stand across the street from the jail and crowd
up around the sheriff's car, damned unique) since it had
also integrated into him whatever it was that had compelled him to stop and listen to a damned highnosed
impudent Negro who even if he wasn't a murderer had
been about to get if not about what he deserved at least
exactly what he had spent the sixty-odd years of his life
asking for—unfolding beneath him like a map in one
slow soundless explosion: to the east ridge on green
ridge tumbling away toward Alabama and to the west
and south the checkered fields and the woods flowing on
into the blue and gauzed horizon beyond which lay at
last like a cloud the long wall of the levee and the great
River itself flowing not merely from the north but out
of the North circumscribing and outland—the umbilicus
of America joining the soil which was his home to the
parent which three generations ago it had failed in blood
to repudiate; by turning his head he could see the faint
stain of smoke which was town ten miles away and
merely by looking ahead he could see the long reach of
rich bottom land marked off into the big holdings, the
plantations (one of which was Edmonds' where the pres-

ent Edmonds and Lucas both had been born, stemming
from the same grandfather) along their own little river
(though even in his grandfather's memory steamboats
had navigated it) and then the dense line of river jungle
itself: and beyond that stretching away east and north
and west not merely to where the ultimate headlands
frowned back to back upon the waste of the two oceans
and the long barrier of Canada but to the uttermost rim
of earth itself, the North: not north but North, outland
and circumscribing and not even a geographical place
but an emotional idea, a condition of which he had fed
from his mother's milk to be ever and constant on the
alert not at all to fear and not actually anymore to hate
but just—a little wearily sometimes and sometimes even
with tongue in cheek—to defy: who had brought from
infancy with him a childhood's picture which on the
threshold of manhood had found no reason or means to
alter and which he had no reason to believe in his old age
would alter either: a curving semicircular wall not high
(anyone who really wanted to could have climbed it; he
believed that any boy already would) from the top of
which with the whole vast scope of their own rich teeming never-ravaged land of glittering undefiled cities and
unburned towns and unwasted farms so long-secured and
opulent you would think there was no room left for
curiosity, there looked down upon him and his countless
row on row of faces which resembled his face and spoke
the same language he spoke and at times even answered
to the same names he bore yet between whom and him
and his there was no longer any real kinship and soon
there would not even be any contact since the very mutual words they used would no longer have the same
significance and soon after that even this would be gone

because they would be too far asunder even to hear one
another: only the massed uncountable faces looking down
at him and his in fading amazement and outrage and
frustration and most curious of all, gullibility: a volitionless, almost helpless capacity and eagerness to believe
anything about the South not even provided it be deroga-
tory but merely bizarre enough and strange enough:
whereupon once more his uncle spoke at complete one
with him and again without surprise he saw his thinking
not be interrupted but merely swap one saddle for
another:

'It's because we alone in the United States (I'm not
speaking of Sambo right now; I'll get to him in a minute)
are a homogeneous people. I mean the only one of any
size. The New Englander is too of course back inland
from the coastal spew of Europe which this country
quarantined unrootable into the rootless ephemeral cities
with factory and foundry and municipal paychecks as
tight and close as any police could have done it, but
there are no longer enough of him just as there are not
of the Swiss who are not a people so much as a neat clean
small quite solvent business. So we are not really resist-
ing what the outland calls (and we too) progress and
enlightenment. We are defending not actually our politics or beliefs or even our way of life, but simply our
homogeneity from a federal government to which in
simple desperation the rest of this country has had to
surrender voluntarily more and more of its personal and
private liberty in order to continue to afford the United
States. And of course we will continue to defend it. We
(I mean all of us: Beat Four will be unable to sleep at
night until it has cancelled Lucas Beauchamp ((or someone else)) against Vinson Gowrie in the same color of

ink, and Beat One and Two and Three and Five who on
heatless principle intend to see that Beat Four makes
that cancellation) dont know why it is valuable. We dont
need to know. Only a few of us know that only from
homogeneity comes anything of a people or for a people
of durable and lasting value—the literature, the art, the
science, that minimum of government and police which
is the meaning of freedom and liberty, and perhaps most
valuable of all a national character worth anything in a
crisis—that crisis we shall face someday when we meet an
enemy with as many men as we have and as much mate-
rial as we have and—who knows?—who can even brag
and boast as we brag and boast.

'That's why we must resist the North: not just to preserve ourselves nor even the two of us as one to remain
one nation because that will be the inescapable by-
product of what we will preserve: which is the very thing
that three generations ago we lost a bloody war in our
own back yards so that it remain intact: the postulate
that Sambo is a human being living in a free country
and hence must be free. That's what we are really defending: the privilege of setting him free ourselves:
which we will have to do for the reason that nobody else
can since going on a century ago now the North tried it
and have been admitting for seventy-five years now that
they failed. So it will have to be us. Soon now this sort
of thing wont even threaten anymore. It shouldn't now.
It should never have. Yet it did last Saturday and it
probably will again, perhaps once more, perhaps twice
more. But then no more, it will be finished; the shame
will still be there of course but then the whole chronicle
of man's immortality is in the suffering he has endured,
his struggle toward the stars in the stepping-stones of his

expiations. Someday Lucas Beauchamp can shoot a white man in the back with the same impunity to lynch-rope or gasoline as a white man; in time he will vote anywhen and anywhere a white man can and send his children to the same school anywhere the white man's children go and travel anywhere the white man travels as the white man does it. But it wont be next Tuesday. Yet people in the North believe it can be compelled even into next Monday by the simple ratification by votes of a printed paragraph: who have forgotten that although a long quarter-century ago Lucas Beauchamp's freedom was made an article in our constitution and Lucas Beauchamp's master was not merely beaten to his knees but trampled for ten years on his face in the dust to make him swallow it, yet only three short generations later they are faced once more with the necessity of passing legislation to set Lucas Beauchamp free.

'And as for Lucas Beauchamp, Sambo, he's a homogeneous man too, except that part of him which is trying to escape not even into the best of the white race but into the second best—the cheap shoddy dishonest music, the cheap flash baseless overvalued money, the glittering edifice of publicity foundationed on nothing like a cardhouse over an abyss and all the noisy muddle of political activity which used to be our minor national industry and is now our national amateur pastime—all the spurious uproar produced by men deliberately fostering and then getting rich on our national passion for the mediocre: who will even accept the best provided it is debased and befouled before being fed to us: who are the only people on earth who brag publicly of being second-rate, i.e., lowbrows. I dont mean that Sambo. I mean the rest of him who has a better homogeneity than we have and

proved it by finding himself roots into the land where
he had actually to displace white men to put them down:
because he had patience even when he didn't have hope,
the long view even when there was nothing to see at the
end of it, not even just the will but the desire to endure
because he loved the old few simple things which no one
wanted to take from him: not an automobile nor flash
clothes nor his picture in the paper but a little of music
(his own), a hearth, not his child but any child, a God
a heaven which a man may avail himself a little of at
any time without having to wait to die, a little earth for
his own sweat to fall on among his own green shoots and
plants. We—he and us—should confederate: swap him
the rest of the economic and political and cultural privi-
leges which are his right, for the reversion of his capacity
to wait and endure and survive. Then we would pre-
vail; together we would dominate the United States;
we would present a front not only impregnable but not
even to be threatened by a mass of people who no longer
have anything in common save a frantic greed for money
and a basic fear of a failure of national character which
they hide from one another behind a loud lipservice to
a flag.

Now they were there and not too long behind the
sheriff. For though the car was already drawn off the road
into the grove in front of the church, the sheriff was still
standing beside it and one of the Negroes was just passing
the pick backward out of the car to the other prisoner
who stood holding both the shovels. His uncle drew in
beside it and stopped and now in daylight he could see
the church, for the first time actually who had lived within
ten miles of it all his life and must have passed it, seen it
at least half that many times. Yet he could not remember

ever having actually looked at it before—a plank steeple-
less box no longer than some of the one-room cabins hill
people lived in, paintless too yet (curiously) not shabby
and not even in neglect or disrepair because he could see
where sections of raw new lumber and scraps and fragments of synthetic roofing had been patched and car-
pentered into the old walls and shingles with a savage
almost insolent promptitude, not squatting nor crouching
nor even sitting but standing among the trunks of the
high strong constant shaggy pines, solitary but not forlorn,
intractable and independent, asking nothing of any, making compromise with none and he remembered the tall
slender spires which said Peace and the squatter utilitarian
belfries which said Repent and he remembered one which
even said Beware but this one said simply: Burn: and he
and his uncle got out; the sheriff and the two Negroes
carrying the tools were already inside the fence and he
and his uncle followed, through the sagging gate in the
low wire enclosure massed with honeysuckle and small
odorless pink and white climbing roses and he saw the
graveyard too for the first time, who had not only violated
a grave in it but exploded one crime by exposing another
—a fenced square of earth less large than garden plots he
had seen and which by September would probably be
choked and almost impenetrable and wellnigh invisible
with sagegrass and ragweed and beggarlice, out of which
stood without symmetry or order like bookmarks thrust
at random into a ledger or toothpicks in a loaf and canted
always slightly as if they had taken their own frozen per-
pendicular from the limber unresting never-quite-vertical
pines, shingle-thin slabs of cheap gray granite of the same
weathered color as the paintless church as if they had been
hacked out of its flank with axes (and carved mottoless

with simple names and dates as though there had been
nothing even their mourners remembered of them than
that they had lived and they had died) and it had been
neither decay nor time which had compelled back into
the violated walls the raw new patching of unplaned
paintless lumber but the simple exigencies of mortality
and the doom of flesh.

He and his uncle threaded on among them to where the
sheriff and the two Negroes already stood above the fresh
raw mound which likewise he who had violated it now
actually saw for the first time. But they hadn't begun to
dig yet. Instead the sheriff had even turned, looking back
at him until he and his uncle came up and stopped too.

'Now what?' his uncle said.

But the sheriff was speaking to him in the mild heavy
voice: 'I reckon you and Miss Eunice and your secretary
were mighty careful not to let anybody catch you at this
business last night, weren't you?'

His uncle answered: 'This is hardly the thing you'd
want an audience at, is it?'

But the sheriff was still looking at him. 'Then why
didn't they put the flowers back?'

Then he saw them too—the artificial wreath, the tedious intricate contrivance of wire and thread and var-
nished leaves and embalmed blooms which someone had
brought or sent out from the florist in town, and the
three bunches of wilted garden and field flowers tied
with cotton string, all of which Aleck Sander had said
last night looked as if they had been thrown at or onto
the grave and which he remembered Aleck Sander and
himself moving aside out of the way and which he knew
they had put back after they filled the hole back up; he
could remember Miss Habersham telling them twice to

put them back even after he himself had protested about
the un-need or at least the waste of time; perhaps he
could even remember Miss Habersham herself helping
to put them back: or then perhaps he didn't remember
them being put back at all but merely thought he did
because they obviously hadn't been, lying now tossed and
inextricable to one side and apparently either he or
Aleck Sander had trodden on the wreath though it didn't
really matter now, which was what his uncle was just
saying:

'Never mind now. Let's get started. Even when we
finish here and are on the way back to town we will still
be only started.'

'All right, boys,' the sheriff said to the Negroes. 'Jump
to it. Let's get out of here——' and there was no sound,
he heard nothing to warn him, he just looked up and
around as his uncle and the sheriff did and saw, coming
not down the road but around from behind the church
as though from among the high windy pines themselves,
a man in a wide pale hat and a clean faded blue shirt
whose empty left sleeve was folded neatly back and
pinned cuff to shoulder with a safetypin, on a small
trim claybank mare showing too much eye-white and
followed by two younger men riding double on a big
saddleless black mule with a rope-burn on its neck and
followed in their turn (and keeping carefully clear of
the mule's heels) by two gaunt Trigg foxhounds, coming
at a rapid trot across the grove to the gate where the man
stopped the mare and swung himself lightly and rapidly
down with his one hand and dropped the reins across
the mare's neck and came with that light wiry almost
springy rapidity through the gate and up to them—a
short lean old man with eyes as pale as the sheriff's and

a red weathered face out of which jutted a nose like the hooked beak of an eagle, already speaking in a high thin strong uncracked voice:

'What's going on around here, Shurf?'

'I'm going to open this grave, Mr Gowrie,' the sheriff said.

'No, Shurf,' the other said, immediate, with no change whatever in the voice: not disputative, nothing: just a statement: 'Not that grave.'

'Yes, Mr Gowrie,' the sheriff said. 'I'm going to open it.'

Without haste or fumbling, almost deliberate in fact, the old man with his one hand unbuttoned two buttons on the front of his shirt and thrust the hand inside, hunching his hip slightly around to meet the hand and drew from inside the shirt a heavy nickel-plated pistol and still with no haste but no pause either thrust the pistol into his left armpit, clamping it butt-forward against his body by the stub of the arm while his one hand buttoned the shirt, then took the pistol once more into the single hand not pointing it at anything, just holding it.

But long before this he had seen the sheriff already moving, moving with really incredible speed not toward the old man but around the end of the grave, already in motion even before the two Negroes turned to run, so that when they whirled they seemed to run full tilt into the sheriff as into a cliff, even seeming to bounce back a little before the sheriff grasped them one in each hand as if they were children and then in the next instant seemed to be holding them both in one hand like two rag dolls, turning his body so that he was between them and the little wiry old man with the pistol, saying in that mild even lethargic voice:

'Stop it. Dont you know the worst thing that could happen to a nigger would be dodging loose in a pair of convict pants around out here today?'

'That's right, boys,' the old man said in his high inflectionless voice. 'I aint going to hurt you. I'm talking to the Shurf here. Not my boy's grave, Shurf.'

'Send them back to the car,' his uncle murmured rapidly. But the sheriff didn't answer, still looking at the old man.

'Your boy aint in that grave, Mr Gowrie,' the sheriff said. And watching he thought of all the things the old man might have said—the surprise, the disbelief, the outrage perhaps, even the thinking aloud: *How do you come to know my boy aint there?*—the rationalising by reflective in which he might have paraphrased the sheriff speaking to his uncle six hours ago: *You wouldn't be telling me this if you didn't know it was so;* watching, even following the old man as he cut straight across all this and he thought suddenly with amazement: *Why, he's grieving:* thinking how he had seen grief twice now in two years where he had not expected it or anyway anticipated it, where in a sense a heart capable of breaking had no business being: once in an old nigger who had just happened to outlive his old nigger wife and now in a violent foulmouthed godless old man who had happened to lose one of the six lazy idle violent more or less lawless a good deal more than just more or less worthless sons, only one of whom had ever benefitted his community and kind and that only by the last desperate resort of getting murdered out of it: hearing the high flat voice again immediate and strong and without interval, inflectionless, almost conversational:

'Why, I just hope you dont tell me the name of the fellow that proved my boy aint there, Shurf. I just hope you wont mention that:'—little hard pale eyes staring at little hard pale eyes, the sheriff's voice mild still, inscrutable now:

'No, Mr Gowrie. It aint empty:' and later, afterward, he realised that this was when he believed he knew not perhaps why Lucas had ever reached town alive because the reason for that was obvious: there happened to be no Gowrie present at the moment but the dead one: but at least how the old man and two of his sons happened to ride out of the woods behind the church almost as soon as he and the sheriff and his uncle reached the grave, and certainly why almost forty-eight hours afterward Lucas was still breathing. 'It's Jake Montgomery down there,' the sheriff said.

The old man turned, immediate, not hurriedly and even quickly but just easily as if his spare small fleshless frame offered neither resistance to the air nor weight to the motive muscles, and shouted toward the fence where the two younger men still sat the mule identical as two clothing store dummies and as immobile, not even having begun yet to descend until the old man shouted: 'Here, boys.'

'Never mind,' the sheriff said. 'We'll do it.' He turned to the two Negroes. 'All right. Get your shovels——'

'I told you,' his uncle murmured rapidly again. 'Send them back to the car.'

'That's right, Lawyer—Lawyer Stevens, aint it?' the old man said. 'Get 'em away from here. This here's our business. We'll attend to it.'

'It's my business now, Mr Gowrie,' the sheriff said.

The old man raised the pistol, steadily and without haste, bending his elbow until it came level, his thumb curling up and over the hammer cocking it so that it

came already cocked level or not quite, not quite pointing at anything somewhere about the height of the empty
belt-loops on the sheriff's trousers. 'Get them out of here,
Shurf,' the old man said.

'All right,' the sheriff said without moving. 'You boys
go back to the car.'

'Further than that,' the old man said. 'Send 'em back
to town.'

'They're prisoners, Mr Gowrie,' the sheriff said. 'I cant
do that.' He didn't move. 'Go back and get in the car,'
he told them. They moved then, walking not back toward the gate but directly away across the enclosure,
walking quite fast, lifting their feet and knees in the
filthy barred trousers quite high, walking quite fast by
the time they reached the opposite fence and half stepping half hopping over it and only then changing direction back toward the two cars so that until they reached
the sheriff's car they would never be any nearer the two
white men on the mule than when they had left the
grave: and he looked at them now sitting the mule
identical as two clothes pins on a line, the identical faces
even weathered exactly alike, surly quick-tempered and
calm, until the old man shouted again:

'All right, boys:' and they got down as one, at the
same time even like a trained vaudeville team and again
as one stepped with the same left leg over the fence, completely ignoring the gate: the Gowrie twins, identical
even to the clothing and shoes except that one wore a
khaki shirt and the other a sleeveless jersey; about thirty,
a head taller than their father and with their father's
pale eyes and the nose too except that it was not the beak
of an eagle but rather that of a hawk, coming up with
no word, no glance even for any of them from the bleak

composed humorless faces until the old man pointed
with the pistol (he saw that the hammer was down now
anyway) at the two shovels and said in his high voice
which sounded almost cheerful even:

'Grab 'em, boys. They belong to the county; if we
bust one it aint anybody's business but the Grand Jury's:'
—the twins, facing each other now at opposite ends of
the mound and working again in that complete almost
choreographic unison: the next two youngest before the
dead one, Vinson; fourth and fifth of the six sons:—
Forrest, the oldest who had not only wrenched himself
free of his fiery tyrant of a father but had even got married and for twenty years now had been manager of a
delta cotton plantation above Vicksburg; then Crawford,
the second one who had been drafted on the second day
of November 1918 and on the night of the tenth (with
a bad luck in guessing which, his uncle said, should not
happen to any man—a point of view in which in fact his
federal captors themselves seemed to concur since his
term in the Leavenworth prison had been only one year)
had deserted and lived for almost eighteen months in a
series of caves and tunnels in the hills within fifteen
miles of the federal courthouse in Jefferson until he was
captured at last after something very like a pitched battle
(though luckily for him nobody was seriously hurt) during which he made good his cave for thirty-odd hours
armed with (and, his uncle said, a certain consistency
and fitness here: a deserter from the United States army
defending his freedom from the United States government with a piece of armament captured from the enemy
whom he had refused to fight) an automatic pistol which
one of the McCallum boys had taken from a captured
German officer and traded shortly after he got home for

a brace of Gowrie foxhounds, and served his year and came home and the town next heard of him in Memphis where it was said he was (1) running liquor up from New Orleans, (2) acting as a special employer-bonded company officer during a strike, but anyway coming back to his father's home suddenly where nobody saw much of him until a few years back when the town began to hear of him as having more or less settled down, dealing in a little timber and cattle and even working a little land; and Bryan, the third one who was the actual force, power, cohering element, whatever you might call it, in or behind the family farm which fed them all; then the twins, Vardaman and Bilbo who spent their nights squatting in front of smoldering logs and stumps while the hounds ran foxes and their days sleeping flat on the naked planks of the front gallery until dark came and time to cast the hounds again; and the last one, Vinson, who even as a child had shown an aptitude for trading and for money so that now, though dead at only twenty-eight, he was not only said to own several small parcels of farmland about the county but was the first Gowrie who could sign his name to a check and have any bank honor it;—the twins, kneedeep then waistdeep, working with a grim and sullen speed, robotlike and in absolute unison so that the two shovels even seemed to ring at the same instant on the plank box and even then seeming to communicate by no physical means as birds or animals do: no sound no gesture: simply one of them released his shovel in a continuation of the same stroke which flung the dirt and then himself flowed effortless up out of the pit and stood among the rest of them while his brother cleaned off what remained of dirt from the top of the coffin, then tossed his shovel up and out with-

out even looking and—as he himself had done last night
—kicked the last of the earth away from the edge of the
lid and stood on one leg and grasped the lid and heaved
it up and over and away until all of them standing along
the rim of the grave could look down past him into
the box.

It was empty. There was nothing in it at all until a
thin trickle of dirt flowed down into it with a whisper-
ing pattering sound.

Chapter Eight

AND HE WOULD REMEMBER IT: the five of them standing at the edge of the pit above the empty coffin, then with another limber flowing motion like his twin's the second Gowrie came up out of the grave and stooped and with an air of rapt displeased even faintly outraged concern began to brush and thump the clay particles from the lower legs of his trousers, the first twin moving as the second stooped, going straight to him with a blind un-hurried undeviable homing quality about him like the other of a piece of machinery, the other spindle say of a lathe, travelling on the same ineluctable shaft to its socket, and stooped too and began to brush and strike the dirt from the back of his brother's trousers; and this time almost a spadeful of dirt slid down across the out-slanted lid and rattled down into the empty box, almost loud enough or with mass and weight enough to produce a small hollow echo.

'Now he's got two of them,' his uncle said.

'Yes,' the sheriff said. 'Where?'

'Durn two of them,' old Gowrie said. 'Where's my boy, Shurf?'

'We're going to find him now, Mr Gowrie,' the sheriff said. 'And you were smart to bring them hounds. Put your pistol up and let your boys catch them dogs and hold them till we get straightened out here.'

'Never you mind the pistol nor the dogs neither,' old Gowrie said. 'They'll trail and they'll ketch anything that ever run or walked either. But my boy and that Jake Montgomery—if it was Jake Montgomery whoever it was found laying in my son's coffin—never walked away from here to leave no trail.'

The sheriff said, 'Hush now, Mr Gowrie.' The old man glared back up at the sheriff. He was not trembling, not eager, baffled, amazed, not anything. Watching him he thought of one of the cold lightblue tearshaped apparently heatless flames which balance themselves on even less than tiptoe over gasjets.

'All right,' the old man said. 'I'm hushed. And now you get started. You're the one that seems to know all about this, that sent me word out to my breakfast table at six oclock this morning to meet you here. Now you get started.'

'That's what we're going to do,' the sheriff said. 'We're going to find out right now where to start.' He turned to his uncle, saying in the mild rational almost diffident voice: 'It's say around eleven oclock at night. You got a mule or maybe it's a horse, anyway something that can walk and tote a double load, and a dead man across your saddle. And you aint got much time; that is, you aint got all of time. Of course it's around eleven oclock, when most folks is in bed, and a Sunday night too when folks have got to get up early tomorrow to start a new week in the middle of cotton-planting time, and there aint any moon and even if folks might still be moving around you're in a lonely part of the country where the chances all are you wont meet nobody. But you still got a dead man with a bullet hole in his back and even at eleven oclock day's going to come sooner or later. All right. What would you do?'

They looked, stared at one another, or that is his
uncle stared—the too-thin bony eager face, the bright
intent rapid eyes, and opposite the sheriff's vast sleepy
face, the eyes not staring, apparently not even looking,
blinking almost drowsily, the two of them cutting without speech across all that too: 'Of course,' his uncle said.
'Into the earth again. And not far, since as you said daylight comes sooner or later even when it's still just eleven
oclock. Especially when he still had time to come back
and do it all over again, alone, by himself, no hand but
his on the shovel.—And think of that too: the need, the
terrible need, not just to have it all to do again but to
have to do it again for the reason he had; to think that
he had done all he possibly could, all anyone could have
asked or expected him to do or even dreamed that he
would have to do; was as safe as he could hope to be—
and then to be drawn back by a sound, a noise or perhaps
he blundered by sheer chance on the parked truck or perhaps it was just his luck, his good fortune, whatever god
or djinn or genie looks after murderers for a little while,
keeps him secure and safe until the other fates have had
time to spin and knot the rope,—anyway to have to
crawl, tie the mule or horse or whatever it was to a tree
and crawl on his belly back up here to lie (who knows?
perhaps just behind the fence yonder) and watch a
meddling old woman and two children who should have
been two hours ago in bed ten miles away, wreck the
whole careful edifice of his furious labor, undo the work
not merely of his life but of his death too . . .' His uncle
stopped, and now he saw the bright almost luminous
eyes glaring down at him: 'And you. You couldn't have
had any idea Miss Habersham was coming with you
until you got home. And without her, you could have
had no hope whatever that Aleck Sander would come

with you alone at all. So if you ever really had any idea of coming out here alone to dig this grave up, dont even tell me——'

'Let that be now,' the sheriff said. 'All right. Somewhere in the ground. And what sort of ground? What dirt digs easiest and fastest for a man in a hurry and by himself even if he has a shovel? What sort of dirt could you hope to hide a body in quick even if you never had nothing but a pocket knife?'

'In sand,' his uncle said immediately, rapidly, almost indifferently, almost inattentively. 'In the bed of the branch. Didn't they tell you at three oclock this morning that they saw him going there with it? What are we waiting for?'

'All right,' the sheriff said. 'Let's go then.' Then to him: 'Show us exactly where——'

'Except that Aleck Sander said it might not have been a mule,' he said.

'All right,' the sheriff said. 'Horse then. Show us exactly where . . . .'

He would remember it: watching the old man clap the pistol again butt-forward into his armpit and clamp it there with the stump of the arm while the one hand unbuttoned the shirt then took the pistol from the armpit and thrust it back inside the shirt then buttoned the shirt again then turned even faster quicker than the two sons half his age, already in front of everybody when he hopped back over the fence and went to the mare and caught reins and pommel all in one hand, already swinging up: then the two cars dropping in second speed against gravity back down the steep pitch until he said 'Here' where the pickup's tracks slewed off the road into the bushes then back into the road again and his uncle stopped: and he watched the fierce old stump-armed man jump the buckskin mare up out of the road into the woods on the opposite side already falling away down toward the branch, then the two hounds flowing up the bank behind him and then the mule with the two identical wooden-faced sons on it: then he and his uncle were out of the car the sheriff's car bumper to bumper behind them, hearing the mare crashing on down toward the branch and then the old man's high flat voice shouting at the hounds:

'Hi! Hi! Hum on boy! At him, Ring!' and then his uncle:

'Handcuff them through the steering wheel:' and then the sheriff:

'No. We'll need the shovels:' and he had climbed the bank too, listening off and downward toward the crashing and the shouts, then his uncle and the sheriff and the two Negroes carrying the shovels were beside him. Although the branch crossed almost at right angles the highway just beyond where the dirt road forked away, it was almost a quarter-mile from where they now stood or walked rather and although they could all hear old Gowrie still whooping at the dogs and the crashing of the mare and the mule too in the dense thicket below, the sheriff didn't go that way, bearing instead off along the hill almost parallel with the road for several minutes and only beginning to slant away from it when they came out into the sawgrass and laurel and willow-choked flat between the hill and the branch: and on across that, the sheriff in front until he stopped still looking down then turned his head and looked back at him, watching him as he and his uncle came up.

'Your secretary was right the first time,' the sheriff said. 'It was a mule.'

'Not a black one with a rope-burn,' his uncle said. 'Surely not that. Not even a murderer is that crassly and arrogantly extrovert.'

'Yes,' the sheriff said. 'That's why they're dangerous, why we must destroy them or lock them up:' and looking down he saw them too: the narrow delicate almost finicking mule-prints out of all proportion to the animal's actual size, mashed pressed deep, too deep for any one mule no matter how heavy carrying just one man, into the damp muck, the tracks filled with water and even as he watched a minute aquatic beast of some sort shot across one of them leaving a tiny threadlike spurt of dissolving mud; and standing in the trail, now that they had found it they could see the actual path itself through the crushed shoulder-high growth in suspension held like a furrow across a field or the frozen wake of a boat, crossing the marsh arrow-straight until it vanished into the jungle which bordered the branch. They followed it, walking in it, treading the two sets of prints not going and returning but both going in the same direction, now and then the print of the same hoof superposed on its previous one, the sheriff still in the lead talking again, speaking aloud but without looking back as though—he thought at first—to no one:

'He wouldn't come back this way. The first time he didn't have time. He went back straight up the hill that time, woods or not and dark or not. That was when he heard whatever it was he heard.' Then he knew who the sheriff was talking to: 'Maybe your secretary was whistling up there or something. Being in a graveyard that time of night.'

Then they stood on the bank of the branch itself—a broad ditch a channel through which during the winter and spring rains a torrent rushed but where now there flowed a thin current scarcely an inch deep and never much over a yard wide from pool to pool along the blanched sand—and even as his uncle said, 'Surely the fool——' the sheriff ten yards or so further along the bank said:

'Here it is:' and they went to him and then he saw where the mule had stood tied to a sapling and then the prints where the man himself had thrashed on along the bank, his prints also deeper than any man no matter how heavy should have made and he thought of that too: the anguish, the desperation, the urgency in the black dark and the briers and the dizzy irrevocable fleeing on seconds, carrying a burden man was not intended to carry: then he was hearing a snapping and thrashing of underbrush still further along the bank and then the mare and then old Gowrie shouted and then another crash which would be the mule coming up and then simple pandemonium: the old man shouting and cursing and the yelping of the hounds and the thudding sound a man's shoe makes against a dog's ribs: but they couldn't hurry anymore, thrashing and crashing their own way through the tearing clinging briers and vines until they could look down into the ditch and the low mound of fresh shaled earth into which the two hounds had been digging and old Gowrie still kicking at them and cursing, and then they were all down in the ditch except the two Negroes.

'Hold up, Mr Gowrie,' the sheriff said. 'That aint Vinson.' But the old man didn't seem to hear him. He didn't even seem aware that anyone else was there; he

seemed even to have forgot why he was kicking the dogs:
that he had merely set out to drive them back from the
mound, still hobbling and hopping after them on one
leg and the other poised and cocked to kick even after
they had retreated from the mound and were merely trying to dodge past him and get out of the ditch into
safety, still kicking at them and cursing after the sheriff
caught him by his one arm and held him.

'Look at the dirt,' the sheriff said. 'Cant you see? He
hardly took time to bury it. This was the second one,
when he was in the hurry, when it was almost daylight
and he had to get it hidden?' and they could all see now
—the low hummock of fresh dirt lying close under the
bank and in the bank above it the savage ragged marks
of the shovel as if he had hacked at the bank with the
edge of the blade like swinging an axe (and again: thinking: the desperation the urgency the frantic hand-to-
hand combat with the massy intolerable inertia of the
earth itself) until enough of it shaled off and down to
hide what he had to hide.

This time they didn't need even the shovels. The body
was barely covered; the dogs had already exposed it and
he realised now the true magnitude of the urgency and
desperation: the frantic and desperate bankrupt in time
who had not even enough of it left to hide the evidence
of his desperation and the reason for his urgency; it had
been after two oclock when he and Aleck Sander, even
two of them working with furious speed, had got the
grave filled back up again: so that by the time the murderer, not only alone but who had already moved six
feet of dirt and then put it back once since the sun set
yesterday, had the second body out and the grave filled
for the second time it must have been daylight, later

than daylight perhaps, the sun itself watching him while
he rode for the second time down the hill and across to
the branch; morning itself watching him while he
tumbled the body beneath the bank's overhang then
hacked furiously from it just enough dirt to hide the
body temporarily from sight with something of that
frantic desperation of the wife flinging her peignoir over
the lover's forgotten glove:—lying (the body) face down
and only the back of the crushed skull visible until the
old man stooped and with his one hand jerked it stiffly
over onto its back.

'Yep,' old Gowrie said in the high brisk carrying voice:
'It's that Montgomery, damned if it aint:' and rose lean
and fast as a tripped watch-spring yelling shouting at
the hounds again: 'Hi boys! Find Vinson!' and then his
uncle shouting too to make himself heard:

'Wait, Mr Gowrie. Wait:' then to the sheriff: 'He was
a fool then just because he didn't have time, not because he is a fool. I just dont believe it twice——' looking around, his eyes darting. Then he stopped them on
the twins. He said sharply: 'Where's the quicksand?'

'What?' one of the twins said.

'The quicksand,' his uncle said. 'The quicksand bed
in the branch here. Where is it?'

'Quicksand?' old Gowrie said. 'Sonabitch, Lawyer.
Put a man in quicksand? my boy in quicksand?'

'Shut up, Mr Gowrie,' the sheriff said. Then to the
twin: 'Well? Where?'

But he answered first. He had been intending to for
a second or so. Now he did: 'It's by the bridge:' then—he
didn't know why: and then that didn't matter either—'It
wasn't Aleck Sander that time. It was Highboy.'

'*Under* the highway bridge,' the twin corrected. 'Where it's been all the time.'

'Oh,' the sheriff said. 'Which one was Highboy?' And he was about to answer that: then suddenly the old man seemed to have forgot about his mare too, whirling, already running before any of them moved and even before he himself moved, running for several strides against the purchaseless sand while they watched him, before he turned and with that same catlike agility he mounted the mare with, clawed himself one-handed up the steep bank and was thrashing and crashing on out of sight before anybody else except the two Negroes who had never quitted it were even up the bank.

'Jump,' the sheriff said to the twins: 'Catch him.' But they didn't. They thrashed and crashed on after him, one of the twins in front then the rest of them and the two Negroes pell mell through the briers and brush, on back along the branch and out of the jungle into the cleared right-of-way below the road at the bridge; he saw the sliding hoof-marks where Highboy had come almost down to the water and then refused, the stream the water crowded over against the opposite concrete revetment flowing in a narrow band whose nearer edge faded without demarcation into an expanse of wet sand as smooth and innocent and markless of surface as so much milk; he stepped sprang over a long willow pole lying above the bank-edge and coated for three or four feet up its length with a thin patina of dried sand like when you thrust a stick into a bucket or vat of paint and even as the sheriff shouted to the twin in front 'Grab him, you!' he saw the old man jump feet first off the bank and with no splash no disturbance of any sort continue right on not through the bland surface but past it as if he had

jumped not into anything but past the edge of a cliff or
a window-sill and then stopping half-disappeared as suddenly with no shock or jolt: just fixed and immobile as
if his legs had been cut off at the loins by one swing of a
scythe, leaving his trunk sitting upright on the bland
depthless milklike sand.

'All right, boys!' old Gowrie cried, brisk and carrying:
'Here he is. I'm standing on him.'

And one twin got the rope bridle from the mule and
the leather one and the saddle girth from the mare and
using the shovels like axes the Negroes hacked willow
branches while the rest of them dragged up other brush
and poles and whatever else they could reach or find or
free and now both twins and the two Negroes, their
empty shoes sitting on the bank, were down in the sand
too and steadily there came down from the hills the
ceaseless strong murmur of the pines but no other sound
yet although he strained his ears listening in both directions along the road, not for the dignity of death because
death has no dignity but at least for the decorum of it:
some little at least of that decorum which should be
every man's helpless right until the carrion he leaves can
be hidden from the ridicule and the shame, the body
coming out now feet first, gallowsed up and out of the
inscrutable suck to the heave of the crude tackle then
free of the sand with a faint smacking plop like the
sound of lips perhaps in sleep and in the bland surface
nothing: a faint wimple wrinkle already fading then
gone like the end of a faint secret fading smile, and then
on the bank now while they stood about and over it and
he was listening harder than ever now with something
of the murderer's own frantic urgency both ways along
the road though there was still nothing: only hearing

recognising his own voice apparently long after everyone
else had, watching the old man coated to the waist with
the same thin patina of sand like the pole, looking down
at the body, his face wrenched and his upper lip
wrenched upward from the lifeless porcelain glare and
the pink bloodless gums of his false teeth:

'Oh gee, Uncle Gavin, oh gee, Uncle Gavin, let's get
him away from the road, at least let's get him back into
the woods——'

'Steady,' his uncle said. 'They've all passed now.
They're all in town now:' and still watching as the old
man stooped and began to brush clumsily with his one
hand at the sand clogged into the eyes and nostrils and
mouth, the hand looking curious and stiff at this which
had been shaped so supple and quick to violence: to the
buttons on the shirt and the butt and hammer of the
pistol: then the hand went back and began to fumble
at the hip pocket but already his uncle had produced a
handkerchief and extended it but that was too late too
as kneeling now the old man jerked out the tail of his
shirt and bending to bring it close, wiped the or at the
dead face with it then bending tried to blow the wet
sand from it as though he had forgotten the sand was
still damp. Then the old man stood up again and said
in the high flat carrying voice in which there was still
no real inflection at all:

'Well, Shurf?'

'It wasn't Lucas Beauchamp, Mr Gowrie,' the sheriff
said. 'Jake Montgomery was at Vinson's funeral yesterday. And while Vinson was being buried Lucas Beauchamp was locked up in my jail in town.'

'I aint talking about Jake Montgomery, Shurf,' old
Gowrie said.

'Neither am I, Mr Gowrie,' the sheriff said. 'Because it wasn't Lucas Beauchamp's old forty-one Colt that killed Vinson either.'

And watching he thought *No! No! Dont say it! Dont ask!* and for a while he believed the old man would not as he stood facing the sheriff but not looking at him now because his wrinkled eyelids had come down hiding his eyes but only in the way they do when somebody looks down at something at his feet so you couldn't really say whether the old man had closed them or was just looking down at what lay on the ground between him and the sheriff. But he was wrong; the eyelids went up again and again the old man's hard pale eyes were looking at the sheriff; again his voice to nine hundred men out of nine hundred and one would have sounded just cheerful:

'What was it killed Vinson, Shurf?'

'A German Luger automatic, Mr Gowrie,' the sheriff said. 'Like the one Buddy McCallum brought home from France in 1919 and traded that summer for a pair of fox hounds.'

And he thought how this was where the eyelids might even should have closed again but again he was wrong: only until the old man himself turned, quick and wiry, already in motion, already speaking peremptory and loud, not brookless of opposition or argument, simply incapable of conceiving either:

'All right, sons. Let's load our boy on the mule and take him home.'

Chapter Nine

AND TWO OCLOCK that afternoon in his uncle's car just behind the truck (it was another pickup; they—the sheriff—had commandeered it, with a slatted cattle frame on the bed which one of the Gowrie twins had known would be standing in the deserted yard of the house two miles away which had the telephone too—and he remembered how he wondered what the truck was doing there, how they had got to town themselves who had left it—and the Gowrie had turned the switch on with a table fork which by the Gowrie's direction he had found in the unlocked kitchen when his uncle went in to telephone the coroner and the Gowrie was driving it) blinking rapidly and steadily not against glare so much as something hot and gritty inside his eyelids like a dust of ground glass (which certainly could and even should have been dust after twenty-odd miles of sand and gravel roads in one morning except that no simple dust refused as this did to moisten at all with blinking) it seemed to him that he saw crowding the opposite side of the street facing the jail not just the county, not just Beat One and Two and Three and Five in their faded tieless khaki and denim and print cotton but the town too—not only the faces he had seen getting out of the Beat Four dusty cars in front of the barbershop and the poolhall Saturday afternoon and then in the barbershop Sunday morning

and again here in the street Sunday noon when the sheriff drove up with Lucas, but the others who except for
the doctors and lawyers and ministers were not just the
town but the Town: merchants and cotton-buyers and
automobile dealers and the younger men who were the
clerks in the stores and cotton offices and salesrooms and
mechanics in the garages and filling stations on the way
back to work from lunch—who without even waiting for
the sheriff's car to get close enough to be recognised had
already turned and begun to flow back toward the Square
like the turn of a tide, already in motion when the sheriff's car reached the jail, already pouring back into the
Square and converging in that one direction across it
when first the sheriff then the truck then his uncle
turned into the alley beyond the jail leading to the loading ramp at the undertaker's back door where the coroner was waiting for them: so that moving not only
parallel with them beyond the intervening block but
already in advance, it would even reach the undertaker's
first; and then suddenly and before he could even turn
in the seat to look back he knew that it had even boiled
into the alley behind them and in a moment a second
now it would roar down on them, overtake and snatch
them up in order: his uncle's car then the truck then
the sheriff's like three hencoops and sweep them on and
fling them at last in one inextricable aborted now-worth-
less jumble onto the ramp at the coroner's feet; still not
moving yet it seemed to him that he was already leaning
out the window or maybe actually clinging to the fleeing
runningboard yelling back at them in a kind of unbearable unbelieving outrage:

'You fools, dont you see you are too late, that you'll
have to start all over again now to find a new reason?'

then turning in the seat and looking back through the
rear window for a second or maybe two he actually saw
it—not faces but a face, not a mass nor even a mosaic of
them but a Face: not even ravening nor uninsatiate but
just in motion, insensate, vacant of thought or even passion: an Expression significantless and without past like
the one which materialises suddenly after seconds or even
minutes of painful even frantic staring from the innocent juxtaposition of trees and clouds and landscape in
the soap-advertisement puzzle-picture or on the severed
head in the news photo of the Balkan or Chinese atroc-
ity: without dignity and not even evocative of horror:
just neckless slack-muscled and asleep, hanging suspended
face to face with him just beyond the glass of the back
window yet in the same instant rushing and monstrous
down at him so that he actually started back and had
even begun to think *In a second more it will* when flick!
it was gone, not only the Face but the faces, the alley
itself empty behind them: nobody and nothing in it at
all and in the street beyond the vacant mouth less than
a dozen people now standing looking up the alley after
them who even as he looked turned also and began to
move back toward the Square.

He hesitated only an instant. *They've all gone around
to the front* he thought rapid and quite calm, having a
little trouble (he noticed that the car was stopped now)
getting his hand onto the door handle, remarking the
sheriff's car and the truck both stopped too at the loading
ramp where four or five men were lifting a stretcher up
to the truck's open endgate and he even heard his uncle's
voice behind him:

'Now we're going home and put you to bed before
your mother has a doctor in to give us both a squirt with

a needle:' then finding the handle and out of the car, stumbling a little but only once, then his heels although he was not running at all pounding too hard on the concrete, his leg-muscles cramped from the car or perhaps even charley-horsed from thrashing up and down branch bottoms not to mention a night spent digging and undigging graves but at least the jarring was clearing his head somewhat or maybe it was the wind of motion doing it; anyway if he was going to have delusions at least he would have a clear brain to look at them with: up the walkway between the undertaker's and the building next to it though already too late of course, the Face in one last rush and surge long since by now already across the Square and the pavement, in one last crash against then right on through the plate glass window trampling to flinders the little bronze-and-ebony membership plaque in the national funeraleers association and the single shabby stunted palm in its maroon earthenware pot and exploding to tatters the sunfaded purple curtain which was the last frail barrier shielding what was left of Jake Montgomery had of what was left of his share of human dignity.

Then out of the walkway onto the sidewalk, the Square, and stopped dead still for what seemed to him the first time since he and his uncle left the supper table and walked out of the house a week or a month or a year ago or whenever it had been that last Sunday night was. Because this time he didn't even need the flick. They were there of course nose-pressed to the glass but there were not even enough of them to block the pavement let alone compound a Face; less than a dozen here too and some most of them were even boys who should have been in school at this hour—not one country face

nor even one true man because even the other four or
five were the man-sized neither men nor boys who were
always there when old epileptic Uncle Hogeye Mosby
from the poorhouse fell foaming into the gutter or when
Willy Ingrum finally managed to shoot through the leg
or loins what some woman had telephoned him was a
mad-dog: and standing at the entrance to the walkway
while his uncle came pounding up it behind him, blinking painfully his painful moistureless eyelids he watched
why: the Square not empty yet because there were too
many of them but getting empty, the khaki and denim
and the printed cotton streaming into it and across it
toward the parked cars and trucks, clotting and crowding
at the doors while one by one they crawled and climbed
into the seats and beds and cabs; already starters were
whining and engines catching and racing and idling and
gears scraping and grinding while the passengers still
hurried toward them and now not one but five or six at
once backed away from the curb and turned and straightened out with people still running toward them and
scrambling aboard and then he could no longer have
kept count of them even if he had ever tried, standing
beside his uncle watching them condense into four
streams into the four main streets leading out of town
in the four directions, already going fast even before they
were out of the Square, the faces for one last moment
more looking not back but out, not at anything, just out
just once and that not for long and then no more, vanishing rapidly in profile and seeming already to be travelling much faster than the vehicle which bore them,
already by their faces out of town long before they had
passed from view: and twice more even from the car;
his mother standing suddenly not touching him, come

obviously through the walkway too from the jail right
past where they were probably still hoicking Montgomery out of the truck but then his uncle had told him
they could stand anything provided they still retained
always the right to refuse to admit it was visible, saying
to his uncle:

'Where's the car?' then not even waiting to be answered, turning back into the walkway ahead of them,
walking slender and erect and rigid with her back looking and her heels clicking and popping on the concrete
as they did at home when he and Aleck Sander and his
father and uncle all four had better walk pretty light for
a while, back past the ramp where only the sheriff's
empty car and the empty truck stood now and on to
the alley where she was already holding open the door
of the car when he and his uncle got there and saw them
again crossing the mouth of the alley like across a stage—
the cars and trucks, the faces in invincible profile not
amazed not aghast but in a sort of irrevocable repudiation, shooting across the alley-mouth so constant and unbroken and so many of them it was like the high school
senior class or maybe an itinerant one-night travelling
troupe giving the Battle of San Juan Hill and you not
only didn't hear you didn't even need to not listen to the
muted confused backstage undersounds to the same as
see the marching or charging troops as soon as they
reached the wings break into a frantic stumbling run
swapping coats and caps and fake bandages as they
doubled back behind the rippling cheesecloth painted
with battle and courage and death to fall in on their own
rear and at heroic attention cross the footlights again.

'We'll take Miss Habersham home first,' he said.

'Get in,' his mother said and one turn to the left into

the street behind the jail and he could still hear them
and another turn to the left into the next cross street
and there they were again fleeing across that proscenium
too unbroken and breakless, the faces rigid in profile
above the long tearing sound of cement and rubber and
it had taken him two or three minutes in the pickup
this morning to find a chance just to get into it and go
the same way it was going; it would take his uncle five
or ten to find a hole to get through it and go back to
the jail.

'Go on,' his mother said. 'Make them let you in:' and
he knew they were not going by the jail at all; he said:

'Miss Habersham——'

'How do I do it?' his uncle said. 'Just shut both eyes
and mash hard with my right foot?' and perhaps did;
they were in the stream too now turning with it toward
home which was all right, he had never worried about
getting into it but getting out of it again before that
frantic pell mell not of flight then if any liked that better
so just call it evacuation swept them on into nightfall to
spew them at last hours and miles away high and dry
and battered and with the wind knocked out of them
somewhere along the county's ultimate scarce-mapped
perimeter to walk back in the dark: saying again:

'Miss Habersham——'

'She has her truck,' his uncle said. 'Dont you remember?'—who had been doing nothing else steadily for five
minutes now, even trying three times to say it: Miss
Habersham in the truck and her house not half a mile
away and all holding her back was she couldn't possibly
get to it, the house on one side and the truck on the
other of that unpierceable barrier of rushing bumper-
locked cars and trucks and so almost as interdict to an

old maiden lady in a second-hand vegetable-peddler's pickup as if it were in Mongolia or the moon: sitting in the truck with the engine running and the gears meshed and her foot on the accelerator independent solitary and forlorn erect and slight beneath the exact archaic even moribund hat waiting and watching and wanting only but nothing but to get through it so she could put the darned clothes away and feed the chickens and eat supper and get some rest too after going on thirty-six hours which to seventy must have been worse than a hundred to sixteen, watching and waiting that dizzying profiled blur for a while even a good while but not forever not too long because she was a practical woman who hadn't taken long last night to decide that the way to get a dead body up out of a grave was to go out to the grave and dig it up and not long now to decide that the way to get around an obstruction especially with the sun already tumbling down the west was to go around it, the truck in motion now running along parallel with the obstruction and in its direction, forlorn and solitary still yet independent still too and only a little nervous, perhaps just realising that she was already driving a little faster than she was used and liked to, faster in fact than she had ever driven before and even then not keeping abreast of it but only beside it because it was going quite fast now: one endless profiled whizz: and now she would know that when the gap came perhaps she would not have the skill or strength or speed or quickness of eye or maybe even the simple nerve: herself going faster and faster and so intent trying to not miss the gap with one eye and watch where she was going with the other that she wouldn't realise until afterward that she had made the turn going not south but east now and not just her

house diminishing rapidly and squarely behind her but
Jefferson too because they or it was not moving in just
one direction out of town but in all of them on all the
main roads leading away from the jail and the undertaker's and Lucas Beauchamp and what was left of Vinson Gowrie and Montgomery like the frantic scattering
of waterbugs on a stagnant pond when you drop a rock
into it: so she would be more desperate than ever now
with all distance fleeing between her and home and
another night coming on, nerving herself for any gap or
crevice now, the battered pickup barely skimming the
ground beside that impenetrable profiled blur drawing
creeping closer and closer beside it when the inevitable
happened: some failure of eye or tremor of hand or an
involuntary flick of the eyelid on alertness's straining
glare or maybe simple topography: a stone or clod in the
path as inaccessible to indictment as God but anyway
too close and then too late, the truck snatched up and
into the torrent of ballbearing rubber and refinanced
pressed steel and hurled pell mell on still gripping the
useless steering wheel and pressing the gelded accelerator
solitary and forlorn across the long peaceful creep of
late afternoon, into the mauve windless dome of dusk,
faster and faster now toward one last crescendo just this
side of the county line where they would burst scattering
into every crossroad and lane like rabbits or rats nearing
at last their individual burrows, the truck slowing and
then stopping a little crossways in the road perhaps where
momentum had spewed it because she was safe now, in
Crossman County and she could turn south again now
along the edge of Yoknapatawpha turning on the lights
now going as fast as she dared along the fringing un-
marked country roads; full night now and in Mott

County now she could even turn west at last watching
her chance to turn north and make her dash, nine and
ten oclock along the markless roads fringing the imagin-
ary line beyond which the distant frantic headlights
flashed and darted plunging into their burrows and
dens; Okatoba County soon and midnight and surely
she could turn north then back into Yoknapatawpha,
wan and spent solitary and indomitable among the
crickets and treefrogs and lightningbugs and owls and
whippoorwills and the hounds rushing bellowing out
from under the sleeping houses and even at last a man
in his nightshirt and unlaced shoes, carrying a lantern:

Where you trying to go, lady?

I'm trying to get to Jefferson.

Jefferson's behind you, lady.

*I know. I had to detour around an arrogant insuffer-
able old nigger who got the whole county upset trying
to pretend he murdered a white man:* when suddenly he
discovered that he was going to laugh, discovering it almost in time, not quite in time to prevent it but in time
to begin to stop it pretty quick, really more surprised
than anything else, until his mother said harshly:

'Blow the horn. Blow them out of the way' and he discovered that it was not laughing at all or anyway not
just laughing, that is the sound it was making was about
the same as laughing but there was more of it and it
felt harder, seemed to be having more trouble getting
out and the harder it felt and sounded the less and less
he could seem to remember what he must have been
laughing at and his face was suddenly wet not with a
flow but a kind of burst and spring of water; anyway
there he was, a hulking lump the second largest of the
three of them, more bigger than his mother than his

uncle was than he, going on seventeen years old and almost a man yet because three in the car were so crowded he couldn't help but feel a woman's shoulder against his and her narrow hand on his knee sitting there like a spanked child before he had even had warning enough to begin to stop it.

'They ran,' he said.

'Pull out, damn you,' his mother said. 'Go around them:' which his uncle did, on the wrong side of the street and going almost as fast as he had driven this morning on the way to the church trying to keep in sight of the sheriff and it wasn't because his mother had rationalised that since all of them were already in town trying their best to get out of it there wouldn't be anybody to be coming toward the Square on that side of the street so it was simply just having one in the car with you even if she wasn't driving it, that's all you needed to do: remembering them once before in a car and his uncle driving and his uncle said then,

'All right, how do I do it, just shut both eyes and mash the accelerator?' and his mother said,

'How many collisions did you ever see with women driving both of them?' and his uncle said,

'All right, touché, maybe it's because one of them's car is still in the shop where a man ran into it yesterday:' then he could no longer see them but only hear the long tearing without beginning or end and leaving no scar of tires and pavement in friction like the sound of raw silk and luckily the house was on the same wrong side of the street too and carrying the sound into the yard with him too and now he could do something about the laughing by taking a moment to put his hand on whatever it was that seemed to have got him started and bringing it out

into the light where even he could see it wasn't that
funny; about ten thousand miles of being funny enough
to set his mother swearing; he said:

'They ran' and at once knew that was wrong, almost
too late even while he was standing right there looking
at himself, walking fast across the yard until he stopped
and not jerked just pulled his arm away and said, 'Look,
I'm not crippled. I'm just tired. I'm going up to my
room and lie down a while:' and then to his uncle: 'I'll
be all right then. Come up and call me in about fifteen
minutes:' then stopped and turned again again to his
uncle: 'I'll be ready in fifteen minutes:' and went on this
time carrying it into the house with him and even in
his room too he could still hear it even through the
drawn shades and the red jumping behind his eyelids
until he started up onto one elbow under his mother's
hand too again to his uncle just beyond the footboard:

'Fifteen minutes. You wont go without me? You promise?'

'Sure,' his uncle said. 'I wont go without you. I'll
just——'

'Will you please get to hell out of here, Gavin?' his
mother said and then to him, 'Lie down' and he did and
there it still was even through even against the hand,
the narrow slim cool palm but too dry too rough and
maybe even too cool, the dry hot gritty feel of his skull
better than the feel of the hand on it because at least
he was used to it by now, he had had it long enough,
even rolling his head but about as much chance to
escape that one frail narrow inevictible palm as to roll
your forehead out from under a birthmark and it was
not even a face now because their backs were toward him
but the back of a head, the composite one back of one

Head one fragile mushfilled bulb indefensible as an egg yet terrible in its concorded unanimity rushing not at him but away.

'They ran,' he said. 'They saved their consciences a good ten cents by not having to buy him a package of tobacco to show they had forgiven him.'

'Yes,' his mother said. 'Just let go:' which was like telling a man dangling with one hand over a cliff to just hold on: who wanted nothing right now but a chance to let go and relinquish into the nothing of sleep what little of nothing he still had who last night had wanted to go to sleep and could have but didn't have time and now wanted more than ever to go to sleep and had all the time in the world for the next fifteen minutes (or the next fifteen days or fifteen years as far as anybody knew because there was nothing anybody could do but hope Crawford Gowrie would decide to come in and hunt up the sheriff and say All right I did it because all they had was Lucas who said that Vinson Gowrie wasn't shot with a forty-one Colt or anyway his, Lucas' forty-one Colt and Buddy McCallum to say or not say Yes I swapped Crawford Gowrie a German pistol twenty-five years ago; not even Vinson Gowrie for somebody from the Memphis police to come and look at and say what bullet killed him because the sheriff had already let old Gowrie take him back home and wash the quicksand off and bury him again tomorrow: where this time Hampton and his uncle could go out there tomorrow night and dig him up) only he had forgotten how: or maybe that was it and he didn't dare relinquish into nothing what little he had left: which was nothing: no grief to be remembered nor pity nor even awareness of shame, no vindication of the deathless aspiration of man by man to

man through the catharsis of pity and shame but instead
only an old man for whom grief was not even a com-
ponent of his own but merely a temporary phenomenon
of his slain son jerking a strange corpse over onto its
back not in appeasement to its one mute indicting cry
not for pity not for vengeance but for justice but just
to be sure he had the wrong one, crying cheery abashless
and loud: 'Yep it's that damned Montgomery damned if
it aint,' and a Face; who had no more expected Lucas to
be swept out of his cell shoulder high on a tide of expiation and set for his moment of vindication and
triumph on the base say of the Confederate monument
(or maybe better on the balcony of the postoffice building beneath the pole where the national flag flew) than
he had expected such for himself and Aleck Sander and
Miss Habersham: who (himself) not only had not wanted
that but could not have accepted it since it would have
abrogated and made void the whole sum of what part he
had done which had to be anonymous else it was valueless: who had wanted of course to leave his mark too on
his time in man but only that, no more than that, some
mark on his part in earth but humbly, waiting wanting
humbly even, not really hoping even, nothing (which of
course was everything) except his own one anonymous
chance too to perform something passionate and brave
and austere not just in but into man's enduring chronicle worthy of a place in it (who knew? perhaps adding
even one anonymous jot to the austerity of the chronicle's brave passion) in gratitude for the gift of his time
in it, wanting only that and not even with hope really,
willing to accept the fact that he had missed it because
he wasn't worthy, but certainly he hadn't expected this:
—not a life saved from death nor even a death saved

from shame and indignity nor even the suspension of a
sentence but merely the grudging pretermission of a
date; not indignity shamed with its own shameful cancellation, not sublimation and humility with humility
and pride remembered nor the pride of courage and
passion nor of pity nor the pride and austerity and grief,
but austerity itself debased by what it had gained, courage and passion befouled by what they had had to cope
with;—a Face, the composite Face of his native kind his
native land, his people his blood his own with whom
it had been his joy and pride and hope to be found
worthy to present one united unbreakable front to the
dark abyss the night—a Face monstrous unravening
omniverous and not even uninsatiate, not frustrated nor
even thwarted, not biding nor waiting and not even
needing to be patient since yesterday today and tomorrow are Is: Indivisible: One (his uncle for this too, an-
ticipating this too two or three or four years ago as his
uncle had everything else which as he himself became
more and more a man he had found to be true: 'It's all
now you see. Yesterday wont be over until tomorrow
and tomorrow began ten thousand years ago. For every
Southern boy fourteen years old, not once but whenever
he wants it, there is the instant when it's still not yet
two oclock on that July afternoon in 1863, the brigades
are in position behind the rail fence, the guns are laid
and ready in the woods and the furled flags are already
loosened to break out and Pickett himself with his long
oiled ringlets and his hat in one hand probably and his
sword in the other looking up the hill waiting for Long-
street to give the word and it's all in the balance, it hasn't
happened yet, it hasn't even begun yet, it not only hasn't
begun yet but there is still time for it not to begin against

that position and those circumstances which made more
men than Garnett and Kemper and Armstead and Wil-
cox look grave yet it's going to begin, we all know that,
we have come too far with too much at stake and that
moment doesn't need even a fourteen-year-old boy to
think *This time. Maybe this time* with all this much to
lose and all this much to gain: Pennsylvania, Maryland,
the world, the golden dome of Washington itself to
crown with desperate and unbelievable victory the
desperate gamble, the cast made two years ago; or to
anyone who ever sailed even a skiff under a quilt sail,
the moment in 1492 when somebody thought *This is it:*
the absolute edge of no return, to turn back now and
make home or sail irrevocably on and either find land
or plunge over the world's roaring rim. A small voice,
a sound sensitive lady poet of the time of my youth said
the scattered tea goes with the leaves and every day a
sunset dies: a poet's extravagance which as quite often
mirrors truth but upside down and backward since the
mirror's unwitting manipulator busy in his preoccupa-
tion has forgotten that the back of it is glass too: because
if they only did, instead of which yesterday's sunset and
yesterday's tea both are inextricable from the scattered
indestructible uninfusable grounds blown through the
endless corridors of tomorrow, into the shoes we will
have to walk in and even the sheets we will have (or try)
to sleep between: because you escape nothing, you flee
nothing; the pursuer is what is doing the running and
tomorrow night is nothing but one long sleepless wrestle
with yesterday's omissions and regrets.'): who had pre-
termitted not even a death nor even a death to Lucas
but merely Lucas, Lucas in ten thousand Sambo-avatars
to scurry unheeding and not even aware through that

orifice like mice through the slot of a guillotine until
at the One unheeding moment the unheeding unwitting
uncaring chopper falls; tomorrow or at least tomorrow
or at most tomorrow and perhaps this time to intervene
where angels fear no white and black children sixteen
and an old white spinster long on the way to eighty; who
ran, fled not even to deny Lucas but just to keep from
having to send up to him by the drugstore porter a can
of tobacco not at all to say they were sorry but so they
wouldn't have to say out loud that they were wrong:
and spurned the cliff away in one long plunge up and
up slowing into it already hearing it, only the most
faintly oscillant now hearing it listening to it, not moving yet nor even opening his eyes as he lay for a moment
longer listening to it, then opened them and then his
uncle stood silhouetted against the light beyond the
footboard in that utter that complete that absolute
silence now with nothing in it now but the breathing of
darkness and the tree-frogs and bugs: no fleeing nor repudiation nor for this moment more even urgency anywhere in the room or outside it either above or below
or before or behind the tiny myriad beast-sounds and the
vast systole and diastole of summer night.

'It's gone,' he said.

'Yes,' his uncle said. 'They're probably all in bed
asleep by now. They got home to milk and even have
time before dark to chop wood for tomorrow's breakfast
too.'

Which made once though still he didn't move. 'They
ran,' he said.

'No,' his uncle said. 'It was more than that.'

'They ran,' he said. 'They reached the point where

there was nothing left for them to do but admit that
they were wrong. So they ran home.'

'At least they were moving,' his uncle said: which made
twice: who hadn't even needed the first cue since not
only the urgency the need the necessity to move again
or rather not really to have stopped moving at all at
that moment four or five or six hours or whatever it had
been ago when he really believed he was going to lie
down for only fifteen minutes (and which incidentally
knew fifteen minutes whether he apparently did or not)
hadn't come back, it had never been anywhere to come
back from because it was still there, had been there all
the time, never for one second even vacated even from
behind the bizarre phantasmagoriae whose ragtag and
bobends still befogged him, with or among which he
had wasted nearer fifteen hours than fifteen minutes; it
was still there or at least his unfinished part in it which
was not even a minuscule but rather a minutecule of his
uncle's and the sheriff's in the unfinishability of Lucas
Beauchamp and Crawford Gowrie since as far as they
knew before he lost track this morning neither of them
knew what they were going to do next even before
Hampton had disposed of what little of evidence they
had by giving it back to old one-armed pistol Gowrie
where even two children and an old woman couldn't get
it back this time; the need not to finish anything but
just to keep moving not even to remain where they were
but just desperately to keep up with it like having to
run on a treadmill not because you wanted to be where
the treadmill was but simply not to be flung pell mell
still running frantically backward off the whole stage
out of sight, and not waiting static for the moment to
flow back into him again and explode him up into

motion but rather already in endless motion like the
treadmill's endless band less than an inch's fraction
above the ultimate point of his nose and chest where the
first full breath would bring him into its snatching orbit,
himself lying beneath it like a hobo trapped between
the rails under a speeding train, safe only so long as he
did not move.

So he moved; he said 'Time:' swinging his legs over:
'What time is it? I said fifteen minutes. You promised——'

'It's only nine-thirty,' his uncle said. 'Plenty of time
for a shower and your supper too. They wont leave
before we get there.'

'They?' he said: up onto his bare feet (he had not undressed except his shoes and sox) already reaching for his
slippers. 'You've been back to town. Before we get there?
We're not going with them?'

'No,' his uncle said. 'It'll take both of us to hold Miss
Habersham back. She's going to meet us at the office. So
move along now; she's probably already waiting for us.'

'Yes,' he said. But he was already unfastening his shirt
and his belt and trousers too with the other hand, all
ready to step in one motion out of both. And this time
it was laughing. It was all right. You couldn't even hear
it. 'So that was why,' he said. 'So their women wouldn't
have to chop wood in the dark with half-awake children
holding lanterns.'

'No,' his uncle said. 'They were not running from
Lucas. They had forgotten about him——'

'That's exactly what I'm saying,' he said. 'They didn't
even wait to send him a can of tobacco and say It's all
right, old man, everybody makes mistakes and we wont
hold this one against you.'

'Was that what you wanted?' his uncle said. 'The can of tobacco? That would have been enough?—Of course it wouldn't. Which is one reason why Lucas will ultimately get his can of tobacco; they will insist on it, they will have to. He will receive installments on it for the rest of his life in this country whether he wants them or not and not just Lucas but *Lucas: Sambo* since what sets a man writhing sleepless in bed at night is not having injured his fellow so much as having been wrong; the mere injury (if he cannot justify it with what he calls logic) he can efface by destroying the victim and the witnesses but the mistake is his and that is one of his cats which he always prefers to choke to death with butter. So Lucas will get his tobacco. He wont want it of course and he'll try to resist it. But he'll get it and so we shall watch right here in Yoknapatawpha County the ancient oriental relationship between the savior and the life he saved turned upside down: Lucas Beauchamp once the slave of any white man within range of whose notice he happened to come, now tyrant over the whole county's white conscience. And they—Beat One and Two and Three and Five—knew that too so why take time now to send him a ten-cent can of tobacco when they have got to spend the balance of their lives doing it? So they had dismissed him for the time. They were not running from him, they were running from Crawford Gowrie; they simply repudiated not even in horror but in absolute unanimity a shall-not and should-not which without any warning whatever turned into a *must*-not. *Thou shalt not kill* you see—no accusative, heatless: a simple moral precept; we have accepted it in the distant anonymity of our forefathers, had it so long, cherished it, fed it, kept the sound of it alive and the very words them-

selves unchanged, handled it so long that all the corners
are now worn smoothly off; we can sleep right in the bed
with it; we have even distilled our own antidotes for it
as the foresighted housewife keeps a solution of mustard
or handy eggwhites on the same shelf with the ratpoison;
as familiar as grandpa's face, as unrecognisable as grandpa's face beneath the turban of an Indian prince, as ab-
stract as grandpa's flatulence at the family supper-table;
even when it breaks down and the spilled blood stands
sharp and glaring in our faces we still have the precept,
still intact, still true: *we shall not kill* and maybe next
time we even wont. But *thou shall not kill thy mother's
child*. It came right down into the street that time to
walk in broad daylight at your elbow, didn't it?'

'So for a lot of Gowries and Workitts to burn Lucas
Beauchamp to death with gasoline for something he
didn't even do is one thing but for a Gowrie to murder
his brother is another.'

'Yes,' his uncle said.

'You cant say that,' he said.

'Yes,' his uncle said. '*Thou shalt not kill* in precept
and even when you do, precept still remains unblemished
and scarless: *Thou shalt not kill* and who knows, perhaps next time maybe you wont. But *Gowrie must not
kill Gowrie's brother*: no maybe about it, no next time
to maybe not Gowrie kill Gowrie because there must
be no first time. And not just for Gowrie but for all:
Stevens and Mallison and Edmonds and McCaslin too;
if we are not to hold to the belief that that point not just
shall not but must not and *can*not come at which Gowrie
or Ingrum or Stevens or Mallison may shed Gowrie or
Ingrum or Stevens or Mallison blood, how hope ever
to reach that one where *Thou shalt not kill at all,* where

Lucas Beauchamp's life will be secure not despite the fact that he is Lucas Beauchamp but because he is?'

'So they ran to keep from having to lynch Crawford Gowrie,' he said.

'They wouldn't have lynched Crawford Gowrie,' his uncle said. 'There were too many of them. Dont you remember, they packed the street in front of the jail and the Square too all morning while they still believed Lucas had shot Vinson Gowrie in the back without bothering him at all?'

'They were waiting for Beat Four to come in and do it.'

'Which is exactly what I am saying—granted for the moment that that's true. That part of Beat Four composed of Gowries and Workitts and the four or five others who wouldn't have given a Gowrie or Workitt either a chew of tobacco and who would have come along just to see the blood, is small enough to produce a mob. But not all of them together because there is a simple numerical point at which a mob cancels and abolishes itself, maybe because it has finally got too big for darkness, the cave it was spawned in is no longer big enough to conceal it from light and so at last whether it will or no it has to look at itself, or maybe because the amount of blood in one human body is no longer enough, as one peanut might titillate one elephant but not two or ten. Or maybe it's because man having passed into mob passes then into mass which abolishes mob by absorption, metabolism, then having got too large even for mass becomes man again conceptible of pity and justice and conscience even if only in the recollection of his long painful aspiration toward them, toward that something anyway of one serene universal light.'

'So man is always right,' he said.

'No,' his uncle said. 'He tries to be if they who use him for their own power and aggrandisement let him alone. Pity and justice and conscience too—that belief in more than the divinity of individual man (which we in America have debased into a national religion of the entrails in which man owes no duty to his soul because he has been absolved of soul to owe duty to and instead is static heir at birth to an inevictible quit-claim on a wife a car a radio and an old-age pension) but in the divinity of his continuity as Man; think how easy it would have been for them to attend to Crawford Gowrie: no mob moving fast in darkness watching constantly over its shoulder but one indivisible public opinion: that peanut vanishing beneath a whole concerted trampling herd with hardly one elephant to really know the peanut had even actually been there since the main reason for a mob is that the individual red hand which actually snapped the thread may vanish forever into one inviolable confraternity of namelessness: where in this case that one would have had no more reason to lie awake at night afterward than a paid hangman. They didn't want to destroy Crawford Gowrie. They repudiated him. If they had lynched him they would have taken only his life. What they really did was worse: they deprived him to the full extent of their capacity of his citizenship in man.'

He didn't move yet. 'You're a lawyer.' Then he said, 'They were not running from Crawford Gowrie or Lucas Beauchamp either. They were running from themselves. They ran home to hide their heads under the bedclothes from their own shame.'

'Exactly correct,' his uncle said. 'Haven't I been saying that all the time? There were too many of them. This

time there were enough of them to be able to run from
shame, to have found unbearable the only alternative
which would have been the mob's: which (the mob) because of its smallness and what it believed was its secret-
ness and tightness and what it knew to be its absolute
lack of trust in one another, would have chosen the
quick and simple alternative of abolishing knowledge of
the shame by destroying the witness to it. So as you like
to put it they ran.'

'Leaving you and Mr Hampton to clean up the vomit,
which even dogs dont do. Though of course Mr Hampton is a paid dog and I reckon you might be called one
too.—Because dont forget Jefferson either,' he said.
'They were clearing off out of sight pretty fast too. Of
course some of them couldn't because it was still only
the middle of the afternoon so they couldn't shut up the
stores and run home too yet; there still might be a chance
to sell each other a nickel's worth of something.'

'I said Stevens and Mallison too,' his uncle said.

'Not Stevens,' he said. 'And not Hampton either. Because somebody had to finish it, somebody with a strong
enough stomach to mop a floor. The sheriff to catch (or
try to or hope to or whatever it is you are going to do)
the murderer and a lawyer to defend the lynchers.'

'Nobody lynched anybody to be defended from it,'
his uncle said.

'All right,' he said. 'Excuse them then.'

'Nor that either,' his uncle said. 'I'm defending Lucas
Beauchamp. I'm defending Sambo from the North and
East and West—the outlanders who will fling him decades back not merely into injustice but into grief and
agony and violence too by forcing on us laws based on
the idea that man's injustice to man can be abolished

overnight by police. Sambo will suffer it of course; there
are not enough of him yet to do anything else. And he
will endure it, absorb it and survive because he is Sambo
and has that capacity; he will even beat us there because
he has the capacity to endure and survive but he will be
thrown back decades and what he survives to may not be
worth having because by that time divided we may have
lost America.'

'But you're still excusing it.'

'No,' his uncle said. 'I only say that the injustice is
ours, the South's. We must expiate and abolish it ourselves, alone and without help nor even (with thanks)
advice. We owe that to Lucas whether he wants it or
not (and this Lucas anyway wont) not because of his
past since a man or a race either if he's any good can
survive his past without even needing to escape from it
and not because of the high quite often only too rhetorical rhetoric of humanity but for the simple indubitable
practical reason of his future: that capacity to survive
and absorb and endure and still be steadfast.'

'All right,' he said again. 'You're still a lawyer and
they still ran. Maybe they intended for Lucas to clean
it up since he came from a race of floor-moppers. Lucas
and Hampton and you since Hampton ought to do something now and then for his money and they even elected
you to a salary too. Did they think to tell you how to
do it? what to use for bait to get Crawford Gowrie to
come in and say All right, boys, I pass. Deal them again.
Or were they too busy being—being . . . .'

His uncle said quietly: 'Righteous?'

Now he completely stopped. But only for a second.
He said, 'They ran,' calm and completely final, not even
contemptuous, flicking the shirt floating away behind

him and at the same moment dropping the trousers and
stepping barefoot out of them in nothing now but shorts.
'Besides, it's all right. I dreamed through all that; I
dreamed through them too, dreamed them away too;
let them stay in bed or milking their cows before dark
or chopping wood before dark or after or by lanterns or
not lanterns either. Because they were not the dream;
I just passed them to get to the dream——' talking quite
fast now, a good deal faster than he realised until it
would be too late: 'It was something . . . somebody . . .
something about how maybe this was too much to expect
of us, too much for people just sixteen or going on eighty
or ninety or whatever she is to have to bear, and then
right off I was answering what you told me, you remember, about the English boys not much older than me
leading troops and flying scout aeroplanes in France in
1918? how you said that by 1918 all British officers
seemed to be either subalterns of seventeen or one-eyed
or one-armed or one-legged colonels of twenty-three?'
—checking then or trying to because he had got the
warning at last quite sharp not as if he had heard suddenly in advance the words he was going to say but as
if he had discovered suddenly not what he had already
said but where it was going, what the ones he had already
spoken were going to compel him to say in order bring
them to a stop: but too late of course like mashing suddenly on the brake pedal going downhill then discovering to your horror that the brake rod had snapped:
'——only there was something else too—— I was trying . . . .' and he stopped them at last feeling the hot
hard blood burn all the way up his neck into his face
and nowhere even to look not because he was standing
there almost naked to begin with but because no clothes

nor expression nor talking either smoke-screened anything from his uncle's bright grave eyes.

'Yes?' his uncle said. Then his uncle said, 'Yes. Some
things you must always be unable to bear. Some things
you must never stop refusing to bear. Injustice and outrage and dishonor and shame. No matter how young you
are or how old you have got. Not for kudos and not for
cash: your picture in the paper nor money in the bank
either. Just refuse to bear them. That it?'

'Who, me,' he said, moving now already crossing the
room, not even waiting for the slippers. 'I haven't been
a Tenderfoot scout since I was twelve years old.'

'Of course not,' his uncle said. 'But just regret it: dont
be ashamed.'

Chapter Ten

PERHAPS EATING had something to do with it, not even pausing while he tried with no particular interest nor curiosity to compute how many days since he had sat down to a table to eat and then in the same chew as it were remembering that it had not been one yet since even though already half asleep he had eaten a good breakfast at the sheriff's at four this morning: remembering how his uncle (sitting across the table drinking coffee) had said that man didn't necessarily eat his way through the world but by the act of eating and maybe only by that did he actually enter the world, get himself into the world: not through it but into it, burrowing into the world's teeming solidarity like a moth into wool by the physical act of chewing and swallowing the substance of its warp and woof and so making, translating into a part of himself and his memory, the whole history of man or maybe even relinquishing by mastication, abandoning, eating it into to be annealed, the proud vainglorious minuscule which he called his memory and his self and his I-Am into that vast teeming anonymous solidarity of the world from beneath which the ephemeral rock would cool and spin away to dust not even remarked and remembered since there was no yesterday and tomorrow didn't even exist so maybe only an ascetic living in a cave on acorns and spring water was really

capable of vainglory and pride; maybe you had to live
in a cave on acorns and spring water in rapt impregnable
contemplation of your vainglory and righteousness and
pride in order to keep up to that high intolerant pitch
of its worship which brooked no compromise: eating
steadily and quite a lot too and at what even he knew
by this time was too fast since he had been hearing it for
sixteen years and put his napkin down and rose and one
last wail from his mother (and he thought how women
couldn't really stand anything except tragedy and poverty
and physical pain; how this morning when he was where
at sixteen he had no business being and doing what
even at twice sixteen he had no business doing: chasing
over the country with the sheriff digging up murdered
corpses out of a ditch: she had been a hundred times less
noisy than his father and a thousand times more valuable, yet now when all he intended was to walk to town
with his uncle and sit for an hour or so in the same office
in which he had already spent a probably elapsed quarter
of his life, she had completely abolished Lucas Beauchamp and Crawford Gowrie both and had gone back
indefatigable to the day fifteen years ago when she had
first set out to persuade him he couldn't button his
pants):

'But why cant Miss Habersham come here to wait?'

'She can,' his uncle said. 'I'm sure she can find the
house again.'

'You know what I mean,' she said. 'Why dont you
make her? Sitting around a lawyer's office until twelve
oclock at night is no place for a lady.'

'Neither was digging up Jake Montgomery last night,'
his uncle said. 'But maybe this time we will break Lucas
Beauchamp of making this constant drain on her gen-

tility. Come along, Chick:' and so out of the house at
last, not walking out of the house into it because he had
brought it out of the house with him, having at some
point between his room and the front door not acquired
it nor even simply entered it nor even actually regained
it but rather expiated his aberration from it, become
once more worthy to be received into it since it was his
own or rather he was its and so it must have been the
eating, he and his uncle once more walking the same
street almost exactly as they had walked it not twenty-
two hours ago which had been empty then with a sort
of aghast recoiled consternation: because it was not
empty at all now, deserted and empty of movement
certainly running as vacant of life from street lamp to
street lamp as a dead street through an abandoned city
but not really abandoned not really withdrawn but only
making way for them who could do it better, only making way for them who could do it right, not to interfere
or get in the way or even offer suggestion or even permit
(with thanks) advice to them who would do it right and
in their own homely way since it was their own grief
and their own shame and their own expiation, laughing
again now but it was all right, thinking: *Because they
always have me and Aleck Sander and Miss Habersham,
not to mention Uncle Gavin and a sworn badge-wearing
sheriff:* when suddenly he realised that that was a part of
it too—that fierce desire that they should be perfect because they were his and he was theirs, that furious in-
tolerance of any one single jot or tittle less than absolute
perfection—that furious almost instinctive leap and
spring to defend them from anyone anywhere so that he
might excoriate them himself without mercy since they
were his own and he wanted no more save to stand with

them unalterable and impregnable: one shame if shame must be, one expiation since expiation must surely be but above all one unalterable durable impregnable one: one people one heart one land: so that suddenly he said, 'Look——' and stopped but as always no more was needed:

'Yes?' his uncle said, then when he said no more: 'Ah, I see. It's not that they were right but that you were wrong.'

'I was worse,' he said. 'I was righteous.'

'It's all right to be righteous,' his uncle said. 'Maybe you were right and they were wrong. Just dont stop.'

'Dont stop what?' he said.

'Even bragging and boasting is all right too,' his uncle said. 'Just dont stop.'

'Dont stop what?' he said again. But he knew what now; he said,

'Aint it about time you stopped being a Tenderfoot scout too?'

'This is not Tenderfoot,' his uncle said. 'This is the third degree. What do you call it?——'

'Eagle scout,' he said.

'Eagle scout,' his uncle said. 'Tenderfoot is, Dont accept. Eagle scout is, Dont stop. You see? No, that's wrong. Dont bother to see. Dont even bother to not forget it. Just dont stop.'

'No,' he said. 'We dont need to worry about stopping now. It seems to me what we have to worry about now is where we're going and how.'

'Yes you do,' his uncle said. 'You told me yourself about fifteen minutes ago, dont you remember? About what Mr Hampton and Lucas were going to use for bait to fetch Crawford Gowrie in to where they could put

Mr Hampton's hand on him? They're going to use Lucas——'

And he would remember: himself and his uncle standing beside the sheriff's car in the alley beside the jail watching Lucas and the sheriff emerge from the jail's side door and cross the dark yard toward them. It was quite dark in fact since the street light at the corner didn't reach this far nor any sound either; only a little after ten oclock and on Monday night too yet the sky's dark bowl cupped as though in a vacuum like the old bride's bouquet under its glass bell the town, the Square which was more than dead: abandoned: because he had gone on to look at it, without stopping leaving his uncle standing at the corner of the alley who said after him: 'Where are you going?' but not even answering, walking the last silent and empty block, ringing his footfalls deliberate and unsecret into the hollow silence, unhurried and solitary but nothing at all of forlorn, instead with a sense a feeling not possessive but proprietary, viceregal, with humility still, himself not potent but at least the vessel of a potency like the actor looking from wings or perhaps empty balcony down upon the waiting stage vacant yet garnished and empty yet, nevertheless where in a moment now he will walk and posture in the last act's absolute cynosure, himself in himself nothing and maybe no world-beater of a play either but at least his to finish it, round it and put it away intact and unassailable, complete: and so onto into the dark and empty Square stopping as soon as he could perceive at effortless once that whole dark lifeless rectangle with but one light anywhere and that in the cafe which stayed open all night on account of the long-haul trucks whose (the cafe's) real purpose some said, the real reason for

the grant of its license by the town was to keep Willy
Ingrum's nocturnal counterpart awake who although the
town had walled him off a little cubbyhole of an office
in an alley with a stove and a telephone he wouldn't
stay there but used instead the cafe where there was somebody to talk to and he could be telephoned there of
course but some people old ladies especially didn't like
to page the policeman in an allnight jukejoint coffee
stall so the office telephone had been connected to a
big burglar alarm bell on the outside wall loud enough
for the counterman or a truck driver in the cafe to hear
it and tell him it was ringing, and the two lighted second-
storey windows (and he thought that Miss Habersham
really had persuaded his uncle to give her the key to
the office and then he thought that that was wrong, his
uncle had persuaded her to take the key since she would
just as soon have sat in the parked truck until they came
—and then added If she had waited because that was
certainly wrong and what had really happened was that
his uncle had locked her up in the office to give the
sheriff and Lucas time to get out of town) but since
the lights in a lawyer's office were liable to burn any time
the lawyer or the janitor forgot to turn them off when
they left and the cafe like the power plant was a public
institution they didn't count and even the cafe was just
lighted (he couldn't see into it from here but he could
have heard and he thought how that, formally shutting
off the jukebox for twelve hours had probably been the
night marshal's first official act besides punching every
hour the time clock on the wall at the bank's back door
since the mad-dog scare last August) and he remembered
the other the normal Monday nights when no loud fury
of blood and revenge and racial and family solidarity

had come roaring in from Beat Four (or Beat One or
Two or Three or Five for that matter or for the matter
of that from the purlieus of the urban Georgian por-
ticoes themselves) to rattle and clash among the old
bricks and the old trees and the Doric capitals and leave
them for one night anyway stricken: ten oclock on Monday night and although the first run of the film at the
picture show would be forty or fifty minutes over now a
few of the patrons who had come in late would still be
passing homeward and all the young men sitting since
that time drinking coca cola and playing nickels into the
drugstore jukebox would certainly be, strolling timeless
and in no haste since they were going nowhere since the
May night itself was their destination and they carried
that with them walking in it and (stock-auction day)
even a few belated cars and trucks whose occupants had
stayed in for the picture show too or to visit and take
supper with kin or friends and now at last dispersing
nightward sleepward tomorrow-ward about the dark
nile-compassing land, remembering no longer ago than
last night when he had thought it was empty too until
he had had time to listen to it a moment and realised
that it was not empty at all: a Sunday night but with
more than Sunday night's quiet, the sort of quiet in fact
that no night had any business with and of all nights
Sunday night never, which had been Sunday night only
because they had already named the calendar when the
sheriff brought Lucas in to jail: an emptiness you could
call emptiness provided you called vacant and empty the
silent and lifeless terrain in front of a mobilised army
or peaceful the vestibule to a powder magazine or quiet
the spillway under the locks of a dam—a sense not of
waiting but of incrementation, not of people—women

and old folks and children—but of men not so much
grim as grave and not so much tense as quiet, sitting
quietly and not even talking much in back rooms and
not just the bath-cabinets and johns behind the barbershop and the shed behind the poolhall stacked with soft
drink cases and littered with empty whiskey bottles but
the stock-rooms of stores and garages and behind the
drawn shades of the offices themselves whose owners
even the proprietors of the stores and garages conceded
to belong not to a trade but a profession, not waiting for
an event a moment in time to come to them but for a
moment in time when in almost volitionless concord they
themselves would create the event, preside at and even
serve an instant which was not even six or twelve or
fifteen hours belated but was instead simply the continuation of the one when the bullet struck Vinson
Gowrie and there had been no time between and so for
all purposes Lucas was already dead since he had died
then on the same instant when he had forfeited his life
and theirs was merely to preside at his suttee, and now
tonight to remember because tomorrow it would be over,
tomorrow of course the Square would wake and stir,
another day and it would fling off hangover, another and
it would even fling off shame so that on Saturday the
whole county with one pierceless unanimity of click and
pulse and hum would even deny that the moment had
ever existed when they could have been mistaken: so
that he didn't even need to remind himself in the absolute the utter the complete silence that the town was
not dead nor even abandoned but only withdrawn giving
room to do what homely thing must be done in its·own
homely way without help or interference or even (thank
you) advice: three amateurs, an old white spinster and a

white child and a black one to expose Lucas' wouldbe
murderer, Lucas himself and the county sheriff to catch
him and so one last time: remembering: his uncle while
he still stood barefoot on the rug with both edges of the
unbuttoned shirt arrested in his hands thirty minutes
ago and when they were mounting the last pitch of hill
toward the church eleven hours ago and on what must
have been a thousand other times since he had got big
enough to listen and to understand and to remember:—
*to defend not Lucas nor even the union of the United
States but the United States from the outlanders North
East and West who with the highest of motives and intentions (let us say) are essaying to divide it at a time
when no people dare risk division by using federal laws
and federal police to abolish Lucas' shameful condition,
there may not be in any random one thousand Southern-
ers one who really grieves or even is really concerned
over that condition nevertheless neither is there always
one who would himself lynch Lucas no matter what the
occasion yet not one of that nine hundred ninety-nine
plus that other first one making the thousand whole
again would hesitate to repulse with force (and one
would still be that lyncher) the outlander who came
down here with force to intervene or punish him, you say
(with sneer) You must know Sambo well to arrogate to
yourself such calm assumption of his passivity and I reply
I dont know him at all and in my opinion no white man
does but I do know the Southern white man not only the
nine hundred and ninety-nine but that one other too
because he is our own too and more than that, that one
other does not exist only in the South, you will see allied
not North and East and West and Sambo against a hand-
ful of white men in the South but a paper alliance of*

*theorists and fanatics and private and personal avengers
plus a number of others under the assumption of enough
physical miles to afford a principle against and possibly
even outnumbered a concorded South which has drawn
recruits whether it would or no from your own back-
areas, not just your hinterland but the fine cities of your
cultural pride your Chicagoes and Detroits and Los An-
geleses and wherever else live ignorant people who fear
the color of any skin or shape of nose save their own and
who will grasp this opportunity to vent on Sambo the
whole sum of their ancestral horror and scorn and fear
of Indian and Chinese and Mexican and Carib and Jew,
you will force us the one out of that first random thousand and the nine hundred and ninety-nine out of the
second who do begrieve Lucas' shameful condition and
would improve it and have and are and will until (not
tomorrow perhaps) that condition will be abolished to
be not forgotten maybe but at least remembered with
less of pain and bitterness since justice was relinquished
to him by us rather than torn from us and forced on him
both with bayonets, willynilly into alliance with them
with whom we have no kinship whatever in defence of
a principle which we ourselves begrieve and abhor, we
are in the position of the German after 1933 who had no
other alternative between being either a Nazi or a Jew
or the present Russian (European too for that matter)
who hasn't even that but must be either a Communist or
dead, only we must do it and we alone without help or
interference or even (thank you) advice since only we can
if Lucas' equality is to be anything more than its own
prisoner inside an impregnable barricade of the direct
heirs of the victory of 1861-1865 which probably did
more than even John Brown to stalemate Lucas' free-*

*dom which still seems to be in check going on a hundred
years after Lee surrendered and when you say Lucas must
not wait for that tomorrow because that tomorrow will
never come because you not only cant you wont then we
can only repeat Then you shall not and say to you Come
down here and look at us before you make up your mind
and you reply No thanks the smell is bad enough from
here and we say Surely you will at least look at the dog
you plan to housebreak, a people divided at a time when
history is still showing us that the anteroom to dissolu-
tion is division and you say At least we perish in the
name of humanity and we reply When all is stricken but
that nominative pronoun and that verb what price
Lucas' humanity then* and turned and ran the short
dead empty block back to the corner where his uncle
had gone on without waiting and then up the alley too
to where the sheriff's car stood, the two of them watching
the sheriff and Lucas cross the dark yard toward them the
sheriff in front and Lucas about five feet behind walking
not fast but just intently, neither furtive nor covert but
exactly like two men simply busy not exactly late but
with no time to dawdle, through the gate and across to
the car where the sheriff opened the back door and said,

'Jump in,' and Lucas got in and the sheriff closed the
door and opened the front one and crawled grunting
into it, the whole car squatting onto its springs and rims
when he let himself down into the seat and turned the
switch and started the engine, his uncle standing at the
window now holding the rim of it in both hands as
though he thought or hoped suddenly on some second
thought to hold the car motionless before it could begin
to move, saying what he himself had been thinking off
and on for thirty or forty minutes:

'Take somebody with you.'

'I am,' the sheriff said. 'Besides I thought we settled all this three times this afternoon.'

'That's still just one no matter how many times you count Lucas,' his uncle said.

'You let me have my pistol,' Lucas said, 'and wont nobody have to do no counting. I'll do it:' and he thought how many times the sheriff had probably told Lucas by now to shut up, which may have been why the sheriff didn't say it now: except that (suddenly) he did, turning slowly and heavily and grunting in the seat to look back at Lucas, saying in the plaintive heavily-sighing voice:

'After all the trouble you got into Saturday standing with that pistol in your pocket in the same ten feet of air a Gowrie was standing in, you want to take it in your hand and walk around another one. Now I want you to hush and stay hushed. And when we begin to get close to Whiteleaf bridge I want you to be laying on the floor close up against the seat behind me and still hushed. You hear me?'

'I hear you,' Lucas said. 'But if I just had my pistol ——' but the sheriff had already turned to his uncle:

'No matter how many times you count Crawford Gowrie he's still just one too:' and then went on in the mild sighing reluctant voice which nevertheless was already answering his uncle's thoughts before even his uncle could speak it: 'Who would he get?' and he thought of that too remembering the long tearing rubber-from-cement sound of the frantic cars and trucks scattering pell mell hurling themselves in aghast irrevocable repudiation in all directions toward the county's outmost unmapped fastnesses except that little island in Beat

Four known as Caledonia Church, into sanctuary: the
old the used the familiar, home where the women and
older girls and children could milk and chop wood for
tomorrow's breakfast while the little ones held lanterns
and the men and older sons after they had fed the mules
against tomorrow's plowing would sit on the front gallery waiting for supper into the twilight: the whippoorwills: night: sleep: and this he could even see (provided that even a murderer's infatuation could bring
Crawford Gowrie ever again into the range and radius
of that nub arm which—since Crawford was a Gowrie
too—in agreement here with the sheriff he didn't believe
—and he knew now why Lucas had ever left Fraser's
store alive Saturday afternoon, let alone ever got out of
the sheriff's car at the jail: that the Gowries themselves
had known he hadn't done it so they were just marking
time waiting for somebody else, maybe Jefferson to drag
him out into the street until he remembered—a flash,
something like shame—the blue shirt squatting and the
stiff awkward single hand trying to brush the wet sand
from the dead face and he knew that whatever the furious
old man might begin to think tomorrow he held nothing
against Lucas then because there was no room for anything but his son)—night, the diningroom perhaps and
again seven Gowrie men in the twenty-year womanless
house because Forrest had come up from Vicksburg for
the funeral yesterday and was probably still there this
morning when the sheriff sent word out for old Gowrie
to meet him at the church, a lamp burning in the center
of the table among the crusted sugarbowls and molasses
jugs and ketchup and salt and pepper in the same labeled
containers they had come off the store shelf in and the
old man sitting at the head of it his one arm lying on the

table in front of him and the big pistol under his hand
pronouncing judgment sentence doom and execution too
on the Gowrie who had cancelled his own Gowriehood
with his brother's blood, then the dark road the truck
(not commandeered this time because Vinson had owned
one new and big and powerful convertible for either
logs or cattle) the same twin driving it probably and the
body boomed down onto the runninggear like a log
itself with the heavy logchains, fast out of Caledonia out
of Beat Four into the dark silent waiting town fast still
up the quiet street across the Square to the sheriff's house
and the body tumbled and flung onto the sheriff's front
gallery and perhaps the truck even waiting while the
other Gowrie twin rang the doorbell. 'Stop worrying
about Crawford,' the sheriff said. 'He aint got anything
against me. He votes for me. His trouble right now is
having to kill extra folks like Jake Montgomery when all
he ever wanted was just to keep Vinson from finding out
he had been stealing lumber from him and Uncle Sudley
Workitt. Even if he jumps onto the runningboard before
I have time to keep up with what's going on he'll still
have to waste a minute or two trying to get the door open
so he can see exactly where Lucas is—provided by that
time Lucas is doing good and hard what I told him to do,
which I sure hope for his sake he is.'

'I'm going to,' Lucas said. 'But if I just had my——'

'Yes,' his uncle said in the harsh voice: 'Provided he's
there.'

The sheriff sighed. 'You sent the message.'

'What message·I could,' his uncle said. 'However I
could. A message making an assignation between a murderer and a policeman, that whoever finally delivers it to
the murderer wont even know was intended for the mur-

derer, that the murderer himself will not only believe he wasn't intended to get it but that it's true.'

'Well,' the sheriff said, 'he'll either get it or he wont get it and he'll either believe it or he wont believe it and he'll either be waiting for us in Whiteleaf bottom or he wont and if he aint me and Lucas will go on to the high way and come back to town.' He raced the engine let it idle again; now he turned on the lights. 'But he may be there. I sent a message too.'

'All right,' his uncle said. 'Why is that, Mr Bones?'

'I got the mayor to excuse Willy Ingrum so he could go out and set up with Vinson again tonight and before Willy left I told him in confidence I was going to run Lucas over to Hollymount tonight through the old Whiteleaf cutoff so Lucas can testify tomorrow at Jake Montgomery's inquest and reminded Willy that they aint finished the Whiteleaf fill yet and cars have to cross it in low gear and told him to be sure not to mention it to anybody.'

'Oh,' his uncle said, not quite turning the door loose yet. 'No matter who might have claimed Jake Montgomery alive he belongs to Yoknapatawpha County now.— But then,' he said briskly, turning the door loose now, 'we're after just a murderer, not a lawyer.—All right,' he said. 'Why dont you get started?'

'Yes,' the sheriff said. 'You go on to your office and watch out for Miss Eunice. Willy may have passed her on the street too and if he did she might still beat us to Whiteleaf bridge in that pickup.'

Then into the Square this time to cross it catacornered to where the pickup stood nosedin empty to the other-wise empty curb and up the long muted groan and rumble of the stairway to the open office door and pass-

ing through it he thought without surprise how she was
probably the only woman he knew who would have
withdrawn the borrowed key from the lock as soon as
she opened the strange door not to leave the key on the
first flat surface she passed but to put it back into the
reticule or pocket or whatever she had put it in when it
was lent to her and she wouldn't be sitting in the chair
behind the table either and wasn't, sitting instead bolt
upright in the hat but another dress which looked exactly like the one she had worn last night and the same
handbag on her lap with the eighteen-dollar gloves
clasped on top of it and the flat-heeled thirty-dollar shoes
planted side by side on the floor in front of the hardest
straightest chair in the room, the one beside the door
which nobody ever really sat in no matter how crowded
the office and only moving to the easy chair behind the
table after his uncle had spent a good two minutes in-
sisting and finally explained it might be two or three
hours yet because she had the gold brooch watch on her
bosom open when they came in and seemed to think that
by this time the sheriff should not only have been back
with Crawford Gowrie but probably on the way to the
penitentiary with him: then he in his usual chair beside
the water cooler and finally his uncle even struck the
match to the cob pipe still talking not just through the
smoke but into it with it:

    '——what happened because some of it we even know
let alone what Lucas finally told us by watching himself
like a hawk or an international spy to keep from telling
us anything that would even explain him let alone save
him, Vinson and Crawford were partners buying the
timber from old man Sudley Workitt who was Mrs Gowrie's second or fourth cousin or uncle or something, that

is they had agreed with old Sudley on a price by the
board foot but to be paid him when the lumber was sold
which was not to be until the last tree was cut and Crawford and Vinson had delivered it and got their money
and then they would pay old Sudley his, hiring a mill
and crew to fell and saw and stack it right there within
a mile of old Sudley's house and not one stick to be
moved until it was all cut. Only—except this part we
dont really know yet until Hampton gets his hands on
Crawford except it's got to be this way or what in the
world were you all doing digging Jake Montgomery out
of Vinson's grave?—and every time I think about this
part of it and remember you three coming back down
that hill to the exact spot where two of you heard him
and one of you even saw riding past the man who already
with one murdered corpse on the mule in front of him
experienced such a sudden and urgent alteration of plan
that when Hampton and I got there hardly six hours
later there was nobody in the grave at all——'

'But he didn't,' Miss Habersham said.

'—What?' his uncle said. '. . . Where was I? Oh yes.—
only Lucas Beauchamp taking his walk one night heard
something and went and looked or maybe he was actually
passing and saw or maybe he already had the idea which
was why he took the walk or that walk that night and
saw a truck whether he recognised it or not being loaded
in the dark with that lumber which the whole neighborhood knew was not to be moved until the mill itself
closed up and moved away which would be some time
yet and Lucas watched and listened and maybe he even
went over into Crossman County to Glasgow and Hollymount until he knew for sure not only who was moving
some of that lumber every night or so, not much at a

time, just exactly not quite enough for anyone who was
not there everyday to notice its absence (and the only
people there everyday or even interested even to that
extent were Crawford who represented himself and his
brother and uncle who owned the trees and the resulting
lumber and so could do what they liked with it, the one
of which was running about the country all day long
attending to his other hot irons and the other an old
rheumatic man to begin with and half blind on top of
that who couldn't have seen anything even if he could
have got that far from his house—and the mill crew who
were hired by the day and so wouldn't have cared even
if they had known what was going on at night as long
as they got their pay every Saturday) but what he was
doing with it, maybe learning even as far as Jake Montgomery though Lucas' knowing about Jake made no
difference except that by getting himself murdered and
into Vinson's grave Jake probably saved Lucas' life.
But even when Hope told me how he had finally got that
much out of Lucas in his kitchen this morning when
Will Legate brought him from the jail and we were driving you home it explained only part of it because I was
still saying what I had been saying ever since you all
woke me this morning and Chick told me what Lucas
had told him about the pistol: But why Vinson? Why
did Crawford have to kill Vinson in order to obliterate
the witness to his thieving? not that it shouldn't have
worked of course since Lucas really should have died as
soon as the first white man came in sight of him standing
over Vinson's body with the handle of that pistol hunching the back of his coat, but why do it this way, by the
bizarre detour of fratricide? so now that we had something really heavy enough to talk to Lucas with I went

straight to Hampton's house this afternoon into the kitchen and there was Hampton's cook sitting on one side of the table and Lucas on the other eating greens and cornbread not from a plate but out of the two-gallon pot itself and I said,

' "And you let him catch you—and I dont mean Craw-ford——' and he said,

' "No. I means Vinson too. Only it was too late then, the truck was done already loaded and pulling out fast without no lights burning or nothing and he said Whose truck is that? and I never said nothing."

' "All right," I said. "Then what?"

' "That's all," Lucas said. "Nothing."

' "Didn't he have a gun?"

' "I dont know," Lucas said. "He had a stick:" and I said,

' "All right. Go on:" and he said,

' "Nothing. He just stood there a minute with the stick drawed back and said Tell me whose truck that was and I never said nothing and he lowered the stick back down and turned and then I never saw him no more."

' "So you took your pistol," I said and he said, "and went——" and he said,

' "I never had to. He come to me, I mean Crawford this time, at my house the next night and was going to pay me to tell him whose truck that was, a heap of money, fifty dollars, he showed it to me and I said I hadn't de-cided yet whose truck it was and he said he would leave me the money anyhow while I decided and I said I had already decided what I was going to do, I would wait until tomorrow—that was Friday night—for some kind of a evidence that Mr Workitt and Vinson had got their share of that missing timber money."

' "Yes?" I said. "Then what?"

' "Then I would go and tell Mr Workitt he better——"

' "Say that again," I said. "Slow."

' "Tell Mr Workitt he better count his boards."

' "And you, a Negro, were going up to a white man
and tell him his niece's sons were stealing from him—and
a Beat Four white man on top of that. Dont you know
what would have happened to you?"

' "It never had no chance," he said. "Because it was the
next day—Sat-dy—I got the message—" and I should
have known then about the pistol because obviously
Gowrie knew about it; his message couldn't have been
*have replaced stolen money, would like your personal
approval, bring your pistol and be sociable*—something
like that so I said,

' "But why the pistol?" and he said,

' "It was Sat-dy," and I said,

' "Yes, the ninth. But why the pistol?" and then I
understood; I said: "I see. You wear the pistol when
you dress up on Saturday just like old Carothers did
before he gave it to you:" and he said,

' "Sold it to me," and I said,

' "All right, go on," and he said,

' "—got the message to meet him at the store
only——" ' and now his uncle struck the match again
and puffed the pipe still talking, talking through the
pipe stem with the smoke as though you were watching
the words themselves: 'Only he never got to the store,
Crawford met him in the woods sitting on a stump beside the path waiting for him almost before Lucas had
left home good and now it was Crawford about the pistol,
right off before Lucas could say good afternoon or were

Vinson and Mr Workitt glad to get the money or anything, saying "Even if it will still shoot you probably
couldn't hit anything with it" and so you can probably
finish it yourself; Lucas said how Crawford finally put
up a half dollar that Lucas couldn't hit the stump from
fifteen feet away and Lucas hit it and Crawford gave him
the half dollar and they walked on the other two miles
toward the store until Crawford told Lucas to wait there,
that Mr Workitt was sending a signed receipt for his
share of the missing lumber to the store and Crawford
would go and fetch it back so Lucas could see it with his
own eyes and I said,

‘ "And you didn't suspicion anything even then?" and
he said,

‘ "No. He cussed me so natural." And at least you can
finish that, no need to prove any quarrel between Vinson
and Crawford nor rack your brains very deep to imagine
what Crawford said and did to have Vinson waiting at
the store and then send him in front along the path since
no more than this will do it: "All right. I've got him.
If he still wont tell whose truck that was we'll beat it out
of him:" because that doesn't really matter either,
enough that the next Lucas saw was Vinson coming down
the path from the store in a good deal of a hurry Lucas
said but probably what he meant was impatient, puzzled
and annoyed both but probably mostly annoyed, probably doing exactly what Lucas was doing: waiting for the
other to speak and explain except that Vinson quit waiting first according to Lucas, still walking saying getting
as far as "So you changed your mind—" when Lucas said
he tripped over something and kind of bucked down onto
his face and presently Lucas remembered that he had
heard the shot and realised that what Vinson had tripped

over was his brother Crawford, then the rest of them
were there Lucas said before he even had time to hear
them running through the woods and I said,

' "I reckon it looked to you right then that you were
getting ready to trip pretty bad over Vinson, old Skipworth and Adam Fraser or not" but at least I didn't say
But why didn't you explain then and so at least Lucas
didn't have to say Explain what to who: and so he was
all right— I dont mean Lucas of course, I mean Crawford, no mere child of misfortune he——' and there it
was again and this time he knew what it was,. Miss
Habersham had done something he didn't know what,
no sound and she hadn't moved and it wasn't even that
she had got any stiller but something had occurred, not
something happened to her from the outside in but
something from the inside outward as though she not
only hadn't been surprised by it but had decreed authorised it but she hadn't moved at all not even to take
an extra breath and his uncle hadn't even noticed that
much '—but rather chosen and elected peculiar and
unique out of man by the gods themselves to prove not
to themselves because they had never doubted it but to
man by this his lowest common denominator that he has
a soul, driven at last to murder his brother——'

'He put him in quicksand,' Miss Habersham said.

'Yes,' his uncle said. 'Ghastly wasn't it.—by the simple
mischance of an old Negro man's insomnambulism and
then having got away with that by means of a plan a
scheme so simple and water-tight in its biological and
geographical psychology as to be what Chick here would
call a natural, then to be foiled here by the fact that four
years ago a child whose presence in the world he was not
even aware of fell into a creek in the presence of that

same Negro insomnambulist because this part we dont
really know either and with Jake Montgomery in his present condition we probably never will though that doesn't
really matter either since the fact still remains, why else
was he in Vinson's grave except that in buying the lumber from Crawford (we found that out by a telephone
call to the lumber's ultimate consignee in Memphis this
afternoon) Jake Montgomery knew where it came from
too since knowing that would have been Jake's nature
and character too and indeed a factor in his middleman's
profit and so when Vinson Crawford's partner tripped
suddenly on death in the woods behind Fraser's store
Jake didn't need a crystal ball to read that either and so
if this be surmise then make the most of it or give Mr
Hampton and me a better and we'll swap, Jake knew
about Buddy McCallum's old war trophy too and I like
to think for Crawford's sake——' and there it was again
and still no outward sign but this time his uncle saw or
felt or sensed (or however it was) it too and stopped and
even for a second seemed about to speak then in the next
one forgot it apparently, talking again: '—that maybe
Jake named the price of his silence and even collected it
or an installment on it perhaps intending all the time to
convict Crawford of the murder, perhaps with his con-
tacts all established to get still more money or perhaps he
didn't like Crawford and wanted revenge or perhaps a
purist he drew the line at murder and simply dug Vinson
up to load him on the mule and take him in to the
sheriff but anyway on the night after the funeral somebody with a conceivable reason for digging Vinson up
dug him up, which must have been Jake, and somebody
who not only didn't want Vinson dug up but had a conceivable reason to be watching the someone who would

have had a conceivable reason for digging him up, knew that he had been dug up within in—you said it was about ten when you and Aleck Sander parked the truck and it got dark enough for digging up graves about seven that night so that leaves three hours—and that's what I mean about Crawford,' his uncle said and this time he noticed that his uncle had even stopped, expecting it and it came but still no sound no movement, the hat immobile and exact the neat precision of the clasped gloves and the handbag on her lap the shoes planted and motionless side by side as if she had placed them into a chalked diagram on the floor: '——watching there in the weeds behind the fence seeing himself not merely betrayed out of the blackmail but all the agony and suspense to go through again not to mention the physical labor who since one man already knew that the body couldn't bear examination by trained policemen, could never know how many others might know or suspect so the body would have to come out of the grave now though at least he had help here whether the help knew it or not so he probably waited until Jake had the body out and was all ready to load it onto the mule (and we found that out too, it was the Gowrie's plow mule, the same one the twins were riding this morning; Jake borrowed it himself late that Sunday afternoon and when you guess which Gowrie he borrowed it from you'll be right: it was Crawford) and he wouldn't have risked the pistol now anyway anymore than he would have used it if he could, who would rather have paid Jake over again the amount of the blackmail for the privilege of using whatever it was he crushed Jake's skull with and put him into the coffin and filled the grave back up—and here it is again, the desperate the dreadful urgency, the loneliness the pariah-hood having not only the horror and repudiation of all man against him but having to struggle with the sheer inertia of earth and the terrible heedless rush of time but even beating all that coalition at last, the grave decent again even to the displaced flowers and the evidence of his original crime at last disposed and secure—' and it would have been again but this time his uncle didn't pause '—— then to straighten up at last and for the first time draw a full breath since the moment when Jake had approached him rubbing his thumb against the tips of the same fingers—and then to hear whatever it was that sent him plunging back up the hill then crawling creeping to lie once more panting but this time not merely in rage and terror but in almost incredulous disbelief that one single man could be subject to this much bad luck, watching you three not only undo his work for the second time but double it now since you not only exposed Jake Montgomery but you refilled the grave and even put the flowers back: who couldn't afford to let his brother Vinson be found in that grave but durst not let Jake Montgomery be found in it when (as he must have known) Hope Hampton got there tomorrow:' and stopped this time waiting for her to say it and she did:

'He put his brother in quicksand.'

'Ah,' his uncle said. 'That moment may come to anyone when simply nothing remains to be done with your brother or husband or uncle or cousin or mother-in-law except destroy them. But you dont put them in quicksand. Is that it?'

'He put him in quicksand,' she said with calm and implacable finality, not moving nor stirring except her

lips to speak until then she raised her hand and opened
the watch pinned to her bosom and looked at it.

'They haven't reached Whiteleaf bottom yet,' his uncle
said. 'But dont worry, he'll be there, my message might
have reached him but no man in this county can possibly
escape hearing anything ever told Willy Ingrum under
the pledge of secrecy, because there's nothing else he can
do you see because murderers are gamblers and like the
amateur gambler the amateur murderer believes first not
in his luck but in long shots, that the long shot will win
simply because it's a long shot but besides that, say he
already knew he was lost and nothing Lucas could testify
about Jake Montgomery or anyone else could harm him
further and that his one last slim chance was to get out
of the country, or say he knew even that was vain, knew
for sure that he was running through the last few pence
and pennies of what he could still call freedom, suppose
he even knew for certain that tomorrow's sun would not
even rise for him,—what would you want to do first, one
last act and statement of your deathless principles before
you left your native land for good and maybe even the
world for good if your name was Gowrie and your blood
and thinking and acting had been Gowrie all your life
and you knew or even only believed or even only hoped
that at a certain moment in an automobile creeping in
low gear through a lonely midnight creek bottom would
be the cause and reason for all your agony and frustration and outrage and grief and shame and irreparable
loss and that not even a white man but a nigger and you
still had the pistol with at least one of the old original
ten German bullets in it.—But dont worry,' he said
quickly: 'Dont worry about Mr Hampton. He probably
wont even draw his pistol, I aint certain in fact that he

has one because he has a way of carrying right along with him into all situations maybe not peace, maybe not abatement of the base emotions but at least a temporary stalemate of crude and violent behavior just by moving slow and breathing hard, this happened two or three terms ago back in the twenties, a Frenchman's Bend lady naming no names at feud with another lady over something which began (we understood) over the matter of a prize cake at a church supper bazaar, whose—the second lady's—husband owned the still which had been supplying Frenchman's Bend with whiskey for years bothering nobody until the first lady made official demand on Mr Hampton to go out there and destroy the still and arrest the operator and then in about a week or ten days came in to town herself and told him that if he didn't she was going to report him to the governor of the state and the president in Washington so Hope went that time, she had not only given him explicit directions but he said there was a path to it knee-deep in places where it had been trodden for years beneath the weight of stopper-full gallon jugs so that you could have followed it even without the flashlight which he had and sure enough there was the still in as nice a location as you could want, cozy and sheltered yet accessible too with a fire burning under the kettle and a Negro tending it who of course didn't know who owned it nor ran it nor anything about it even before he recognised Hampton's size and finally even saw his badge: who Hope said offered him a drink first and then did fetch him a gourd of branch water and then made him comfortable sitting against a tree, even chunking the fire up to dry his wet feet while he waited for the owner to come back, quite comfortable Hope said, the two of them

there by the fire in the darkness talking about one thing
and another and the Negro asking him from time to time
if he wouldn't like another gourd of water until Hampton said the mockingbird was making so confounded
much racket that finally he opened his eyes blinking for
a while in the sunlight until he got them focussed and
there the mockingbird was on a limb not three feet
above his head and before they loaded up the still to
move it away somebody had gone to the nearest house
and fetched back a quilt to spread over him and a pillow
to put under his head and Hope said he noticed the pillow even had a fresh slip on it when he took it and the
quilt to Varner's store to be returned with thanks to
whoever owned them and came on back to town. And
another time——'

'I'm not worrying,' Miss Habersham said.

'Of course not,' his uncle said. 'Because I know Hope
Hampton——'

'Yes,' Miss Habersham said. 'I know Lucas Beauchamp.'

'Oh,' his uncle said. Then he said, 'Yes.' Then he
said, 'Of course.' Then he said, 'Let's ask Chick to plug
in the kettle and we'll have coffee while we wait, what
do you think?'

'That will be nice,' Miss Habersham said.

Chapter Eleven

FINALLY HE EVEN GOT up and went to one of the front
windows looking down into the Square because if Monday was stock-auction and trade day then Saturday was
certainly radio and automobile day; on Monday they
were mostly men and they drove in and parked the cars
and trucks around the Square and went straight to the
sales barns and stayed there until time to come back to
the Square and eat dinner and then went back to the
sales barns and stayed there until time to come and get
in the cars and trucks and drive home before full dark.
But not Saturday; they were men and women and children too then and the old people and the babies and the
young couples to buy the licenses for the weddings in
the country churches tomorrow, come in to do a week's
shopping for staples and delicacies like bananas and
twenty-five-cent sardines and machine-made cakes and
pies and clothes and stockings and feed and fertilizer
and plow-gear: which didn't take long for any of them
and no time at all for some of them so that some of the
cars never really became permanently stationary at all
and within an hour or so many of the others had joined
them moving steadily processional and quite often in
second gear because of their own density round and
round the Square then out to the end of the tree-dense
residential streets to turn and come back and circle round

and round the Square again as if they had come all the way in from the distant circumambient settlements and crossroads stores and isolate farms for that one purpose of enjoying the populous coming and going and motion and recognising one another and the zephyr-like smoothness of the paved streets and alleys themselves as well as looking at the neat new painted small houses among their minute neat yards and flowerbeds and garden ornaments which in the last few years had come to line them as dense as sardines or bananas; as a result of which the radios had to play louder than ever through their supercharged amplifiers to be heard above the mutter of exhausts and swish of tires and the grind of gears and the constant horns, so that long before you even reached the Square you not only couldn't tell where one began and another left off but you didn't even have to try to distinguish what any of them were playing or trying to sell you.

But this one seemed to be even a Saturday among Saturdays so that presently his uncle had got up from behind the table and come to the other window too, which was why they happened to see Lucas before he reached the office though that was not yet; he was still standing (so he thought) alone at the window looking down into the Square thronged and jammed as he couldn't remember it before—the bright sunny almost hot air heavy with the smell of blooming locust from the courthouse yard, the sidewalks dense and massed and slow with people black and white come in to town today as if by concert to collect at compound and so discharge not merely from balance but from remembering too that other Saturday only seven days ago of which they had been despoiled by an old Negro man who had got him-

self into the position where they had had to believe he
had murdered a white man—that Saturday and Sunday
and Monday only a week past yet which might never
have been since nothing of them remained: Vinson and
his brother Crawford (in his suicide's grave and strangers
would be asking for weeks yet what sort of jail and sheriff
Yoknapatawpha County had where a man locked in it
for murder could still get hold of a Luger pistol even if
it didn't have but one bullet in it and for that many
weeks nobody in Yoknapatawpha County would still be
able to tell him) side by side near their mother's headstone in Caledonia churchyard and Jake Montgomery
over in Crossman County where somebody probably
claimed him too for the same reason somebody did
Crawford and Miss Habersham sitting in her own hall
now mending the stockings until time to feed the chickens and Aleck Sander down there on the Square in a
flash Saturday shirt and a pair of zoot pants and a hand-
ful of peanuts or bananas too and he standing at the
window watching the dense unhurried unhurryable
throng and the busy almost ubiquitous flash and gleam
on Willy Ingrum's cap-badge but mostly and above all
the motion and the noise, the radios and the automobiles
—the jukeboxes in the drugstore and the poolhall and
the cafe and the bellowing amplifiers on the outside
walls not only of the record-and-sheetmusic store but
the army-and-navy supply store and both feed stores and
(that they might falter) somebody standing on a bench
in the courthouse yard making a speech into another
one with a muzzle like a siege gun bolted to the top of
an automobile, not to mention the ones which would be
running in the apartments and the homes where the
housewives and the maids made up the beds and swept

and prepared to cook dinner so that nowhere inside the town's uttermost ultimate corporate rim should man woman or child citizen or guest or stranger be threatened with one second of silence; and the automobiles because explicitly speaking he couldn't see the Square at all: only the dense impenetrable mass of tops and hoods moving in double line at a snail's crawl around the Square in a sharp invisible aura of carbon monoxide and blatting horns and a light intermittent clashing of bumpers, creeping slowly one by one into the streets leading away from the Square while the other opposite line crept as slowly one by one into it; so dense and slow dowelled into one interlocked mosaic so infinitesimal of movement as to be scarcely worthy of the word that you could have crossed the Square walking on them—or even out to the edge of town for that matter or even on a horse for that matter, Highboy for instance to whom the five- or six-foot jump from one top across the intervening hood to the next top would have been nothing or say the more or less motionless tops were laid with one smooth continuous surface of planks like a bridge and not Highboy but a gaited horse or a horse with one gait: a hard-driving rack seven feet in the air like a bird and travelling fast as a hawk or an eagle: with a feeling in the pit of his stomach as if a whole bottle of hot sodapop had exploded in it thinking of the gallant the splendid the really magnificent noise a horse would make racking in any direction on a loose plank bridge two miles long when suddenly his uncle at the other window said,

'The American really loves nothing but his automobile: not his wife his child nor his country nor even his bank-account first (in fact he doesn't really love that bank-account nearly as much as foreigners like to think because he will spend almost any or all of it for almost anything provided it is valueless enough) but his motorcar. Because the automobile has become our national sex symbol. We cannot really enjoy anything unless we can go up an alley for it. Yet our whole background and raising and training forbids the subrosa and surreptitious. So we have to divorce our wife today in order to remove from our mistress the odium of mistress in order to divorce our wife tomorrow in order to remove from our mistress and so on. As a result of which the American woman has become cold and undersexed; she has projected her libido onto the automobile not only because its glitter and gadgets and mobility pander to her vanity and incapacity (because of the dress decreed upon her by the national retailers association) to walk but because it will not maul her and tousle her, get her all sweaty and disarranged. So in order to capture and master anything at all of her anymore the American man has got to make that car his own. Which is why let him live in a rented rathole though he must he will not only own one but renew it each year in pristine virginity, lending it to no one, letting no other hand ever know the last secret forever chaste forever wanton intimacy of its pedals and levers, having nowhere to go in it himself and even if he did he would not go where scratch or blemish might deface it, spending all Sunday morning washing and polishing and waxing it because in doing that he is caressing the body of the woman who has long since now denied him her bed.'

'That's not true,' he said.

'I am fifty-plus years old,' his uncle said. 'I spent the middle fifteen of them fumbling beneath skirts. My ex-

perience was that few of them were interested in love or
sex either. They wanted to be married.'

'I still dont believe it,' he said.

'That's right,' his uncle said. 'Dont. And even when
you are fifty and plus, still refuse to believe it.' And that
was when they saw Lucas crossing the Square, probably
at the same time—the cocked hat and the thin fierce
glint of the tilted gold toothpick and he said,

'Where do you suppose it was all the time? I never
did see it. Surely he had it with him that afternoon, a
Saturday when he was not only wearing that black suit
but he even had the pistol? Surely he never left home
without the toothpick too.'

'Didn't I tell you?' his uncle said. 'That was the first
thing he did when Mr Hampton walked into Skipworth's
house where Skipworth had Lucas handcuffed to the
bedpost—gave Hampton the toothpick and told him to
keep it until he called for it.'

'Oh,' he said. 'He's coming up here.'

'Yes,' his uncle said. 'To gloat. Oh,' he said quickly,
'he's a gentleman; he wont remind me to my face that
I was wrong; he's just going to ask me how much he
owes me as his lawyer.'

Then in his chair beside the water cooler and his
uncle once more behind the table they heard the long
airy rumble and creak of the stairs then Lucas' feet
steadily though with no haste and Lucas came tieless and
even collarless this time except for the button but with
an old-time white waistcoat not soiled so much as
stained under the black coat and the worn gold loop of
the watchchain—the same face which he had seen for
the first time when he climbed dripping up out of the
icy creek that morning four years ago, unchanged, to

which nothing had happened since not even age—in the act of putting the toothpick into one of the upper waistcoat pockets as he came through the door, saying generally,

'Gentle-men,' and then to him: 'Young man—' courteous and intractable, more than bland: downright cheerful almost, removing the raked swagger of the hat: 'You aint fell in no more creeks lately, have you?'

'That's right,' he said. 'I'm saving that until you get some more ice on yours.'

'You'll be welcome without waiting for a freeze,' Lucas said.

'Have a seat, Lucas,' his uncle said but he had already begun to, taking the same hard chair beside the door which nobody else but Miss Habersham had ever chosen, a little akimbo as though he were posing for a camera, the hat laid crownup back across his forearm, looking at both of them still and saying again,

'Gentle-men.'

'You didn't come here for me to tell you what to do so I'm going to tell you anyway,' his uncle said.

Lucas blinked rapidly once. He looked at his uncle. 'I cant say I did.' Then he said cheerily: 'But I'm always ready to listen to good advice.'

'Go and see Miss Habersham,' his uncle said.

Lucas looked at his uncle. He blinked twice this time. 'I aint much of a visiting man,' he said.

'You were not much of a hanging man either,' his uncle said. 'But you dont need me to tell you how close you came.'

'No,' Lucas said. 'I dont reckon I do. What do you want me to tell her?'

'You cant,' his uncle said. 'You dont know how to say

thank you. I've got that fixed too. Take her some flowers.'

'Flowers?' Lucas said. 'I aint had no flowers to speak of since Molly died.'

'And that too,' his uncle said. 'I'll telephone home. My sister'll have a bunch ready. Chick'll drive you up in my car to get them and then take you out to Miss Habersham's gate.'

'Nemmine that,' Lucas said. 'Once I got the flowers I can walk.'

'And you can throw the flowers away too,' his uncle said. 'But I know you wont do one and I dont think you'll do the other in the car with Chick.'

'Well,' Lucas said. 'If wont nothing else satisfy you ——' (And when he got back to town and finally found a place three blocks away to park the car and mounted the stairs again his uncle was striking the match, holding it to the pipe and speaking through with into the smoke: 'You and Booker T. Washington, no that's wrong, you and Miss Habersham and Aleck Sander and Sheriff Hampton, and Booker T. Washington because he did only what everybody expected of him so there was no real reason why he should have while you all did not only what nobody expected you to but all Jefferson and Yoknapatawpha County would have risen in active concord for once to prevent you if they had known in time and even a year from now some (when and if they do at all) will remember with disapproval and distaste not that you were ghouls nor that you defied your color because they would have passed either singly but that you violated a white grave to save a nigger so you had every reason why you should have. Just dont stop:' and he:

'You dont think that just because it's Saturday afternoon again somebody is hiding behind Miss Habersham's

jasmine bush with a pistol aimed at her waiting for
Lucas to walk up to the front steps. Besides Lucas didn't
have his pistol today and besides that Crawford Gowrie
——' and his uncle:

'Why not, what's out yonder in the ground at Caledonia Church was Crawford Gowrie for only a second
or two last Saturday and Lucas Beauchamp will be carrying his pigment into ten thousand situations a wiser
man would have avoided and a lighter escaped ten
thousand times after what was Lucas Beauchamp for a
second or so last Saturday is in the ground at his Caledonia Church too, because that Yoknapatawpha County
which would have stopped you and Aleck Sander and
Miss Habersham last Sunday night are right actually,
Lucas' life the breathing and eating and sleeping is of
no importance just as yours and mine are not but his
unchallengeable right to it in peace and security and in
fact this earth would be much more comfortable with a
good deal fewer Beauchamps and Stevenses and Mal-
lisons of all colors in it if there were only some painless
way to efface not the clumsy room-devouring carcasses
which can be done but the memory which cannot—that
inevictible immortal memory awareness of having once
been alive which exists forever still ten thousand years
afterward in ten thousand recollections of injustice and
suffering, too many of us not because of the room we
take up but because we are willing to sell liberty short
at any tawdry price for the sake of what we call our own
which is a constitutional statutory license to pursue
each his private postulate of happiness and contentment
regardless of grief and cost even to the crucifixion of
someone whose nose or pigment we dont like and even
these can be coped with provided that few of others who

believe that a human life is valuable simply because it
has a right to keep on breathing no matter what pigment
its lungs distend or nose inhales the air and are willing
to defend that right at any price, it doesn't take many
three were enough last Sunday night even one can be
enough and with enough ones willing to be more than
grieved and shamed Lucas will no longer run the risk
of needing without warning to be saved:' and he:

'Maybe not three the other night. One and two halves
would be nearer right:' and his uncle:

'I said it's all right to be proud. It's all right even to
boast. Just dont stop.')——and came to the table and
laid the hat on it and took from the inside coat pocket
a leather snap-purse patina-ed like old silver and almost
as big as Miss Habersham's handbag and said,

'I believe you got a little bill against me.'

'What for?' his uncle said.

'For representing my case,' Lucas said. 'Name whatever your fee is within reason. I want to pay it.'

'Not me,' his uncle said. 'I didn't do anything.'

'I sent for you,' Lucas said. 'I authorised you. How
much do I owe you?'

'Nothing,' his uncle said. 'Because I didn't believe you.
That boy there is the reason you're walking around
today.'

Now Lucas looked at him, holding the purse in one
hand and the other hand poised to unsnap it—the same
face to which it was not that nothing had happened but
which had simply refused to accept it; now he opened
the purse. 'All right. I'll pay him.'

'And I'll have you both arrested,' his uncle said, 'you
for corrupting a minor and him for practising law without a license.'

Lucas looked back to his uncle; he watched them staring at one another. Then once more Lucas blinked twice. 'All right,' he said. 'I'll pay the expenses then. Name your expenses at anything within reason and let's get this thing settled.'

'Expenses?' his uncle said. 'Yes, I had an expense sitting here last Tuesday trying to write down all the different things you finally told me in such a way that Mr Hampton could get enough sense out of it to discharge you from the jail and so the more I tried it the worse it got and the worse it got the worse I got until when I came to again my fountain pen was sticking up on its point in the floor down here like an arrow. Of course the paper belongs to the county but the fountain pen was mine and it cost me two dollars to have a new point put in it. You owe me two dollars.'

'Two dollars?' Lucas said. He blinked twice again. Then he blinked twice again. 'Just two dollars?' Now he just blinked once, then he did something with his breath: not a sigh, simply a discharge of it, putting his first two fingers into the purse: 'That dont sound like much to me but then I'm a farming man and you're a lawing man and whether you know your business or not I reckon it aint none of my red wagon as the music box says to try to learn you different:' and drew from the purse a worn bill crumpled into a ball not much larger than a shriveled olive and opened it enough to read it then opened it out and laid it on the desk and from the purse took a half dollar and laid it on the desk then counted onto the desk from the purse one by one four dimes and two nickels and then counted them again with his forefinger, moving them one by one about half an inch, his lips moving under the moustache, the purse

still open in the other hand, then he picked up two of
the dimes and a nickel and put them into the hand
holding the open purse and took from the purse a quarter and put it on the desk and looked down at the coins
for a rapid second then put the two dimes and the nickel
back on the desk and took up the half dollar and put it
back into the purse.

'That aint but six bits,' his uncle said.

'Nemmine that,' Lucas said and took up the quarter
and dropped it back into the purse and closed it and
watching Lucas he realised that the purse had at least
two different compartments and maybe more, a second
almost elbow-deep section opening beneath Lucas' fingers
and for a time Lucas stood looking down into it exactly
as you would look down at your reflection in a well then
took from that compartment a knotted soiled cloth tobacco sack bulging and solid looking which struck on
the desk top with a dull thick chink.

'That makes it out,' he said. 'Four bits in pennies. I
was aiming to take them to the bank but you can save
me the trip. You want to count um?'

'Yes,' his uncle said. 'But you're the one paying the
money. You're the one to count them.'

'It's fifty of them,' Lucas said.

'This is business,' his uncle said. So Lucas unknotted
the sack and dumped the pennies out on the desk and
counted them one by one moving each one with his forefinger into the first small mass of dimes and nickels,
counting aloud, then snapped the purse shut and put it
back inside his coat and with the other hand shoved the
whole mass of coins and the crumpled bill across the
table until the desk blotter stopped them and took a
bandana handkerchief from the side pocket of the coat

and wiped his hands and put the handkerchief back and stood again intractable and calm and not looking at either of them now while the fixed blaring of the radios and the blatting creep of the automobile horns and all the rest of the whole County's Saturday uproar came up on the bright afternoon.

'Now what?' his uncle said. 'What are you waiting for now?'

'My receipt,' Lucas said.

WILLIAM FAULKNER, born New Albany, Mississippi, September 25, 1897—died July 6, 1962. Enlisted Royal Air Force, Canada, 1918. Attended University of Mississippi. Traveled in Europe 1925-1926. Resident of Oxford, Mississippi, where he held various jobs while trying to establish himself as a writer. First published novel, *Soldiers' Pay*, 1926. Writer in Residence at the University of Virginia 1957-1958. Awarded the Nobel Prize for Literature 1950.

Intruder in the Dust, Faulkner's fourteenth novel, was published in September, 1948, twenty-two years after the publication of his first (*Soldiers' Pay*). Six years fell between the publication of *Intruder in the Dust* and the previous novel, *Go Down, Moses*—by far the longest interval between books in Faulkner's entire career—mainly because he was also hard at work on *A Fable* (published in 1954) and doing film work through economic necessity.

VINTAGE CRITICISM,
LITERATURE, MUSIC, AND ART